A DEADLY DIVERSION

David Barry

ACORN BOOKS
www.acornbooks.co.uk

D1634574

04220863

This edition published in 2014 by
Acorn Books
www.acornbooks.co.uk

Acorn Books is an imprint of
Andrews UK Limited
www.andrewsuk.com

Copyright © 2014 David Barry

The right of David Barry to be identified as the author
of this work has been asserted by him in accordance
with the Copyright, Designs and Patents Act 1988

All rights reserved. No part of this publication may be
reproduced, stored in or introduced into a retrieval
system, or transmitted, in any form, or by any means
(electronic, mechanical, photocopying, recording or
otherwise) without the prior written permission of the
publisher. Any person who does any unauthorised act
in relation to this publication may be liable to criminal
prosecution and civil claims for damages.

All characters appearing in this work are fictitious. Any
resemblance to real persons, living or dead, is purely
coincidental.

Contents

A DEADLY DIVERSION

Prologue

Friday 19 July 2002

He had no illusions about the way he looked, knowing how he blended into the background - a featureless person no one would remember, and that was useful in this line of work. Which was why he felt safe staying in the same hotel as the target, secure in the knowledge that people barely gave him a second glance. And his real identity had disappeared somewhere in the dismal past, dropped like a stone into a lake, and it was highly unlikely his false identity could be compromised.

He had followed them from just outside Guildford in Surrey. Not that he had to follow close behind them all the way from the south of England, as the electronic tracker on the target's BMW gave a fairly precise location, allowing him to keep a safe distance.

He knew they were heading for Inverness, and it was unlikely they would attempt the six-hundred mile journey in one day. And he'd been right. Hence the stopover at a location not far from Carlisle at a five star hotel. Years ago it would have been way beyond his budget. But not anymore. Now he could afford life's luxuries, and in any case the hotel needn't come out of his commission and would be classed as expenses.

He sat in the dining room as far away from his target as possible. Even so, it was unnerving the way their son glanced in his direction every so often and studied him closely. Instinctively, his hand went to his neck. He had always had an inferiority complex about his protruding Adam's apple, and now the boy kept staring at him as he ate his continental breakfast, watching the bobbing of his protrusion as he swallowed. The kid was only ten-years-old, and he should have known better than to stare like that. Not that it mattered. Because of the electronic tail, he could track them at a distance. Then, once he had them in a secluded spot...

Twenty minutes later, after settling his hotel bill, he sat in his van in the car park waiting for the family to leave. He watched from a distance as they got back into their silver BMW. The boy sat in the front passenger seat and his mother sat at the back. He gave them a ten minute start before following. His motorcycle leathers lay on the seat next to him, the helmet on the floor by the passenger seat, and the revolver was in the glove compartment. Although it was late July, it felt too hot, because he had wrongly assumed that this far north, especially in Scotland, it was always at least four or five degrees cooler than the south of England. But not now - not now he needed to wear stifling hot motorcycle leathers. At least he'd had the sense to wear a light T-shirt, grey and nondescript, drawing little attention to himself.

It was still many miles and hours until Inverness and he hoped they would stop off for some lunch or pull into a beauty spot to admire the scenery. That's when he would do it. He couldn't let them get as far as Inverness. It had to be somewhere fairly secluded; but there were many tourists around at this time of the year, and he couldn't be sure there wouldn't be any visitors who might witness the execution. Not that it mattered. All anyone would see was a motorcyclist in a black helmet, an unrecognisable figure who would vanish into nowhere. Even if there were no witnesses to the hit, he was well enough informed on police procedure, knowing forensics would soon identify the motorcycle tracks. But by then he would probably be back south of the border with the motorbike inside the van, with all the time in the world to get rid of it, along with the weapon.

By late morning, their BMW drove along the A82 west of Loch Lomond. He was only about five minutes behind them, and when they reached the village of Crianlarich, he saw they had stopped. He carried on driving and noticed they had parked outside a store, presumably to buy provisions for lunch. He carried on driving through the village and parked in a lay-by to wait. Ten minutes later their BMW past his van, but he didn't follow. He guessed they would very soon find somewhere to enjoy their picnic lunch. Hopefully, somewhere remote.

They couldn't have gone more than seven or eight miles when he picked up the tracker on his mobile, informing him they had turned west. He consulted his map and saw they had taken a B-road and were in the Glen Orchy area. About halfway to the area where they had turned off the main road, he saw there was a village called Tyndrum, so he used his BlackBerry to check it out on the internet, which seemed to take forever. But eventually he learnt there was an old lead mine outside the village, with a Forestry Commission warning that it could be a dangerous place to go walking. It seemed an ideal place to park the van.

It took him less than ten minutes to find a secluded spot where he could unload the motorbike quickly down the ramp. By now he was sweating profusely, and the leather motorcycle jacket felt uncomfortably clammy, so he left it unzipped as far down as his stomach, knowing the breeze would cool him as he sped to his destination to carry out the contract. As he lowered the helmet onto his head, a feeling of power swept over him - power and anticipation, like a matador stepping into the bullring.

He covered the distance from where he had parked the van to their picnic site in less than five minutes. As he came over the brow of a hill, he saw them sitting by a river, enjoying the tranquillity of the valley as they ate their sandwiches. The boy sat on the bank with his bare feet cooling off in the water. As they heard the roar of his engine, all three turned and looked up at him. The father stood up, his food spilling onto the ground, his body stiffening with fear, aware there was a price on his head.

The motorbike's engine revved once before speeding down the incline towards them, their terrified images getting larger as he neared them in seconds, like the zoom on a telephoto lens. He saw the panicking father pushing his wife towards the car, and waving at his son to get away from the bank and into the passenger seat.

But they were too late. He skidded to a stop only a yard away from the father, took the gun from inside his leather jacket and, without a moment's hesitation, shot him in the middle of the forehead, the bullet going clean through the man's skull. A stream of blood from the back of his head spurted across the roof of the car. His wife opened her mouth to scream but the second bullet caught her in the mouth. In case she survived by some miracle, he put a third bullet through her head as she slid down the car, leaving a bloody trail along the bodywork.

He glanced towards the shocked boy. He had no intention of killing him. Not children. Never. It was a rule of his.

But knowing he had no time to waste, he kicked the stand of the bike, swung his leg over the seat, then hurriedly crouched beneath the back of the BMW. His hand felt for the tracker and tugged hard on the strong magnet attaching it to the car. He shoved the small black box into his pocket and got back on the bike. Then kicked the stand away, and was about to rev up and turn away from the scene but a glance at the boy stopped him accelerating right away. The kid was in a state of shock, frozen with fear, staring at him with uncomprehending eyes. Then he realised his jacket wasn't zipped up, and his neck and chest were unshielded. Without thinking, he took his left hand off the handlebar accelerator and it flew to his throat, concealing this vulnerable area from the kid. He felt exposed, like he'd made a grave error.

So there was only one way to rectify this mistake. His decision was instant, because he was a professional and couldn't leave anything to chance.

He put two bullets into the boy's head. He regretted having to do it. But by staring at him during breakfast, the kid had signed his own death warrant.

Not only that, the boy had witnessed him retrieving the tracker and it wasn't something he wanted the police to know about.

As he sped from the scene of carnage, he thought the boy's death was unfortunate but necessary. Justifiable in the circumstances.

***

The youngsters in the school party were baking hot and getting fractious. Some of the girls had started bickering and were hungry and thirsty, having spent the day walking round the ruins of Pompeii with no shade from the unrelenting sun. By the time they got back to their accommodation, they were tired and desperately in need of energy-giving nourishment.

While one of the volunteers poured them ice cold drinks, Miss Mitchell, one of the teaching staff, had a call on her mobile. It was from the girls' school and it was the head teacher calling. Puzzled, wondering what was so urgent for the head teacher to call halfway through the trip, she took the call.

As she listened intently, her puzzled frown cut deeper scars into her forehead. She struggled, fighting back tears, until one huge tear rolled out of her left eye, which she wiped away quickly as she struggled to remain self-controlled.

As she ended the almost one-sided conversation, promising she would explain to the pupil as gently as possible what had happened, the pupils who were present in the dining area, all focused their attention on her, knowing she was a messenger of bad news. There was an expectant pause, every eye on her, as she struggled and fought back tears.

Eventually, she spoke in a voice choked with emotion, looking at one of the girls, who felt a stab of alarm as she was singled out, scared and knowing she was to be the recipient of brutal news.

'Alice, do you think I could have a quiet word alone?'

The girl felt herself crumble, everything suddenly becoming unreal, as if it was happening to someone else.

'What is it, Miss?'

'Please, Alice. If you could just come into my room for one minute. There's something I have to tell you.'

As the teacher led the way out of the dining room and along the hall to her room, followed by the pupil, how she hated her responsibility, her duty in having to explain to her pupil the worst news that anyone should ever hear. How her whole family had been wiped out, killed by a crazed gunman.

Chapter 1

Monday 23 September 2013

Feeling nervous and apprehensive, I slept fitfully, and woke in the early hours. As I lay on my back, staring at the ceiling, I felt uneasy and questioned whether my partner Bill Turner and I had taken on something two geezers in their mid-fifties should have left to younger men. Starting a private investigation agency suddenly seemed foolhardy, a venture that smacked of Walter Mitty absurdity. On the other hand, I kept telling myself, as I lay there gnashing my teeth and feeling an uncomfortable tension in my neck, the two of us had come through countless escapades unscathed.

I suppose my nervousness was due to it being our first day in our brand new office, and already we had two potential client appointments, one in the morning and one just after lunch.

I picked up my mobile from the bedside cabinet and checked the time. It was just gone five and I was wide awake. So as not to disturb Michelle, I turned back the duvet carefully and gently swung my legs out of bed; but as I padded quietly across the room, I heard her stir.

'I can't sleep either,' she mumbled. 'So I think I might as well get up. If you can't beat them, join them.'

'I hope it wasn't my fault you couldn't sleep,' I said from the bathroom door.

Michelle blinked the sleep from her eyes and focused on mine. 'I think I'm as worried as you are about your first day as a private eye.'

It was said in a mocking tone.

I sighed. 'Oh, come on, sweetheart, it's not like the movies. It's about getting information; stuff like info about employees ripping off their employers with false expenses claims and suchlike.'

'But knowing you, Freddie, and your propensity for getting into hot water...'

'Propensity,' I said. 'Good word for this time of the morning. I'm just going to shower, then I'll have an early breakfast.'

'I might join you. And I've also got a busy day.'

'What are you up to?'

'I'm looking for a cheaper venue for my dance classes. The Catholic church hall knows how to charge.'

'Well, the Pope didn't get where he is today - ' I said.

As I showered, I thought about Michelle's dancing school, which was taking off in a big way. The dancing school our daughter Olivia attended during the last school year closed down, and Michelle saw an opening and went for it. Word soon got around, and she went from one evening a week to three in less than a month. But Olivia, almost a star pupil at the previous school, seemed to have suddenly lost interest and often said she felt too tired or too ill to attend. At first, Michelle and I thought it was because she was reluctant to be taught by her mother, and when we asked her this, she became uncommunicative and shrugged it off, mumbling that it was nothing to do with 'Mum'. We thought she might get over it, but there was no sign that her dancing, which had once meant so much to her, was about to light up her day as it had in the past.

It was worrying, and I was determined to get to the bottom of it.

***

Michelle and I had already eaten a substantial breakfast by the time Olivia came into the kitchen for her usual crunchy nut cereal, the same breakfast she has eaten every morning for the past year. She avoided eye contact with us and stared into her cereal bowl. Her inscrutable expression wouldn't fool anyone and I was convinced it masked feelings of shame, though I had no inkling of any reason she should feel guilty. But her eyes said it all, downcast and withdrawn, and Michelle and I knew this was a volatile teenage situation and things would soon come to a head.

There was no clock in our kitchen, but I fancied a ticking highlighted the silence.

As our daughter reached automatically for the milk jug, still careful to avoid meeting our eyes, the silence stretched unbearably, and the imaginary ticking in my head got louder. I heard Michelle quietly clearing her throat, careful not to disturb the delicate balance of the unpredictable. And then Olivia, spoon poised immobile over the cereal, as if dreading the act of eating, made eye contact with Michelle.

'Where's Jackie?' she asked.

I was relieved. Asking after her sister was a good sign. Perhaps she could confide in big sister, tell her things she wouldn't want to tell her parents.

'Surely you haven't forgotten,' Michelle replied. 'She spent last night at Claire'shouse, and they're going straight from there to college this morning.'

Olivia stared uncomprehendingly into the distance, desperately trying to work something out in her mind. I could see the confusion in her eyes, the strain in trying to understand something that lay just out of her grasp. And then she crumpled. From deep inside her came a gurgling sound as her shoulders trembled and shook, and she was racked with heaving sobs.

Michelle had seen it coming, and within an instant she held our daughter in a firm embrace. 'Olivia! Sweetheart! What is it? Tell Mummy what's wrong? Please sweetheart. We can't help you if you don't tell us.'

I rose, feeling helpless and awkward, and a little extraneous seeing as Michelle was already comforting Olivia, cuddling, caressing and nuzzling her. I walked over to them and stood the other side of Olivia, desperately hoping my presence wouldn't stop her from unloading whatever was troubling her. I thought perhaps it was a daughter to mother scenario, an unburdening of womanly problems, and males were strictly off-limits in these female confidences. But I was wrong, because Olivia suddenly blurted out:

'That man won't leave me alone.'

I felt a wave of coldness pass through my body.

'Which man?' Michelle asked.

Sobbing and heaving, Olivia spluttered as she tried to speak. 'He won't leave me... leave me alone. He's always there. At first he was friendly... but now... now he's said nasty things about my friends. And I'm frightened of him.'

'Who is this bastard?' I said, trying to soften the harshness in my voice.

Olivia looked up at me, her eyes veiled with tears. 'I don't know, Dad. I don't know.'

'But you must have some idea.'

'That's just it. I haven't a clue.'

Michelle straightened up, but kept her arm draped around Olivia's shoulders. 'I don't understand, sweetheart. Is it someone round here? Someone we know? Or someone at school?'

'He's called Eclipse.'

'What sort of name's that?' Michelle asked, looking across at me, frowning.

Suddenly, I began to understand what this was about.

'Is this someone on the internet?' I said. 'Someone you don't really know?'

'We just got chatting on this forum. A chat room. He seemed quite nice at first. We just talked about our interests and made jokes. Then my friend Diane got an email from me, telling her she was too fat to dance and saying lots of horrible things about her dancing. Only it wasn't from me. Not really. He must have found a way of sending her an email as if it came from me.'

Michelle leaned over Olivia and spoke quietly and intensely. 'Have you explained to Diane it wasn't you?'

'I tried, but she wouldn't believe me. Now she won't speak to me at all. Nor will Chrissie or Jessica. And now he's starting to say disgusting things, and sending pictures of...'

'Pornographic pictures?' I questioned.

Olivia shook her head. 'Not really. Some of the women had no clothes on but they weren't doing anything. They were tied up or handcuffed, and wearing weird masks. You know, like that bondage stuff. In a torture chamber. And then, this morning, when I checked my emails I got a scary, horrible...'

Olivia broke off again and tried to control her tears. She wiped her nose with the back of her hand and sniffed loudly.

'Can you show us?' I asked. 'Maybe we can trace his email.'

She shook her head intensely. 'Anyone can have an email account, Dad, and you can send emails from an internet café or anywhere. You must know that.'

'Even so, I'd like to see what he sent you.'

She nodded her agreement and seemed relieved to be unburdening herself. She grabbed some sheets of kitchen roll to blow her nose, and then we followed her upstairs and into her bedroom. The lid of her laptop was open on her desk. She sat on her swivel chair in front of the desk and clicked the laptop on.

'It'll just take a moment to boot up,' she said.

While we waited, I glanced around at the familiar room, a room which still looked like a young child's. There were soft toys and teddy bears propped comfortably in various places, like a family of comforting characters, and girlie emblems decorating the walls. But far from comforting me, it had the opposite effect of heightening the way I felt sickened and disturbed by the thoughts of a pervert targeting my little girl on the internet.

'When did this start happening, Olivia?' Michelle asked.

'Just over two weeks ago. Maybe a bit longer. Nearer three weeks.'

She clicked on the email that had been sent. Her swivel chair was on castors and she propelled it back a foot, as if the threat of what was on her computer was tangible and could reach out and harm her physically.

Most of the email was an image of an elderly man I recognised from the newspapers a while back. And next to his picture was the script:

'Josef Fritzl. Wow! What a man. My hero. Imagine locking his daughter in a cellar for 24 years. Now that's what I call fun. Would you like to have some long term fun, Olivia? I bet you would. Don't worry, kid. We'll get there in the end. One day I'll come and I'll find you. You can bet on it. Whatever it takes, I'll find you.'

I saw Michelle shiver and cross her arms over her chest. It was an instinctive gesture of self-preservation, and a moment later she unfolded them and placed her hands on Olivia's shoulders, massaging gently. My throat felt dry, and I felt utterly helpless. What the hell could I do about a message that came from Christ knows where? How could I protect my family from this type of disgusting violation? But I knew I had to do something to set her mind at ease. I looked at the email address, which was from someone calling himself Eclipse, but what caught my eye was the country suffix following the dot com. It was PL.

'That email address,' I said. 'I've never seen that suffix before. Which country signs itself PL?'

'I looked it up, Dad. It's Poland.'

Michelle and I exchanged looks, both at a loss, wondering what we could do about this. Michelle was the first to verbalise what I'd been thinking.

'If this is someone from another country, then why not change your email address?'

Olivia shook her head. 'I've done that already. Several times. But whoever it is seems to find out. And I've used different passwords every time, but it doesn't do any good. I just wish whoever it is would go away.'

'At least,' I said, gently smoothing Olivia's hair, 'knowing this person is in another country - a long way from here - means this is not physically threatening. It's probably some geeky nutter who gets his thrills from frightening kids on the internet. I know it's not much comfort me saying this, but you're probably not the only one he's latched on to.'

'Assuming it's a man,' Michelle said.

I chuckled humourlessly. 'Oh, come on, Michelle. How many female computer geeks d'you know? These sad bastards are usually blokes.'

'I don't care who it is,' Olivia shouted, staring at the screen with loathing. 'I just wish it would stop. And my friends hate me because of it.'

She burst into tears again and buried her head in her hands. Michelle cuddled her, and spoke just above a whisper.

'Sweetheart, this man's a long way off and can't harm you. I'm sure if you explain to your friends, and show them your emails, they'll know it's not you sending them out.'

'But I don't get a chance to speak to them. They don't want to know me.'

Michelle straightened up and looked me in the eye, as though she was seeking approval for what she was about to say, then leant forward again and spoke quietly to Olivia. 'I've got a suggestion to make. I've got to go and see some new venues for my dance classes. Why don't I ring up the school, tell them you're not feeling well - I mean, it's only a few weeks into the new term - and you can come with me to look at some of these halls. We can have lunch out, and then we can make an appointment to see one of the staff at the school to tell them what's been going on. They can help explain to some of your friends that these nasty emails haven't come from you. We can open up your emails at the school and show them what's been happening. How does that sound?'

There was a pause while Olivia thought about this. Through her sniffles she mumbled, 'If you're sure - '

'Of course, I'm sure. What do you think, Freddie?'

'Sounds like a good idea.' I clicked my fingers as another idea came to me. 'It's our first day at Weston and Turner today, and our secretary Nicky's a wiz on computers - which is why we employed her - she might be able to sort something out, and she might know how to stop this bastard from contacting you.'

'How can she?' Olivia sniffed.

'I haven't a clue. But she's been the one to organise our system in the office - real state-of-the-art stuff - and the bloke who's done our system's apparently brilliant. Knows all there is to know about IT. I'll have a word with Nicky about this, and if she can't help, she can put me in touch with her expert. How does that sound?'

Olivia nodded. 'Yeah. Thanks, Dad.'

'Good girl.' I glanced at my watch. 'I'd better head off. If Nicky gets into the office early, as I think she might, I'll have a word with her before we start. The sooner we get this business sorted, the better.'

I kissed them both before leaving, and Michelle squeezed my hand and whispered, 'Thanks, Freddie.'

It was just gone seven-thirty when I left the house, and it felt strange to be up and about at this time. Normally I'm a night bird, but the job of supplying doormen to London clubs could now be run from my computer and smart phone, with occasional visits just for appearances sake. And once our investigation agency was up and running, we could leave Nicky in charge of the early morning administration of the business, while Bill and I got on with the job of investigating... well, whatever needed investigating.

Our office was situated just off Chalk Farm Road, not far from the Tube station. We had looked at premises in a more central location, but the rents were crippling. Even Chalk Farm was bad enough, but we didn't want to move any further than this out of central London. And we needed somewhere smart; somewhere that gave the impression to potential clients that we were successful operators. The building we chose was spacious, had recently housed theatre wig suppliers and was somewhat rundown, but we soon converted it into two stylish offices, the outer one being Nicky's and the reception area. The most useful element of the premises, though, was the small parking space at the side, just space enough for one car. Nicky and Bill travelled to Chalk Farm on the Tube, so I was the only one who needed to park, although if the business took off, Bill would need a company car so we could work independently of each other. But we would cross that bridge later.

As I set off from Wanstead to Chalk Farm, although it was probably no more than twelve miles distant, I guessed it would probably take a good forty-five minutes because it was bang in the middle of rush hour. Normally, I don't mind driving, but on this particular morning I found it difficult to concentrate. As I thought about Olivia's anonymous tormenter, my mood darkened. I kept thinking about all the evil computer geeks who enjoy wrecking people's lives. And for what? Just because they get a kick out of it? Invading unsuspecting internet user's privacy, spying on them, feeding them false information, and threatening and frightening them for no reason other than a desire to play sadistic games.

Feeling impotent, and knowing I was powerless to protect my daughter from something that was activated hundreds of miles away, my mood got even darker. Because I drifted into a fantasy scenario, dishing out a vicious beating to a perverted computer geek, I lost concentration and had to slam on the brakes, nearly hitting the back of a black cab who had spotted a fare and pulled up suddenly.

I tooted angrily and yelled obscenities at the cab. He couldn't have heard me, and I felt no better for having discharged my anger in this way.

Chapter 2

I was first to arrive at our workplace, but it was still only ten past eight, so I wasn't expecting either Bill or Nicky for a good twenty minutes yet. I made a cafetiére of coffee and sat at my desk surveying the surroundings. Comfortable brown leather chairs, a dark grey carpet, framed pictures on the wall, photographs of Bill and me in army gear when we were in our early twenties, and a shelf on which stood a camera with a telephoto lens to show we were in the business of surveillance.

I should have been pleased with the way our office looked, but my thoughts were still morbidly stuck in the internet bullying groove, thinking about the predator who had singled out my daughter for harassment.

Nicky arrived just before Bill and immediately noticed how down I was. I didn't want to go through the story twice, so I told her I had a problem and could she wait for Bill to arrive before I unloaded my worries.

Although I didn't know Nicky that well - Bill and I had interviewed her for the job three weeks ago - she struck us both as being highly efficient and bright. She was certainly charming and personable. I didn't know whether she was a genuine blonde or if her hair was dyed. If the latter, it was expensively treated and had a beautiful sheen to it that you only get in television commercials. She was an attractive forty-five, although she had knocked five years off at the interview. Going by her CV, it was clearly a blatant lie, but what the hell! - she could easily have passed for late-thirties. She had once been a high-flyer in an advertising agency, rising to creative director level, but she had always had an ambition to act and gave up the daytime job to train at a drama school for two years. After leaving, she got one or two jobs in touring theatre shows, mainly understudying, and after a gruelling three years she decided she had left it too late to realise her ambitions and, accepting defeat, she decided to start over again. At her interview she said she liked the idea of being in sole charge of the office as a manager rather than just a secretary, so we promoted her immediately to office manager and upped the advertised salary from four- to five-hundred a week.

Although this Monday morning was the first day we were open for business, Nicky had already worked more than a fortnight for us, organising the office, and choosing our furniture and fixtures. She suggested that two desks, positioned in an L-shape, might prove intimidating to clients, so we ended up with just the one large desk, which Bill and I decided to share, depending on who was doing what and when. Nicky also spent time liaising with her computer expert, getting our system up and running, our website designed and ordering any surveillance equipment we might need. So we were raring to go. And I would have enjoyed the anticipation of setting off on this great adventure were it not for the Olivia business.

Bill arrived five minutes after Nicky and they both came into the inner sanctum and sat and listened to the desperate account of my daughter's online persecution. After I had finished Bill looked at me and shrugged, and I wondered if this was to indicate that he felt helpless, knowing as much about computers as I did - which was very little.

'If this arsehole is in Poland,' he said, 'at least Olivia's not in any real danger. I mean, I know it must be upsetting for her, and even a bit scary, but someone in East Europe's not going to...'

I interrupted him. 'Yeah, Bill, but - and I'm only guessing - I would think you could fly from Poland to London in well under three hours.'

'Olivia wouldn't have provided him with her address, I hope.'

'Even so, she's got lots of friends at school. They're always emailing and texting. If he can read her emails, I dread to think what he can find out about her.'

It was then I noticed Nicky was disturbingly quiet, staring at her nails and frowning thoughtfully.

'What do you think, Nicky?' I asked.

I noticed the nervousness in her voice as she spoke.

'Freddie, I don't want to frighten you, but anyone with the requisite knowledge of computers can mask the physical location of a computer.'

'You mean, give a Polish address and the person could be right here in London.'

'It's possible.'

'Oh, Jesus!'

She saw me wiping my fingers across my forehead, trying to wipe away the fear, and said with a tentative smile of reassurance, 'But this person may well be a sad weirdo hacking away from some dank hole in Gdansk, who gets his kicks from scaring people a long way away.'

'Even so...' I began, but she didn't let me finish.

'Why don't I give Ricky Lee a ring? He knows much more than I do about computing. He's a good programmer, so he's pretty shit-hot. I'll tell him it's urgent and ask if he can meet you late this afternoon, after our second meeting.' Nicky stood up purposefully and walked towards her own office and reception area, saying as she went, 'I've just got time to call him before our first meeting. Try not to worry, Freddie. I'm sure Ricky Lee can help us out.'

It eased my concerns for the moment. Now that I felt something was being done, I could concentrate on our first client's investigation. None of us knew what his problem was, and he said he was reluctant to discuss it with Nicky over the phone.

Chapter 3

Piers Granville-Aston had a voice to match his posh name, plummy and rich. I guessed he was somewhere in his late twenties or early thirties. He wore a dark blue suit and an expensive-looking mauve-striped shirt, open at the collar. His brown hair was longish and curly, and a one-sided fringe flopped above his right eye. Nicky announced him, and gestured for him to take a seat, but he shook hands with me and Bill first while we introduced ourselves. Nicky carried a notebook and pencil but, before sitting down, he stared pointedly at her notebook.

'Nicky will take notes in shorthand,' I explained. 'So we don't have to rely on our memories for all the little details.'

He looked slightly uncomfortable, shifting his weight from one foot to another. 'I don't think,' he began hesitantly, 'I don't think I want you to take notes at this stage. I'll just give you an overview of what the problem is. It won't be difficult to understand what it is I want you to do. It's quite straightforward in fact. But I would sooner...' He hesitated, glancing at Nicky. 'Would sooner talk man-to-man in private.' He chuckled nervously. 'Delicate matter and all that.'

Nicky looked to me for guidance and I said, 'That's OK, Nicky. I'm sure we can deal with Mr Granville-Aston's enquiry for the moment.'

Once Nicky had gone, closing the door behind her, our potential client relaxed, flopped into a leather chair, crossed his legs elegantly and asked us to call him Piers.

'Well, Piers,' I began, what can we do for you?'

'I've been arrested. I've been bailed, and if I'm sentenced after the trial, I could face a lengthy prison term. That's if it goes horribly wrong.'

'What are you charged with?'

He paused before answering. 'Attempted rape.' He made a childish face, as if he was a naughty boy. Nothing more than a silly prank.

'That sounds to me quite serious,' Bill said. 'Would you care to fill us in on the details, right from the beginning?'

Our upper class client laughed confidently. 'Oh, it's not that serious when you hear the truth about what went on between the three of us.'

I shot him a puzzled frown. 'Three of you?'

He glanced at my business partner and said, 'Bill is right. Let me start at the very beginning. An old school chum of mine, Clive Westbourne - we were at Eton together - and we were in high spirits...' He broke off to chortle at his own private joke before resuming his tale. 'In other words, we were pissed as rats, and we'd been knocking them back all lunchtime at this pub in Ealing. We chatted the barmaid up, probably behaved quite outrageously but she didn't seem to mind. Far from it. We thought she might be up for it, if you catch my drift.' He broke off to give us a familiar brotherhood leer before continuing. 'Anyway, she finished work around three, so we invited her for some Chinky chow. Of course, by the time the food arrived at this restaurant, where they were quite happy to take our money but clearly wanted to close for the afternoon, we had ordered several bottles of wine, and the food wasn't good, so we had a bit of fun with it instead.'

'How d'you mean?' I asked.

He laughed, clearly pleased with his behaviour in the Chinese restaurant, and mimed throwing something small. 'We bombarded the waiters with their pork balls.'

I kept my expression deadpan. I didn't wanted to encourage the tosser, but at this stage didn't want to upset a potential client either. But if there's one thing I can't stand, it's the way the upper classes throw food around contemptuously, because they never have to worry about going without.

He giggled again while he relived the scene, and I suddenly wanted to reach across the desk and smack this arsehole. It took an enormous effort to restrain myself.

'So there we were, chucking this disgusting pig-swill grub about. Clive told them not to mind; we'd pay for any mess we made. When we paid the bill, tipping them handsomely, I swear their slit eyes grew wider. Anyway, by now we were both legless, and we propositioned the filly - invited her back to Clive's flat.'

Bill interrupted the story to ask, 'Does this girl have a name? Or is she just an object?'

The obnoxious double-barrelled twat threw a look at my partner that was a mixture of confusion and irritation, as if he couldn't quite work out if Bill was being critical or humorous in a deadpan style. After all, he was the man from a privileged background who could click his fingers and pay for any favour he liked.

'Her name is Christine Smarden,' he said. 'Or is it Marden?' He waved a dismissive hand. 'Anyway, it's not important. So we jumped in a cab to Clive's flat in South Ealing, with the filly sitting between us in the back. We had a bit of a fumble, and she didn't seem to mind, which was how we knew she was up for it.'

'How old was this girl?' I asked.

'I don't know. Does it matter?'

'It could be important.'

He flushed, and his irritation surfaced. 'Oh, she was old enough. Not under age, if that's what you mean. She was at least eighteen-years-old.'

'How can you be so sure? I've known loads of fifteen-year-olds who could pass for older.'

'Look, she was working in a pub, for Christ's sake,' he bellowed, then glanced over his shoulder in case Nicky heard him and came in to see what was wrong. 'She was at least sixteen. Perfectly legal. Her choice to come back to Clive's place. OK?'

'Go on.'

He paused for a second, while he composed himself. 'Well, Clive's flat is a first floor maisonette, and he lives above an elderly lady. We hadn't long arrived, and we were really legless by now. Giggling and falling over. I suppose we were making a hell of a racket. In our cups, we thought we were up for a ménage a trois.'

He grinned, and when I didn't respond, he explained, 'That's a threesome.'

Patronising bastard.

'Yes,' I said, 'I know perfectly well what it means. So what happened next?'

'It's all a bit hazy. I think Clive started to undress her. He was fumbling so much she helped him. She was lying on the floor, half naked. I remember her knickers and trousers were all tangled up round her ankles, and then all I could see was Clive's hairy arse on top of her. He was swearing and saying things like, "Come on, you bastard, I know you can do it." While I was watching, I fell over quite a few times. I remember crashing onto the floor. And then I think Clive said, "Oh this is no good. I can't get it up, Piers. See if you can do it." So he got off her and I got on. But even though I tried to get the dog into the kennel, it just didn't want to go.' He sniggered dirtily, preening himself at this turn of phrase.

I stifled a sigh, wanting to get rid of this unpleasant oaf but at the same time wanting to hear the entire story.

'So how come you were arrested for this, especially if as you say she's not under age and this was consensual?'

'Well, that's where the police come into it,' he replied. 'Because we were so drunk, we didn't realise how long we must have been creating havoc and pissing about with the girl. And Clive had left his front door open. Because of all the noise, the woman downstairs called the police. Anyway, Clive's standing at the window, stark naked, and he saw them pull up outside. He warned me the police were there but I thought it was a wind up, and I was still laughing and trying to get it up as the police barged in. Clive had hidden in the wardrobe. And that was when the girl started to struggle and push me off "These men have tried to rape me," she said. But at the time I was too drunk to take it in. They made us get dressed, took us to the police station and I was arrested. Later, when the girl told her story, they arrested Clive.'

'Why did she claim you tried to rape her?' Bill asked.'

'She was probably ashamed at being caught *in flagrante* with two fellahs.'

'But she said "these men" when the police walked in. Did the police know your friend was hiding in the wardrobe?'

'No, but making Sherlock Holmes deductions is beyond the ordinary plod.'

'So what exactly do you want Weston and Turner to do?' I asked.

'Well, it's clear the little cow lied about our attempts to rape her. So I thought you could investigate her. Find out if he she's had many licentious assignations, one-night stands and such. We can afford a good barrister who will discredit her. You might also speak to her informally, and get her to admit she lied. No doubt you can record these conversations?'

From the corner of my eye I saw Bill shaking his head. He didn't need to demonstrate to me his reluctance to represent this arsehole because I had already made up my mind. But I was glad we were of the same mind. I stood up.

'Thank you for coming to see us. I regret we cannot represent you in this matter.'

Was it my imagination, but did his face lose its colour? This was not a man who was used to being turned down. He stood up, so that he was on the same level with me, and I could see a cat-like viciousness in his eyes.

'Why the hell not?' he demanded, his lower lip stretched taut as his face turned ugly from rejection.

I shrugged hugely, knowing it would wind him up even more. 'Bad time,' I said.

His eyes blazed with anger. 'What's that supposed to mean? Are you in the habit of turning down business? And it's not as if I haven't told you the truth. There was no attempt to rape the little cow. She was perfectly willing to be fucked by both of us and...'

I raised a hand to silence him. 'I don't give a monkey's. It's not a good case for us to start off with - not with everything that's going on in the media right now.'

'I don't follow you.'

'It kicked off with the Jimmy Savile disgrace, and it's been escalating ever since. There's not a day goes by without some celebrity being accused of sexual harassment, whether it's with someone under age or not. So two drunken, public school wankers trying to have it off with a young barmaid -' I spread my arms in a gesture of resignation - 'is not the sort of business we welcome right now.'

'Oh, so that's it,' he sneered. 'Inverted fucking snobbery. Well, let's see if you're as fussy about turning down business in six months' time, when you'll no doubt be ready to visit the Job Centre with the rest of the great unwashed.'

He turned sharply, threw open the door and exited through the reception area without so much as a glance at Nicky.

'What a prick,' Bill said with a wide grin.

I nodded agreement. 'But we've just turned down our first client. We can't do that too often.'

Nicky entered the office and handed me a sheet from a notebook. 'I had a word with Ricky Lee Bishop and that's his address in Finchley. It's not half-eleven yet, so I said you'd be over to see him at twelve noon. It's not that far away, so you'll be back here well in time for the two-thirty appointment. I explained briefly what it's about and he said he can't promise but he'll do anything he can to help.'

'That's brilliant, Nicky. Thanks.'

'What happened with client numero uno?'

'We had a disagreement.'

'Don't tell me he wound you up the wrong way. Mind you, I thought that cut-glass accent was a bit OTT.'

Bill laughed. 'Yeah, you should have heard the conversation between Freddie and him. It was like listening to Michael Caine talking to Prince Charles.'

Chapter 4

The computer programmer's home was a large two-storey terrace house in a cul-de-sac in Finchley. The outside looked as if it could have done with a lick of paint; apart from that it looked as if it was homely and belonged to a family who hadn't much time to worry about D-I-Y. In the porch stood a multi-coloured golf umbrella next to a kid's tricycle. I rang the bell and waited, and after a moment I heard pounding feet coming downstairs. I saw his shape through the stained-glass of the front door dashing towards me, and then he threw the door open wide and thrust out his hand.

'Hi!' he said. 'You must be Freddie.'

He was fresh-faced and good looking, with bright intelligent eyes, and dishevelled blond hair like Boris Johnson. Although he must have been in his early thirties, he dressed like a teenager: a T-shirt with some sort of weird fantasy image on it, and military camouflage long shorts and trainers.

I shook his hand and said, 'Good to meet you Ricky Lee.'

'Please. Call me Rick. Deep down I think my parents were rednecks giving me two Christian names like that. Come on in, and we'll go to my office upstairs. Watch the toys as you go. It's sometimes like walking through a minefield. I nearly broke my neck coming downstairs last week.'

As I followed him up to the first floor, I asked him how many children he had.

'Just the one so far. Matthew who's four, and he's at a pre-school nursery at the moment. My wife Sarah works part time as a speech therapist.

He ushered me into a spacious room, which was a clutter of shelves, manuals, gadgets and an enormous desk with a flat screen monitor, then took a folding director chair from the side of his desk, opened it up for me, got another one for himself, and sat in front of the desk facing me. I thanked him for seeing me at short notice.

'Funny we never met,' he said. 'Seeing as I organised your system and designed your website.'

'It's Nicky who's dealing with that side of things,' I explained. 'I'm OK on computers, but just OK if you know what I mean. And I have another business to run, so I was out a great deal during the first week or so the office was being organised. But you met my partner Bill.'

'I did. Seems a nice guy.'

He frowned and leant forward, a serious look on his face. 'Sorry to hear about the problem you're having with this troll upsetting your daughter. All these sorts of intrusions are worrying and I don't blame you for being concerned. So these emails have been sent with a Poland suffix?'

I nodded. 'That's right. The name of the sender is Eclipse. And prior to the dot.com the provider is given as hacking republic. One word.'

Rick stared into the distance thoughtfully. 'Hmm. The name of Eclipse suggests his host is masked, and may be almost impenetrable. Some hosts now are what they call "bulletproof", and not many people know how to infiltrate them.'

'So if they're impenetrable,' I said, my hopes spiralling out of control, 'is there nothing anyone can do about it?'

'I said "*almost* impenetrable." No system has a one-hundred percent guarantee of freedom from being penetrated. Look at the way Gary McKinnon invaded the Pentagon's security system. But out in this vast internet world there are thousands of blackhats who far outnumber the whitehats.'

He saw the confused look on my face and went on to explain: 'Blackhats are the criminal hackers. Whitehats are the ones who try to solve security issues. But it's a minefield out there, and often whitehats have to resort to illegal methods to resolve certain issues.'

'And presumably you're a whitehat, Rick, and might be able to reveal who it is that's doing this to my daughter.'

Rick frowned deeply and shook his head. 'I'm sorry, Freddie. I'm a programmer and web designer. I set up systems for companies such as yourself, designing bespoke operations for what suits a company best. But the sophisticated hacking is - well, it's beyond me. Most of these hackers are really bright geeks who have played computer games since they came out of the womb and know exactly what they're doing. It might seem odd to someone who doesn't have a huge knowledge of IT, but these kids learn their skills from fantasy games. Stuff like *Grand Theft Auto*. But I got my IT skills through more conventional methods and much later in life. So, by comparison, I'm limited in my knowledge.'

I wondered why I was wasting my time coming to see Nicky's so-called expert, and I felt irritated by the way she had raised my hopes.

'However,' Rick added with a smile, and patted my knee, 'I do know someone who knows someone who might be able to help. I'm not certain where he lives, but I know how and where you can contact him. His name's Trevor Reagan, but everyone knows him as "Trev the Rev".'

'Rev?' I questioned. 'Rev as in vicar?'

Rick grinned. 'Exactly. He was a genuine vicar years ago, in a suburb of Colchester. Which is where I know him from. Perhaps I should explain: I was a committed Christian. I still am.'

Following this statement, he looked at me as if he expected an objection of some sort.

'I'm not religious myself,' I said. 'But my motto is live and let live. So tell me about Trev the Rev.'

'Well, Trev was a really trendy vicar, a genuine person, kind hearted, generous, and heavily involved in supporting youngsters in the community. He ran the youth club at the church hall, and some of the youngsters smoked dope. While he didn't encourage it, he didn't try to ban it either, and considered it a better option than alcohol. And just to prove how non-judgemental he was, on a few occasions he joined in and smoked the odd joint, which was passed around in true fashion. To cut a long story short, an outraged parent shopped him, he lost his job and was sentenced to nine months in an open prison on the Isle of Sheppey in Kent.'

'Nine months prison!' I exclaimed, thinking of my occasional snorts of the white powder. 'Nine months, just for smoking a joint. How come?'

'It was a little more complicated. He actually bought some puff in bulk and sold it on to the kids.'

'Ah! So he was dealing.'

'Yes and no. He didn't make a profit. He did it to keep the kids off the streets, stop them from mixing with dealers and gravitating towards Class A drugs. But the judiciary didn't see it that way, so they gave him a custodial sentence.

Anyway, he served just over four months of his sentence. I intended to pay him a visit, but somehow the time flew by and I never got around to it. Though I did write to him while he was in prison, and he wrote back. He enjoyed writing, and I'm ashamed to admit he wrote far, far longer letters than the ones I sent him.'

'Well, he would have had more time on his hands,' I said. 'Sorry. Go on with the story.'

'In one of his letters, he told me about this interesting American chap he met in prison. The man had almost served his time, and intended staying on the island after his release. This man - I can't remember his name - was sentenced to eighteen months for computer fraud. Hacking. He was something of a genius, Trev said, as far as computers were concerned. So if he can't help you out, no one can.'

'So where can I get in touch with this American bloke?'

Rick tugged at his lower lip with a thumb and forefinger before answering. 'Ah, that's just it. It will involve a bit of legwork. You'll need to find him via Trevor.'

'And how do I find Trevor?'

Rick half rose, leant across the desk, grabbed a scrap of paper and pen, and scribbled down some instructions which he handed me.

'"The Oasis Hostel, Tottenham",' I read. 'Is that it?'

'Yes. Sorry I can't be more specific. That's as much as I know. I always intended going to visit him, but what with starting a family -'

'I know how it is,' I said, and got up. 'Well, thanks for your help, Rick.'

'I'll see you to the door. Sorry I couldn't be more help.'

'No, that's been very helpful.'

I must have sounded negative because when we got to the front door he put a hand on my shoulder and said, 'Perhaps I can really help, Freddie. Sarah's got loads of evening therapy sessions coming up, so once Matthew's asleep, maybe I'll try and improve my hacking skills. If I identify this evil troll, I'll be in touch.'

'Yeah, thanks.,' I said. 'Much appreciated.'

As I walked to the car, I felt a peculiar sense of unreality, as if I was passing through a portal into a strange and alien world of myth and sorcery.

Chapter 5

At two-thirty, on hearing voices from Nicky's office, I glanced at my watch. The small hand was on the two, the large hand on the six, as you would expect for a two-thirty appointment, but what I found extraordinary was that just at the very moment the potential client entered our premises, the second hand hit the twelve. It was punctual perfection, and I guessed this client would expect some exacting standards. Her name was Mrs Alice Egerton, and she had explained to Nicky on the phone that she sought solutions about her family - solutions the police had been unable to resolve.

I sat behind the desk, with Bill sitting to my right, and there was another chair placed to my left for Nicky to sit on and take notes, with the client's chair directly ahead of mine, so we would form a circle. Nicky opened the door for Mrs Egerton and Bill and I shot to our feet.

Her face was familiar. I had seen her before but I couldn't quite place where from. I guessed she was somewhere in her mid twenties. She had dark hair, cut short, and her skin was pale, smooth and unblemished. There was something androgynous about her. She was slightly boyish but at the same time attractively feminine. She wore trainers and a track suit, and her figure was healthily athletic, as if she worked out regularly, but her body seemed robust rather than undernourished. She carried a beige cardboard folder and a bottle of Evian water.

Nicky asked her if she would like a coffee before we started, but she shook her head and offered up the water bottle. We then shook hands, made the introductions, and sat down.

Staring at her with a certain amount of intensity, I thought I had better apologise and explain the awkwardness I felt. 'I'm sorry, Mrs Egerton, forgive my rudeness, but your face seems very familiar - '

She shrugged casually, as if she was used to virtual recognition.

'I expect you would be more familiar with my unmarried name. Bayne. Alice Bayne. Ring any bells?'

It shot through my brain like a speeded up film, running backwards over the years, through newspapers, televised press conferences and magazine articles. Now I knew exactly where I'd seen her before.

'About ten or twelve years ago,' I began, my voice sounding slightly hoarse, 'your family was killed somewhere in Scotland. They were murdered, I believe.'

She nodded and looked down at the folder in her lap. 'It happened eleven years last July. I was sixteen-years-old at the time, and was on a school trip, otherwise I'd have been shot as well, along with my mother, father and young brother. He was only ten.' As the emotional memory of this horrendous event gripped her, she struggled to control the tears that threatened to overwhelm her. When she recovered enough to continue, there was a tremor in her voice. 'I'm sure you're all aware, from the media coverage, what happened.'

'It looked like a professional killing, didn't it?' Bill said 'They reckon the killer was a motor cyclist, and it's a common method for a hitman to use.'

She looked at Bill and nodded. 'The police have seen thousands of CCTV hours, trying to find a motor bike that followed them for a distance. But any motor cyclists that did appear to follow Dad's car were eliminated from the enquiry. The Strathclyde police worked in conjunction with Surrey police and neither force could find anything from CCTV footage in either country. In any case, once they were north of Glasgow in the Loch Lomond area, there were no CCTV cameras.'

'From what I can remember reading about the case, Mrs Egerton, ' I said, 'there wasn't much forensic evidence.'

As she unscrewed the top of her Evian water, she said, 'Please call me Alice.'

I nodded, remembering how the media had always referred to her as Alice. She had become the celebrity victim, so it was always headlines using her first name in bold letters.

Alice took a small sip of water before acknowledging my observation. 'The only forensic evidence was the motor cycle tracks, the tyre marks which could have belonged to several makes and models of bikes.'

Nicky stopped writing to ask, 'What about eyewitnesses? Surely someone in nearby villages must have noticed a motor cyclist.'

'Yes, there were a few people who saw motorcyclists around that time, but as they weren't aware any crime had been committed, they didn't take much notice. Eyewitnesses described one particular biker who travelled north through Bridge of Orchy at an incredibly high speed. Police identified the man but later eliminated him from their enquiries.'

'I'm trying to remember the newspaper reports,' Bill said. 'Did the killer use an automatic weapon?'

'No, there were no ejected casings found at the scene. Ballistics identified the weapon used as a .38 Smith and Wesson.'

I knew what Bill was thinking. A professional hitman is unlikely to use an automatic weapon and risk it jamming. A revolver is far more reliable. And if a hitman ever uses an automatic, it's a case of life imitating art. They've watched too many movies.

'Didn't the Strathclyde police check your father's background going back years?' I queried.

'Yes. Dad was born and bred in Glasgow, and as a student he studied at Glasgow School of Art, so there was nothing untoward about that period of his life. He met and married his first wife, decided it was time he got a proper job and took a degree in electrical engineering. Then, after they divorced, he moved to south east England, and met Mum in the 1980s. I was born in 1985 and my brother was born six years later.'

As soon as she mentioned her brother, I saw the effort it took her to remain in control. The struggle was fleeting, and I guessed she had managed to quell the constant battle against the intensity of her emotions during the eleven years since her family's tragic death.

'So the police never found a motive,' I said, 'And I seem to remember the media describing your father as a successful businessman. Did they never find a connection with his business interests?'

'None at all.'

'I've forgotten what his company did.'

'He had his own software company which he ran from his offices in Guildford.'

'So he must have been something of a computer expert then.'

She nodded fervently. 'One of the very best. There was nothing he couldn't do on computers. Even when he got home, he would spend hours surfing the net. It used to drive Mum nuts. He was sometimes like a man possessed.'

A warning switch clicked in my head as she explained about her father's obsession with computers. It was an uncomfortable feeling I had, an instinctive fear of the unknown. I couldn't explain it, but it was like experiencing déjà vu in reverse, my instinct alerting me to some catastrophic event in the future. Or maybe, because of my daughter's harassment on the internet, I was being paranoid, seeing ghosts in those machines we've become so dependent on.

'What sort of software did your father's company design?' Nicky asked.

'In the early days, I believe, 'Alice began, looking up at the ceiling as she tried to recollect, 'it was small-scale things like designing your own stationery or educational stuff. But the lucrative material came much later when he put his art skills to good use and his company went into the games market.'

'So what happened to the company when he was so tragically killed?' I asked.

'It was disbanded. All the employees got redundancy payments. It was pretty much my father's company. Without him running it, I don't think it could have survived. Although Ed Warren seemed to think otherwise.'

'Who is Ed Warren?'

'He was manager at Dad's firm, and was about to be offered a directorship. But that never happened. He was paid off along with the other employees. I think he became very bitter about that. But as far as winding up the company was concerned, for a long time I was too upset to get involved and left it in the hands of our solicitors. But if my father's legacy is anything to go by, that company was making a small fortune. His estate was worth twenty million.'

'All of which you inherited?'

Her eyes flashed angrily, as if I had accused her of a crime.

'Seeing as I'm the next of kin,' she snapped, 'and the only living relative, yes I inherited Dad's fortune. But I saw that money as a curse, and would have given away every penny to live in poverty for the rest of my life if I could only have my family back. For years that fortune has remained untouched in the bank, and I've been living off the interest. But now all that is about to change.'

'In what way?'

'Because in eleven years the police have discovered nothing. I still want justice for my family and I'm willing to pay whatever it costs to find my family's murderers.' She looked at Bill. 'On the other hand, your website describes you as tough and resilient, and I had expected perhaps some younger, fitter men...'

Bill held up a hand in protest. 'OK, I'll admit we're not getting any younger, but we're still fit for a good few years yet. And experience must count for something. Wouldn't you agree, Freddie?'

I knew why Bill had bounced the ball back into my court and took up the pitch.

'I know what it's like to lose someone close, Alice. Forty-six years ago my father was being blackmailed by an East End gangster and ended up topping himself. Just by chance, nine months ago, I got the proof I needed. This gangster was in his late-sixties but was protected by a mob of thugs. Bill and I managed to snatch him one night and... well, put it this way: revenge is sweet. We may be getting on a bit, Alice, but we've survived many battles by using our loafs rather than just brawn; although, believe me, Bill may not look it, but there's no one tougher than him in a sticky situation.'

She threw Bill another look, examining him like a specimen, and then she smiled for the first time in our meeting. 'I don't doubt it, Bill. I don't think I'd tangle with you if we were on opposite sides.'

He grinned back at her, saying nothing. Nicky stopped scribbling to ask if she was interested in using our services.

'Just tell me one thing,' Alice replied. 'What makes you think you can get answers where the police failed?'

'You would be too young to remember,' I said. 'Years ago Granada Television made excellent documentaries called *World in Action*. Some of the episodes exposed miscarriages of justice. One of them was about the Birmingham Six who had been wrongly accused and sentenced for the Birmingham IRA bomb atrocity. The television company in the making of the film revealed the true culprit who planted the bomb. So if a few TV journalists can get it right, when the police get it wrong...And then there was the more recent case of Barri White who was wrongly convicted...'

She didn't let me finish and held up her hand. 'You don't have to convince me any further. I had already accepted your pitch when you told me about your father and the East End gangster. But if you take on this job, I want you to agree to certain conditions.'

'What sort of conditions?'

'While you're investigating the murder of my family, I would like exclusivity. You take on no other commission but mine.'

There was a deathly silence in the office while Bill and I considered this proposal, and from the corner of my eye I saw that Nicky had stopped writing.

'Naturally,' Alice continued, 'you will need to be recompensed for the loss of any other business. So what I propose is this: let me have your bank details, and by tomorrow morning I will have deposited half a million in your account. That should be sufficient to keep your business running for a good year at least, and pay for expenses you will incur during the investigation. It means that, unlike the police, you can be lavish when it comes to buying information.' Eyebrows raised, she looked enquiringly from me to Bill and back again to me. 'How does that sound? Of course, if you would like time to discuss it...'

I interrupted her with a laugh. 'To be honest, I think that's the best offer we're going to get all day. It's more than generous.' I stared at my partner. 'And I don't know about you, Bill, but - '

'Nothing to discuss, Freddie,' Bill interrupted. 'So count me in.'

I parted my arms, giving Alice a gesture of acceptance. 'That's agreed then.'

'However,' she said, 'Not entirely settled. There will be certain demands that I will make.'

I thought there might be, and I guessed that she wouldn't part with so much money without making certain stipulations. I knew she would expect us to perform like true professionals, provide her with some answers as to why her father had been targeted, and possibly arrive at some justice for her dead family. I nodded and waited to hear the conditions she planned to impose on the investigation.

'I will need progress reports at every step of the investigation, and I would like to become involved.'

'When you say "involved",' I started to say, but she waved it aside and interrupted me.

'There may be odd occasions when getting information out of someone is better coming from a female, which is when I may become involved. And having become frustrated by the police investigation, and their reluctance to give me clear updates, I would like to know exactly what goes on with your investigation.'

'I'm sure we have no problem with that, Alice,' I smiled. 'It will be good to have you on board, and - who knows? - you could discover things we might otherwise miss. But there is just one small thing I would like to know. Your name is Mrs Egerton now. Will paying our firm half a million for this investigation cause marital problems or has your husband readily agreed to it?'

She shook her head. 'Mark doesn't come into it. We've split up.'

She saw me frown, and added hastily. 'But don't worry: it was amicable. Mark won't make waves. We're still on good terms, and he's not short of money himself. The reason for our separation - and we will eventually get divorced - is because Mark is desperate to have children. Whereas I... I don't think I want to bring another family into this God-awful world. I may feel differently when I reach my thirties and my biological clock starts its countdown, but for now...' She broke off and stared at our office manager. 'What about you, Nicky? Do you have a family?'

'No, and I'm now past the deadline.'

'You certainly don't look it. And do you have any regrets about not having children?'

'None at all.'

'I know this might seem like an obvious question,' Bill said loudly, commanding everyone's attention. 'This Ed Warren, who was about to become a director in your father's company, did the police investigate him?'

'Of course they did. Although I never liked the man, he was cleared. There was no motive whatsoever. He didn't stand to gain from my father's death. Quite the opposite in fact: because when my father was killed, he lost out on becoming a director and he lost his job.'

She rose and placed her folder on the desk in front of me. 'All the details, as much as I know, are in that file. So if you need to speak with Ed Warren, or any of Dad's old employees, you can - but I don't think you'll learn anything new. Now if you'd like to give me your bank details, Freddie.'

I scribbled our sort code and account number on a scrap of paper and pushed it toward her. While she took a smart phone out of her handbag and keyed in some instructions, we all waited quietly, and I fancied I could her my partner's heart beating a tattoo as half a million pounds headed towards our account. Or perhaps it was my own heartbeat, as out expectations soared, and what had started out as a terrible day was improving by the minute. I knew I still had to investigate my daughter's internet tormentor, and although we had agreed to work exclusively for Alice, I figured the business with Olivia was a private and personal matter.

Before she left, I explained to our wealthy client that first of all Bill and I needed to do some brainstorming but we wouldn't waste much time in starting our investigation. We saw her out into the reception area, and were just about to shake hands with her when a motorcycle messenger barged in through the door. He was in the process of removing his helmet, as most messengers are instructed to do before entering premises, but he hadn't completed the action and I saw the effect this had on Alice, who tensed and stepped back on her right foot. I could understand her fear, because she had been badly affected by images of motorcycle hitmen. But there was more than just fear in her spontaneous reaction. She looked as if she was taking up a defensive position, balanced on the back foot, ready to move forward at lightning speed, her arms hard and taut, in a classic martial arts stance.

As soon as the messenger had removed his helmet, and she saw he was young and acne-scarred, she relaxed and stood normally. Then, while Nicky signed for the messenger's package, we shook hands with Alice, and she wished us the best of luck as she left the building.

There was a brief hiatus after she and the messenger had departed, and then the three of us grinned, whooped for joy and hugged each other. We couldn't believe our luck. Our first day as private investigators and we had landed the biggest catch of all. But as Bill pointed out:

'We've got our work cut out. After eleven long years of police investigation, what hope do we have?'

Not what I wanted to hear. My expectations took a sudden dive as I contemplated failure, while Nicky ignored the sudden switch from optimism to pessimism and opened the package.

'Never mind,' she said cheerfully, 'perhaps some of these little gadgets will help you to solve the crime.'

I wasn't sure if she intended irony or not, but the knowledge that we had absolutely nowhere to begin this investigation filled me with dread. We were amateurs up against the professionals, and the prospect didn't look good. Then Bill, intrigued by one of the gadgets, held it up and grinned.

'Look at this brilliant little gizmo. An electronic tracker you attach by magnet underneath a car.'

A sudden flash in my head. 'What did you say, mate?'

'I said this brilliant little gizmo...'

'Yes, I heard what you said. But just thinking out loud for a moment: suppose you wanted to follow someone from Surrey up to Scotland, and didn't want to get too close...'

'You could stick one of these on your target's car,' Bill said, completing my sentence. 'But our client said the police viewed thousands of hours of CCTV looking for motorcycles, except there was no CCTV up in them there hills. But presumably they would have looked for motorbikes coming back down south towards Glasgow about the time it would have taken a motorcyclist to travel that distance.'

'Yes, but supposing he wasn't on a motorbike,' I surmised. 'Suppose he transported the bike in another vehicle - a van, for instance. An old mate of mine used to compete in motocross events, and they would always transport their bikes either on a trailer or in a van, which could easily be unloaded down a ramp. Yes, that has to be what happened.' I picked up the little black box tracker and examined it. 'There can't be many companies in the UK that market this type of surveillance equipment. So Alice has given us the file, which will have the time and date of the murders. What we need to do is find out who bought this sort of equipment back then. And it uses GPS, the same as a satnav, so someone would have to be registered with a company.'

Bill scratched his chin thoughtfully. 'You know, even if we find out who the killer is, it doesn't tell us who issued the orders. There's got to be a reason; a motive. Her father either did something illegal, or was involved in some sort of enterprise that could compromise a lot of dangerous people.'

Nicky raised her hand like a schoolgirl. 'Can I make a suggestion? Why not interview this Ed Warren chap? You might get to learn something about the father from him.'

'Good idea, Nicky,' I agreed. 'We'll put both those things top of our list. We might find it difficult getting the information about the tracker by telephone, so we'll make a point of calling in person.'

'Yes, that way we can offer them an inducement to part with the information,' Bill said. 'Let's hope we get lucky. For all we know, the killer might have used the same company as we're using to buy this equipment. And as we happen to be good customers, we might get the info gratis.'

'Not that we need worry our pretty little heads about that,' I replied. 'By this time tomorrow we'll be rolling in it.'

I spotted a glint in Bill's eye, and he actually parodied Fagin by rubbing his hands together. I chuckled, then asked Nicky to get the names and addresses of all the electronic surveillance equipment suppliers, and to try and make an appointment for us to meet the ex-manager of the software company, while Bill and I went into the office to study the information in the file she had given us.

We agreed that we would start our investigation first thing the next day. I still hadn't forgotten that I needed to sort out the disturbing internet assault on my daughter's computer, and I intended to spend the evening searching for a trendy pot-smoking ex-vicar known as Trev the Rev.

Chapter 6

Before going to North London in search of the defrocked vicar, I phoned Michelle and she told me Jackie would be back for dinner, so I stopped off on the way home and picked up a dinner for four at an Indian takeaway.

Olivia felt better about the internet situation, calmer now she had spent the day with Michelle. In the afternoon, after Michelle had successfully negotiated better rates at a new venue for her dance school, they visited Olivia's comprehensive to explain about the internet problems. The school agreed to have a word with her friends the next day, and bring them in to the office during a break, so that Olivia could show them the emails and the chat room threats.

Over dinner I told them about the ex-vicar I had to find in Tottenham, and then explained about the American on the Isle of Sheppey, someone I could hopefully meet tomorrow night to see if he could help us to eliminate the troll. When they asked me if I'd had a good first day at work and about my potential clients, first I told them about the public school oaf, and they approved of the way I'd kicked him into touch. Then, when I began to describe our next client, I realised I had to play it down, telling them it was a profitable assignment but merely involved some tedious enquiries we needed to make about a software company. I knew if I told them the whole truth, they would worry about the risks it involved in tracking down a ruthless killer.

Not long after dinner I set off for Tottenham, hoping to find Trev the Rev's homeless shelter without much difficulty. I thought my best bet was to enquire at the police station, and sure enough the uniformed copper at the desk knew where it was and gave me directions on how to find it. Just as I was getting back in the car, my mobile rang. It was an unknown number and it turned out to be Rick, our computer expert. I made a mental note to transfer his number into my phonebook once the call ended.

'Freddie!' he yelled, sounding breathless with excitement. 'I decided I would make this troll of your daughter's my mission this evening and, guess what? I seem to be getting somewhere. I can't spend any more time on it tonight but I'll see what I can do tomorrow and hopefully come up with some answers for you.'

'That's great, Rick,' I told him. 'But when we know who it is, what do we do?'

'We can expose the cheeky sod. It sounds like he's gone too far in harassing your daughter, and he's making criminal threats. Once I have the info, we'll have him.'

'That's fantastic, Rick. If you come up with anything tomorrow, give me a bell. It might save me a trip to the Isle of Sheppey.'

'I can't guarantee anything though, Freddie.'

'No problem. I'm in Tottenham right now, and just about to find Trev the Rev to get this American's address.'

'Give Trevor my regards, will you?'

'Will do,' I promised, and cut the call.

***

The street the homeless shelter was in was gloomy and forbidding, with semi-detached council houses on one side, some boarded up, and many with discarded junk in the front gardens, or paved over to make room for cars and motor bikes.

Along the other side of the street was a row of small shops, including a drab-looking hairdresser's, a squat Asian-run general store, its windows protected by metal shutters, and a Chinese takeaway called Oriental Palace, a name that was ironically inappropriate seeing as no attempt had been made to decorate the premises. The only thing about it that looked pristine was the flashing fruit machine inside the waiting area. At the end of the row of shops was a derelict patch of land with a part-demolished building on it that looked is if it might have been a small public library at one time. Beyond this was the homeless shelter, which may once have been a community centre.

I pulled up outside, careful to avoid a pile of broken glass, although I heard a skeleton rattle and clank as I flattened some discarded beer cans. When I got out of the car I realised the Jag looked ostentatious, which stood out in this street like a doner kebab in a five star Michelin restaurant. And just to prove a point, three youngsters, two white and one black, materialised from the gloom and stood in front of me, barring my way. They couldn't have been more than nine or ten years old, swaggering with the affected pimp-roll of their gangster idols.

'Couple of quid to look after your car, mister,' one of the white kids said, a statement rather than a question, giving me little choice other than to acquiesce in this protection racket. There wasn't a shred of doubt in my mind that if I didn't comply, when I returned to my Jag there would be a nice juicy scratch across the paintwork. I know I shouldn't have subscribed to this racket, encouraging youngsters to live unscrupulous lives, but I thought about the quarter of a million heading for our business account, and I really didn't want my car damaged, so I coughed up. But they didn't look like such bad kids, and I had to admit this little scheme of theirs was enterprising. If Maggie Thatcher had still been alive she'd have been proud of them.

I took a two-pound coin out of my trouser pocket and handed it to the one who'd made the demand. 'If you do a good job and protect my car,' I said, 'there'll be another two quid for you when I get back. I shouldn't be more than ten minutes.'

The kid's eyes lit up. 'Yeah, thanks, mister. See you later then.'

I made my way along the front path towards the hostel door which was inside a porch under a triangular slate roof. The building was grey and pebble-dashed, and to the left of the door there was a large board on which was painted in bold red the name OASIS SHELTER, and underneath in black italic lettering were the usual biblical words of wisdom, "*Jesus Christ the same yesterday, and today, and for ever*".

I stepped inside the porch and saw there was a speakerphone entry with a push button. I pressed the bell and waited, and then a female voice asked brightly, 'Who is it?'

'I'm looking for Trevor Reagan,' I said.

'Are you looking for a bed for the night?'

'No, I just want to speak to Trevor.'

'Do you know him?'

'We have a mutual acquaintance.'

'Who's that?'

I was becoming irritated by her questions. 'A man called Ricky Lee Bishop. Just tell Trevor I'm a friend of his and I wish to speak with him, will you?'

There was a pause while I thought she might be relaying this message to the man himself. Then she said, 'He'll be with you in just a minute.'

Rick's name must have carried weight because after a moment the door opened wide and a tall, thin man with dark designer stubble and receding hair greeted me with an outstretched hand. He was in his mid-thirties and wore a voluminous bright red T-shirt which came to halfway down his thighs, with some sort of strange logo on it, what looked like a silhouette of zombies on the march. He wore this underneath a blue bomber jacket in a shiny material, and from his appearance I understood why his young parishioners had nicknamed him Trev the Rev.

'So you're a friend of Ricky Lee?' he queried.

I nodded as we shook hands. 'Actually, I've only just met him. He designed the website for our business. He sends his regards, by the way.'

'Thank you. But why did he put you in touch with me?'

'He told me you could help with some problems I've been having with an internet troll.'

He frowned and ran a hand over his stubble. 'I don't understand. Ricky Lee knows much more about computers than I do.'

'He said you know an American chap on the Isle of Sheppey who might be able to help.'

His eyes narrowed, perhaps not wanting to be reminded of his disgraced past.

'It's my daughter,' I added quickly, hoping to reel him in with the account of her distress. 'She's scared of someone who's sending her frightening and disgusting messages. And I believe the American guy is a brilliant hacker who might be able to discover who's doing this to my girl.'

43

His eyes softened, and his teeth tugged at his bottom lip, displaying genuine concern and sympathy. Then he stood aside and pulled the door a little wider. 'You'd better come in. We'll go into the office and see what we can sort out.'

As I entered I wavered slightly, unsettled by the smell, a cocktail of sweat, urine and school dinners. Noticing my reaction, Trevor patted me on the shoulder as he shut the door.

'I suppose I'm used to the smell. I know how disconcerting it can be on a first visit.'

I nodded and took in the gloomy surroundings. The walls of the building looked solid, painted beige from ceiling to floor, and were covered in posters giving information about everything from how to contact the Samaritans and where to get advice if you had an alcohol problem, although I didn't think many of the floating population using this hostel would bother with advice on alcoholism. Too late for that.

On a table next to a giant radiator, were piles of leaflets, and two crumpled Special Brew cans. Ahead of me was a door that was slightly ajar, and from this room came shuffling, coughing and wheezing noises, with an occasional gruff voice, unintelligible and loud.

'This way,' Trevor said, and I followed him through another door marked Private. This was his office, and I've never seen anywhere so cluttered with paperwork. Stacks of folders and files lay in untidy piles taking up a great deal of floor space, and sitting behind a desk, working on a computer keyboard that looked sticky with grime, was a young girl with hennaed hair, large lime-green plastic earrings, and a multi-coloured sweater. Trevor introduced her as Marie and she acknowledged me with a nod and brief 'Hi!' before focusing on the computer monitor again, squinting closely at the screen as if she was short-sighted.

Trevor gestured for me to sit in a folding, black metal chair, while he perched on the edge of the desk, looking down on me. There wasn't another chair in the tiny office, so I knew this was not a classic domination technique.

'So,' he began, 'your daughter's having trouble on the internet.'

'That's right. Some sick bastard's been hounding her, and the last message that really freaked her out said he admired Josef

Fritzl, the man who locked his daughter in a cellar for twenty-four years, the poor girl who became an unwilling sex object for her father. This pervert who's been pestering my daughter said he'd like to do the same to her.'

Trevor shivered and shook his head as he spoke. 'Another hateful monster. No wonder you're worried.'

His assistant stopped tapping the keyboard to comment, 'Women haters. That's what they are. Because they fear women, they hate them and want to destroy them, even if it's only with words.'

'I think you're right,' I agreed. 'It all boils down to feelings of insecurity. But if I find out who this pervert is who's targeted my daughter, he'll really have something to feel insecure about.'

'The trouble is,' Trevor said, 'these trolls can be anywhere in the world; close by or hundreds of miles away.'

'The email address of this one gives the country as Poland, but I'm told that need not necessarily be the case.'

'That's right. I believe a group of computers can share an IP address and be anywhere in the world, but appear to be in another area. I think they're called proxy servers. Of course, I don't know that much about them, but...' He stopped and shrugged.

'But you know a man who does,' I concluded.

'Which is why you're here.' He got up and walked to the other side of the desk, slid open the top drawer, took out an address book, leant over the desk, and scribbled on a sheet of A4 paper. As he came over and handed it to me, he said, 'His name's Brad Shapiro I'm sorry, but I don't have his phone number; just his address.'

'How will I know he's at home?'

'You won't. But he doesn't usually go very far. His whole life is computing.'

'Another geek,' I said.

Trevor smiled. 'Yes but this one's the best there is. He's got a brain ten times bigger than anyone else.'

I returned his smile. 'And does he have an ego to match?'

'Haven't they all. Although when I spent time with him in jail, he was helpful and charming.'

I looked toward his assistant to observe her reaction to the jail disclosure, but she carried on typing and didn't appear to be listening.

'It's all right,' he smiled. 'Marie knows about my blunder. And although I'm no longer a part of the church - I haven't even been in one since I went inside - I think I can still contribute something to society. Hence our small homeless shelter, which relies on the goodwill of others - small donations here and there.'

Not only did I not doubt his sincerity, I didn't doubt he was hinting for a contribution as well. As I stuffed Brad Shapiro's address into my pocket, I took my wallet out and gave him three twenty pound notes.

'Thank you,' he said. 'That's most generous, and it'll go a long way to feed some of our unfortunates. Can you believe some of them may not have eaten anything for three or four days when they come in here? So we make sure they get a hot meal. We have a kitchen out the back.'

I thanked him for the American's address, said goodbye to his assistant, and then he walked me to the front door and we shook hands.

'Good luck,' he said solemnly. 'I hope Brad's able to solve the problem. If anyone can, he can. And when you see Ricky again, please give him my very best wishes.'

When I got to my car, the kids who were supposed to be protecting it had disappeared. I had been away less than ten minutes and they couldn't be bothered to wait that long for the other two pounds. So much for enterprise. Maggie would have been deeply disappointed.

Chapter 7

As soon as we arrived at the office Nicky presented us with a list of companies in the south east who supplied electronic surveillance equipment, including the address of the company we had purchased our equipment from. Most of the security equipment firms didn't deal with the sort of spy stuff we were searching for, so we were left with a list of four just outside the London area. But it would still take us quite a bit of time, as the company from where we got our equipment was just off the M4 near Reading, another two were just off the M1, near Luton and Hemel Hempstead respectively, with the fourth just off the M25 near Woking. Of course, the sensible thing would have been to split the workload, visiting two firms each. Apart from the fact we hadn't yet organised a car for Bill, we decided it would be better if we worked together to begin with, especially as we were both new to this game and we could bounce ideas off each other during the journeys.

As we drove along the M4 to our first port of call, Bill was quiet and thoughtful and I asked him if anything was wrong.

'I don't know, mate,' he replied. 'I just hope we're not going on a wild goose chase. This killer might be based in Scotland. I mean, there's plenty of scum in Glasgow who'd do a hit for a few quid. So if the killer used an electronic tracker, it could have been purchased north of the border. And even if it is someone who bought the tracker down south, he ain't going to purchase it in his own name, is he?'

'But we know the Bayne family stayed the night at a hotel near Carlisle to break the journey. If they were followed from the south, maybe the killer also stayed at the hotel. He would have needed to register, using a false name and address.'

'Which gets us nowhere.'

I tried to sound optimistic, even though I didn't feel it. 'Listen, Bill, at least it's a start. Even a false name is something to go on, as it could lead who knows where.'

'Convince me.'

'The thing that puzzles me is why the police never followed up on the Bayne's overnight stop to get the guest list from the hotel. There was nothing in Alice's file about that.'

'They probably got too hung up on the motorcycle angle. Bit like the Yorkshire Ripper case when they focused their enquiries on a Geordie because of the accent on the hoax tape.'

'Yeah, all those man hours wasted. Think what it must have cost Strathclyde police in time and effort to search the CCTV for motorcycles.'

Bill exhaled noisily, displaying frustration. 'But we're only guessing about the killer using a van and tracker. We have yet to get any evidence. And as it happened eleven years ago - '

'Listen,' I said. 'She's paid half a million into our bank, so we'll do our best to come up with some answers. More than that she cannot expect.'

'Call me old fashioned, Freddie, but I'd expect a lot more for that sort of money.'

'Cheer up, mate. Here's the turn off. We're nearly there.'

***

At the firm near Reading we drew a blank. As we were good customers, having spent over two grand with them on equipment, they were helpful and we didn't have to drop them a backhander for information. It took them a while to scroll back eleven years, but in this instance, thank God for computers. But all they could tell us was that apart from a contract with Thames Valley Police for some vehicle trackers, and two large organisations who wanted to check the legitimate mileage of their sales reps, there was not a single tracker sold to an individual around that time.

The outcome was the same at the next two firms. No individual trackers sold, except for one of the companies selling just two units, but they were sold to a very reliable and long-established private enquiry agency in central London. This left us with the company in Woking, which we had already noted was not far from Guildford where Tim Bayne's firm was located, and his house was equidistant between the two towns.

The firm, Tech-Intelligence, was a unit in the centre of a small industrial estate on the outskirts of Woking. Like most of these technical surveillance firms, most of their business was mail order, and in front of their unit stood a small van, its back doors open, displaying piles of boxes, clearly being loaded for deliveries. We parked in the road, walked up the slight incline and parking space, and entered their reception area, which wasn't dissimilar to the other three we had visited. I pressed the bell on the counter and we thumbed through their catalogues while we waited.

'So what we gonna do about next year?' Bill said.

I threw him an enquiring look and waited for him to elaborate.

'There'll be a change in the law. Private investigator's will have to be licensed. How the hell will we get accreditation for our company?'

I banged the counter lightly with my fist, demonstrating a positive attitude. 'If we solve this case - bearing in mind that we could succeed where the police have failed - we'll be flavour of the month. It'll open doors for us.'

'And if we don't solve the case?'

I was about to give him my answer, but we were interrupted by a door behind the counter opening and a middle-aged man slithered across the floor to greet us. I'm not exaggerating when I say slithered, because the man had a shifty demeanour, and sidled from door to counter like a reptile. I almost expected him to hiss when he spoke.

'Yes, what can I do for you?'

He was middle-aged, of medium height, and wore a thick tweed jacket with striking checks, a striped shirt and tie, resulting in a combination of clashing patterns and colours, as if this display of sartorial hideousness was a deliberate attempt at irony. If that wasn't enough, it was difficult to take my eyes off his balding head, thinly disguised with the worst comb-over I've ever seen, greasy strands of dark hair plastered in strips onto his head, fooling no one but himself.

I didn't dare look at Bill, otherwise we might have lost it completely.

Like the other surveillance firms we had visited earlier, I put our business card on the counter in front of him. 'I regret we're not here to purchase any equipment,' I said. 'But we'd like some information if possible.'

He sniffed loudly. 'What about?'

'About a product you may or may not have sold about eleven years ago.'

'Sorry. No can do.'

'Oh? And why's that?'

'We don't give out information about our customers.'

'Perhaps I could have a word with the manager then.'

He sniggered and pointed at the window behind me. 'See that van just leaving - whoops! - there it goes round the corner.' He giggled again, enjoying some sort of private joke. 'That van contains our manager, a personal delivery for an important customer. So you've just missed him.'

I restrained my impulse to grab the little squirt around the throat, and gave him a strained smile as I took my wallet out. His eyes lit up and he glanced over his shoulder furtively, perhaps afraid of another employee entering to queer his pitch.

Bill leant forward and dropped his voice to a conspiratorial whisper. 'We can pay for this information. Providing, of course, the information we require is available. We are talking eleven years ago.'

'That's not a problem. If we sold something, and you can give me the rough idea of the date, I can look it up. So how much are you prepared to offer for this obviously important information?'

I took out three twenties and put them on the counter. He stared at me and ran a reptilian tongue over his thin lips.

'I think you can do better than that. I'm taking a huge risk, and passing on confidential information could get me into serious trouble. So that's got to be worth at least a hundred.'

I looked him in the eye, letting him know what I thought of him before I took out another two twenties and placed them on top of the other three. As he went to pick them up, I slammed a hand over them.

'Information first.'

'But what if I don't have the information you require? After going to all the trouble of searching our records...'

'You'll still get your money,' I interrupted him. 'We just want to know if you sold a car tracking device to an individual rather than a company, sometime around July in two-thousand and two.'

He frowned deeply and stared into the distance. 'I know it's a long time ago, but I seem to remember - hang on a second. I'll look it up to make sure.'

He glanced at the door, probably hoping he wasn't going to be disturbed, then slithered hurriedly to the other end of the counter and began clicking a computer keyboard while staring intently at the monitor. After a nail-biting five minutes, with the tension and excitement growing inside me, I watched as he scribbled something on a scrap of paper.

'Yes, I can vaguely remember this man. I was the one who sold him the tracker. And I have his name and address here.'

Feet scuffing the floor, he sidled back along the counter and handed me the paper. On it was written the name: "Peter Chapmays,. 9 Coach Road, London SE1 2XT."

Peering over my shoulder, Bill said, 'We made enquiries at some other surveillance equipment firms, and they said they often sell to customers who probably give false names and addresses.

The salesman shrugged. 'Not a lot we can do about that, is there?'

'Did he pay cash?'

'I think he did, yes.'

'I don't suppose you can remember what this man looked like.'

'Not really. I seem to think he was fairly ordinary-looking. Except - '

I released my hold on the money and pushed it towards him. 'Except what? What can you remember?'

'Well, I happened to be outside, loading one of our vehicles. He drove up in a van, parked alongside it and came into the office. As I was about to follow, I happened to glance inside his van and I saw a motorbike in the back. At first I thought he might be some sort of racer - scrambling or motocross. But I think it was a road bike.'

I exchanged a look with Bill and saw the faint glimmer of a smile.

'I think that's why I remembered him so clearly,' the gadget salesman went on as he pocketed the money, 'because I thought it was unusual to transport a motorbike, when he could so easily have driven it to pick up the electronic tracker in half the time. Our trackers are only this big.' He held his hands together, indicating a space between his fingers of three or four inches. 'It could easily have fitted into his pocket.'

I saw him tap his own pocket, the one with the money in it, and his lips pursed into a prissy little smile. Much as I disliked the man, I had to admit the information he'd given us was good. And if his memory was that reliable going back eleven years -

'Hang on to my business card,' I told him. 'And if you should remember anything else about this customer, give us a bell.'

I was about to turn away when I spotted a crafty glint in his eye.

'And would this information be worth another little tickle?'

I knew then that he'd probably feed me any old codswallop just to get his greedy little mitts on the necessary. So I said before we exited, 'I was hoping you might provide any supplementary information as compensation for my generosity.'

I heard him snigger just before I closed the door. Back in the car, I asked Bill what he thought as I tapped in to the internet on my smart phone.

'Hmm. Suppose I didn't want to give away my identity,' he reflected, 'I'd call myself Brown, Smith or Jones. If it is the man who killed the Bayne family, why would he pick such an unusual name, drawing attention to himself?'

'Maybe,' I replied, 'it's because he's got a false ID which looks official. A passport and bona fide-looking documents in that name.'

'An identity stolen from someone else perhaps.'

'Could be,' I said, as I got the UK Streetmap up on the screen, then tapped in Coach Road and the postcode.

'Have you found it?' Bill asked.

'There's no such address.'

'I could have told you that without looking.'

I sighed. 'But we still needed to check it out. Now let's go and have a word with this Ed Warren.'

Chapter 8

Next stop was Kingston-upon-Thames. By now it was gone half-two and we were feeling hungry and thirsty. We decided we could grab something after we'd spoken to Ed Warren, especially as Nicky had made the appointment to see him at three and it would take us about thirty minutes to get to his place.

Halfway up Kingston Hill we turned off into Park Road, and took the third street on the left, and his street was on the right, an area of small Edwardian terrace houses, most of them neat with a modest appearance of comfort and faded elegance, stained glass above the doors, with many houses proudly showing-off abundant hanging baskets. The sort of houses which could have been bought for a song back in the sixties, and would now fetch three-hundred thousand - and the rest.

If the street seemed a trifle overdone in it's ostentatious display of floral symbols of affluence, there was no such flamboyance at Warren's house, which was the most rundown in the street. The windows needed cleaning and, instead of curtains in the front room, there was a venetian blind, jammed at an oblique angle, as though someone had attempted to open it hurriedly and then abandoned the attempt. The ill-chosen brown paint on the front door, chipped and curling at the edges, resembled potato peelings, and a green wheelie bin, crammed to bursting with old newspapers and garbage wrapped in plastic supermarket bags, stood slipshod in the small front garden, highlighting the building's aura of neglect, a sneering carbuncle in an otherwise immaculate street.

I rang the front doorbell and we waited, listening for the sounds of footsteps. We heard a female voice shouting something unintelligible, followed by a man yelling, 'All right! I'm going! I'm going!'

After a few minutes the door was thrown open. While the neglect of the building had prepared us for perhaps a single man, too busy and industrious to lavish attention on domestic matters and his property, we were unprepared for what greeted us.

'You must be the private detectives,' he slurred and grinned. 'Super sleuths. I hope you're not packing a rod.' He giggled at his own wit.

I was shocked to find the man whose newspaper photograph I'd seen in Alice's file had changed drastically. Although the picture was probably taken ten or more years ago, this overweight man, with a bulbous nose, red-rimmed eyes, and badly in need of a shave, was nothing like the businessman and manager of the software company.

'Mr Warren?' I enquired, to make sure it was him.

'Yes, but please call me Ed. I'm sorry, I've forgotten your names.'

'I'm Freddie Weston and this is my colleague Bill Turner.'

He didn't offer his hand, but stood aside and gestured along the hall. As we walked inside, squeezing past his bulk, I caught a stale sweet smell of liquor on his breath, and I wondered how far gone he was. He pointed to the door on the right.

'Go into the front room. Bit crowded in there but it'll have to do. Though I don't see what else I can tell you about Delphic Digital, other than what a stupid fucking name it is for a software company.'

We entered his living room which was a tip. Brown padded envelopes lay in heaps beneath the window, stacks of audio CDs were strewn across the floor, and cardboard boxes were piled high along one wall. The only furniture in the room was a desk with a laptop and printer, a two-seater mock-leather sofa with frayed arms, and an upright chair with a high back.

I sat on the settee next to Bill, and Ed Warren sat in the upright chair facing us. 'As you can see,' he said, waving an uncoordinated arm about, 'this is my office. I run our business from here. When I got my redundancy payment from Bayne's software company, I bought this small existing business. Mail order. Music CDs for the specialist market. Medieval chants, madrigals, harpsichords - that sort of thing. Very esoteric.'

'D'you sell much of it?' Bill asked politely.

Warren shrugged and was about to answer when a woman with enormous sagging breasts lurched through the open door. 'Do we fuck!' she slurred, and almost tripped over a box of CDs, which she attempted to kick, missed and staggered sideways, grabbing the wall for support. Her waistline was a revoltingly mushy spare tyre which wobbled from the effort it took her to keep from falling over.

'Angela!' Warren admonished, but with a laugh. 'Get back in your cage. You know you're not allowed in here when we have visitors.'

'Well fuck you!'

He laughed again, as if this was all part of a well-rehearsed double-act. 'Such repartee. You've been reading Oscar Wilde again, haven't you?'

She ignored him and stared at Bill and me. 'So sorry.' *It came a out as show shorry.* 'I didn't know we had guests.'

'I told you, Angela,' Warren yelled. 'How many more times? They've come to ask me about the Delphic company.'

'Ask about what?'

'The company I used to work for.'

'Until the bastards sacked you.'

'They didn't sack me. I was made redundant when the company disbanded.'

He might have saved his breath. She was too far gone to comprehend rational explanations. Eyes glassy, she leaned towards Bill and me, and made a drinking gesture.

'Would you lie-kadrink?'

We shook our heads in unison. 'I've got a long drive,' I explained. 'And we're both working really. That's very kind of you but - no thanks.'

'Oh, well suit yourselves.'

She staggered out of the room and I let my breath out gently, relieved we could now question Warren on his own. We heard her stumbling along the hall, and Warren called out, 'Don't open another bottle. It's too early yet.' A door slammed, and then

Warren explained apologetically, 'It's Angela's birthday, so we thought we'd celebrate. We're not usually like this.'

And there really is a Gotham City.

'I know you probably explained all this to the police in two-thousand and two,' I said, 'but was there anything going on in Bayne's company that made you suspicious? Something dodgy going on?'

A rasping sound as Warren scratched his unshaven chin before answering. 'Nothing that would make you think someone would want to kill him.'

'But anything else suspicious? Or maybe suspicious is too strong a word. Something minor? Something going on that wasn't quite kosher?'

He thought for a bit. Then: 'Well, the company seemed to be making far more money than it deserved. It's hard to explain. I knew we were turning over millions each year, but the firm was quite small and didn't employ that many staff.'

'Is it possible,' Bill said, 'that he could have been making his money criminally, and using the software company to launder the proceeds?'

Warren smirked, indicating we were stating the obvious. 'Don't you think the police went into all that at the time? They had to find a good fucking motive for his death and they never could. The only thing I could think of were the games he created.'

'Games?' I questioned.

'Yes, I often wondered if he created games which he sold to other companies.'

'But why would he do that?'

'So that he could retain the royalties personally, and it wouldn't have to go through the company.'

'But that doesn't make any sense. If he received one-hundred per cent royalties, he'd be taxed on the full amount; whereas if he put it through the company - '

Warren mimed tipping a hat low over his eyes. 'Well, you're the private eyes, you tell me. And the police asked all these sorts of questions back then. If you ask me, the longer this goes on, the less likely anyone is of finding a motive.' He suddenly tapped the side of his nose and smirked. 'And maybe it wasn't him who was the target. Maybe it was his wife. Or the son.'

'What!' Bill exclaimed. 'Why would a killer target a ten-year-old kid?'

Warren snorted. 'Ah hah! Maybe he was going to be the next Harry Potter, and the old one paid to have him eliminated.'

He laughed loudly, a laugh that rumbled revoltingly with phlegm. I thought it was time we left, and I was just about to stand up when Warren said, 'Seriously though, I found it odd why the police didn't follow up on Tim's mysterious visitor just a week or so before he died.'

My ears pricked up and I leant forward on the edge of my seat. 'Any idea who this might have been, Ed?'

'Not a clue. And no one else in the firm did either. Maybe Tim's life was being threatened and this visitor was a cop or a detective. If he was a cop, he must have been an important one, because I watched him leave, sitting in the back seat of a Mercedes like Lord Muck.'

'Nothing unusual in that, is there?' Bill commented. 'A certain rank of detective would almost certainly be driven by a subordinate.'

Warren shook his head slowly. 'Ah-ah. This was different. I noticed his driver was more of a chauffeur than a detective. Wearing something dark and navy. More like the sort of driver who runs a Scotland Yard commissioner about.'

'So after the murders,' I said, 'when the police came to question you, did they ask about this visitor?'

'Yes, and I gave them as much information as I could. Even told them about him looking like a high-ranking police officer.'

'And what did they say to that?

'Nothing. They just made a note of everything I said, and sort of glossed over it. Most of their questions concerned the running of the company, trying to find out if any of the staff knew of anything untoward going on. But nobody did.

Whoever this unknown visitor was, the police knew about it, because he came back with them. I can't be absolutely certain, but as they were leaving, I went to my office window, which looked out over the car park, and I saw the Merc parked near the entrance, a long way from the building. It was too far away to see who was inside it. But the detective chief inspector who questioned me, instead of getting into the car he arrived in with his colleague, walked over to the Merc and climbed into the back seat.'

'Didn't this strike you as peculiar?'

'Not really. Because, like I said, I thought the mysterious visitor was a copper come about Tim receiving death threats. If it *was* him who returned - and I can't really be sure - I thought maybe he was a senior officer who wanted an update from his colleagues.'

'It's still very odd.'

'If you want answers, try the paranormal,' Warren sniggered, rolling his hands palms down over an imaginary ball.

'Psychic help,' Bill said sniffily. 'As reliable as a punctured condom.'

Warren shrugged hugely. 'Well, there you are. Heaven and earth, Horatio, and all that.'

I was just about to rise prior to leaving, but there was one more thing I needed to know. 'Did the media ever mention this mysterious visitor?'

Warren gazed rheumy-eyed into the distance before answering. 'Now you come to mention it, I don't think they did. Not the papers or TV, or any of the press conferences the police gave.'

So that was why there was nothing about it in the file Alice had given us. She probably had no knowledge of the visitor, especially if the police had kept it to themselves. Ed Warren and some of the other staff who worked at the software company would have been the only ones to have known. And once they told the police about it, they wouldn't have seen any reason to mention it again. But I decided to probe a little further.

'Didn't it strike you as odd, this strange visitor, being airbrushed out of the picture following the murders?'

'I never gave it much thought. What with worrying about redundancy and all that. I hated the idea of starting over, even though I was only thirty-two.'

I tried not to catch flies with my mouth. Now only forty three, and he didn't look a day under sixty. I exchanged a look with Bill, and we both knew the meeting was well and truly over. There was nothing more to be gained by talking to Ed Warren. It was time to leave and let him get back to hitting the bottle.

Chapter 9

After we left Ed Warren's house we found a pub called the Albert Arms on Kingston Hill where we both had a pint of Young's Special and ordered brie and bacon sandwiches. While we waited for the food to arrive, I phoned the office and asked Nicky to get a list of the games produced by Delphic Digital, then to telephone some games retailers to find out how well they sold. I told her to expect us back in the office, if we didn't hit any major traffic snarl-ups, around four-thirty.

Feeling refreshed after our beer and sandwiches, we had another brainstorming session in the car. We both agreed in our suspicions that Bayne was involved in something criminal, but why a high-ranking police officer visited him prior to the murder was anyone's guess. We kept asking ourselves the same damned questions, going round in circles and getting nowhere fast. The build up of traffic when we came off Westway and drove through Camden Town, meant we were getting somewhere - but slowly. We got back to the office at quarter-to-five.

I gave Nicky a brief rundown on the information we'd gleaned so far, then asked her about the games. She read off a list of names, bizarre-sounding futuristic geek games, none of which meant anything to a couple of dinosaurs like Bill and me.

'Most of these games got excellent reviews,' she said. 'But - ' She paused and tapped the top of her notebook with her pen, and looked at us with a twinkle in her eye, indulging in creating a dramatic effect.

'But what?' I said impatiently.

'None of them sold very well. Most of the stores stopped stocking them, and much of the stock they did have they got rid of, selling them at a loss. Even online sales at Amazon were poor.'

'Thanks, Nicky.' Bill said. 'At least that tells us he made his fortune in another way. And one that wasn't legit, which is probably why he wound up dead, with his wife and son as collateral damage.'

Nicky, her pen gripped tightly in anger, said, 'How could anyone cold-bloodedly kill two innocent...' She stopped as she thought about it and I saw her shiver.

'It's worse for the living,' I said. 'Never able to get over... or come to terms with it. It's the cruellest blow, left without an answer. Always left wondering why.'

Bill, perhaps thinking I'd been dragged back to my father's suicide, patted my shoulder. 'Cheer up, Freddie. If we can get some answers for our client, it might ease her pain.'

I forced a grin, shaking off our morbid thoughts, and looked at Nicky. 'You went to drama school and became an actress for a while. How's your Scottish accent?'

She frowned, wondering where this was leading. 'I think it's OK. Why?'

'In the file Alice gave us, there's the name of the hotel her family stayed in the night before the murder. I'd like you to find out if a Peter Chapmays is also registered for that same night.'

'So why do I need to have a Scottish accent?'

'Well, they'll need to go back eleven years. I think you'll get more co-operation if you say you're a detective inspector from Strathclyde police investigating a cold case; that tragic murder from two-thousand and two.'

Nicky nodded thoughtfully. 'Yeah, that makes sense. I could do a reasonable Morningside dialect.'

'Where's that?'

'Edinburgh. Sort of a posh Scottish accent. As in mae gels are the crème de la crème.'

I laughed. 'Whatever. But try not to camp up the Maggie Smith. If that's possible. And if they say they'll call you back, tell them you're on the road, give them your mobile number, and say you need the information urgently.'

'Will do.'

Nicky sat behind her desk, got the hotel number from a Google search on her computer, then dialled the number on her mobile. It was answered almost immediately and we watched her performing. Her Scottish accent might not have fooled a genuine native, but it sounded convincing enough to English ears like mine.

'Hello. I wonder if you can help me please. My name is Detective Inspector Barbara Watson from Strathclyde Police, D Division, Glasgow.'

"D Division, Glasgow." Nice touch. I exchanged a look with Bill, who smiled and nodded approval. Nicky's improvisation skills were impressive.

'Eleven years ago, on Thursday the 18th of July, a Mr Timothy Bayne and family stayed at your hotel, which was the night before they were tragically murdered, gunned down near Loch Lomond.' There was a brief pause, and then Nicky said, 'You do?'

She caught my eye, raised her eyebrows, and I could tell the person on the other end admitted remembering the incident.

'Yes, it was a terrible tragedy,' Nicky continued in a soft lilting dialect. 'And I know my colleagues will have spoken to staff at your hotel back when it happened, but new evidence has come to light. Is it possible for you to find out the name of someone who may have checked in the same day as the Bayne family?. Of course, I'm not suggesting this person may have had anything to do with the murders. We may just want to eliminate him from our enquiries.'

Nicky was cooking on gas now and I could see she was enjoying this.

'You can? No I don't mind holding. The name of the person is Peter Chapmays and it was a Thursday. July eighteen. Yes, thank you. I'd be most grateful. I'll hang on while you look it up.'

Nicky waited, but this time she didn't look at us. She stared at her computer monitor and a tremor of excitement ran through the room as we waited for the information to be keyed into the hotel's system. Eventually, Nicky made eye contact with us as she listened intently to the information she was given.

'Thank you, yes, that's very useful. I know it's a long time ago, but any chance you could describe this person for me?' Pause. 'Just a rough age would be helpful.'

I stared at Nicky's notebook and read the message upside down. She had written "40-ish".

'And what address did he give in the hotel register?' Scribbling in her notebook furiously, Nicky pulled a face and shook her head. 'No, that's terrific. Thank you for that. That's been most helpful.'

As soon as she hung up, Bill said, 'I assume that address is the same as the false one we were given at Tech-Intelligence.'

'That's right. Coach Road and an SE1 address. Which doesn't exist.'

'That was quite a performance, Nicky,' I said. 'Well done. At least we know the killer stayed at that hotel, using the same name as before.'

Nicky chewed the end of her pen thoughtfully before removing it to say, 'Wonder if they have CCTV at that hotel.'

'It's a strong possibility,' I replied. 'But I doubt they would hand something like that over to anyone other than the police. In any case, ordinary tapes going back eleven years. I would have thought they'd have been wiped years ago.'

Bill looked at me. 'You would think the cops would have checked the CCTV at the time.'

'What if,' I said, thinking aloud, 'they questioned the staff to see if there were any motor cyclists who checked in that night? And maybe there weren't, so they didn't bother checking the CCTV.'

'How fucking stupid can you be, to overlook a thing like that?'

'I suppose they fixated on the bike theory, like the Yorkshire police did with the Geordie tape.'

'At least *we* know this Chapmays character's the killer, whoever he is. And we know he stayed at the hotel, and drove north with his motor bike in the back of his van. This is evidence now, not speculation.'

'But if this man's got a false ID,' Nicky said, 'where does that leave you?'

Silence. Struck dumb as we considered the problem. Bill was the first to break it.

'Well, we've made some progress. More than the police did, that's for sure. So at least we'll have some news to give Alice.'

Bang on cue, the telephone rang on Nicky's desk.. She picked it up and said, 'Weston and Turner,' followed by, 'Hello, Alice. Yes, Freddie and Bill have made progress and have some news to report. I'll hand you over to Freddie and he can tell you what's happened.'

She handed me the phone and I told Alice most of everything that had gone on with our day. She seemed impressed that we had at least discovered what had happened, and commented on how the police seemed to have overlooked what now seemed obvious. She then wanted to know how we intended to proceed, and I told her we had to have another brainstorming session to see how we could discover a motive. If we find a motive, I told her, we're halfway there. I was trying to convince myself as much as her, but I realised it sounded hollow. So I mentioned the games her father's company sold - or, more to the point, didn't sell. I'd been saving this revelation till last, not knowing how she might react. Implying her old man was involved in a criminal activity might go down like a lead balloon. But I was wrong. She said it had crossed her mind years ago that he may have made his money from something illegal. I asked her if she ever found out about his company's games selling badly, and she told me she had no interest in computer games whatsoever, and didn't ever remember playing one or taking any interest in them, in spite of it being supposedly the way her father earned his living. The only reason she thought he was involved in something unlawful, she said, was after her family was murdered and because of the way the crime was committed, carrying all the hallmarks of a professional hitman.

I asked her to think back to long before the killings. 'Was there anything about your father's behaviour, however insignificant it might seem, that seemed peculiar in any way?'

There was a long pause while she thought about it. Bill and Nicky looked at me intently, waiting to see my reaction to her answer.

'Now I come to think of it,' Alice said, 'there was a time when I was about fourteen, and I sneaked quietly into Dad's study when he was on the phone. When he saw me, he reacted like he'd been stung. Well, I suppose I made him jump, and he ended the call.

He said "I've got to go," and slammed the phone down. Then he lost his temper and shouted at me. How dare I walk into his study without knocking and that sort of thing. He over-reacted and I've no idea why.'

Guilt? I wondered. *Caught out in some dodgy deal.*

'What did he say just before he noticed you entering? Can you remember?'

'Nothing that seemed to make much sense. Something about control of the skimming. I had no idea what it meant. I still don't.'

Something stirred in my brain. I had the germ of an idea, but I didn't want to share it with her right now. I needed more time to think about it.

'Have you any idea what it might mean, Freddie?'

'Christ knows,' I replied. 'But I'll talk it over with Bill, and we'll see what we can come up with. Meanwhile, if you think back to any conversations - even from when you were much younger - which might throw some light on our investigations, let us know, would you, Alice?'

'Of course I will. There was one other name which might be significant.'

'What was that?'

I heard her sigh. 'That's just it. I can't remember. It was all so long ago. From when I was only eight. I guess because I was so young he probably didn't care about speaking openly in front of me. I remember it being a strange name - like a nickname. If only I could remember what it was. Maybe it'll come back to me. I'll let you know if it does. I'll call you tomorrow. And well done, Freddie - all of you - you've found out more in a day than the police did in eleven years.'

'I guess we got lucky.'

'No such thing as good or bad luck, Freddie. Either way, you become responsible for what happens. I've always believed, you make your own luck, good or bad.'

I knew she was referring to her father, for the way his illegal activities might have brought bad luck to the family. So I mumbled goodbye and hung up.

Bill and Nicky looked at me expectantly, waiting to be copied in on Alice's information about her father's conversation.

'What does skimming mean to you, Bill?'

He shrugged. 'Flat stones you chuck across the water, to see how many times they bounce.'

It was Nicky who verified my suspicions.

'I think I know. I had a mate who was skimmed - if there's such a past tense verb - skimmed at an ATM he was. Cleaned out his bank account.' She looked at Bill and made a Tommy Cooper gesture. 'Just like that. I think skimmers are machines positioned above ATMs that read the data on the magnetic strip of a customer's bank card, and probably the pin number as well.'

I nodded. 'Exactly, Nicky. That's just what I thought it was. Alice interrupted her father on the phone when he said something like "control of the skimming" and he went absolutely ape.'

'So he was probably involved in bank fraud,' Bill said. 'Would that explain a fortune of twenty million?'

'Why not? Especially if he was heavily involved in organised crime, doing it on a massive global scale. And Alice told us how her father was always on the computer and it used to drive her mother nuts. Using online methods, that's how these criminals keep in touch and keep their identities secret.'

A cold tremor ran through my body as I was reminded of Olivia's threatening troll, and how her hacker's identity might be unbreakable. I glanced at my watch. Nearly five-thirty.

'I think we need to sleep on this. We'll start fresh tomorrow morning at nine and see what the next plan of action is. Meanwhile, I've got to see a man on the Isle of Sheppey.'

Bill pulled a face. 'Lucky you. What a karsey that place is. Don't bother to send me a postcard.'

I laughed, in spite of my dread of the journey across London and down to east Kent, which right now I could have done without. 'Can I leave you to lock up?' I said.

'Sure, mate. Nicky and I'll see to it. You dash off - or crawl off - in the rush hour traffic.'

I tapped the wallet in my back pocket. 'Is there an ATM close by. I may need to get some cash?'

Bill chuckled. 'There's one just round the corner past the tube station. But watch out for the skimmers. A half a million's a lot to lose.'

Chapter 10

There was no quick way across London and Kent in the rush hour, so I flipped a metaphorical coin in my head and plumped for a route via Islington, then over London Bridge and east along the Old Kent Road. It took me about forty-five minutes to get as far as Borough High Street, just across the other side of the river, when I felt my mobile vibrating. I stuck the hazard lights on and pulled over. I saw it was a text message from Rick.

The text read: "Urgent. Might know who Eclipse is. Vital u meet me. Matthew in bed by 8. Sarah home at 9. Meet me Joiners Arms, Ballards Lane, Finchley 9.30. Rick."

I wondered why it was so crucial for Rick to want to meet me this evening. If this Eclipse who was frightening Olivia was in Poland, why the urgency? On the other hand, as it had already been pointed out to me, the address might be a smokescreen and the bastard could be in London.

I put the car back into drive and accelerated sharply into the traffic. A blast of a horn from an irate cabbie, so I raised a hand of apology in my rear view mirror. I was starting to feel anxious about the situation with Olivia, and uneasy about Rick's message and having to wait until nine-thirty to discover what was so urgent. On the other hand, I was relieved I no longer had to journey to Sheppey.

Instead of going left at the end of Borough High Street, I did a right, and returned north of the river across Blackfriars Bridge. I toyed with the idea of going home first, but I had already driven what seemed like hundreds of miles today already, and I also needed to check out on a few of my club doormen, so I decided I would get a drink and a bite to eat in a pub just off Farringdon

Road, somewhere like Clerkenwell Green, where I could make one or two phone calls and keep my other business flowing steadily.

***

By the time I got to the Joiners Arms in Finchley, my mood was dark, savagely angry as I thought about the internet pervert intimidating my daughter. And why did they have to call them trolls? I asked myself. Trolls I thought of as fictional monsters from fairy stories and pantomimes, nothing more than a string of harmless wicked witches, ogres or giants, about as real as Father Christmas. But the threat to my daughter was from a very real sick mind and I wanted nothing more than to find the person responsible and beat him to a pulp.

This being a Tuesday night, I was relieved to find the Joiners Arms was relatively quiet. I didn't think I could cope with any forced hilarity tonight, or a pub quiz droning on and on.

I ordered a large Bushmills and sat in a quiet corner. Nine-twenty on the pub clock. Just ten minutes to go, and then I would find out what this was all about and hopefully put a stop to this twisted bastard threatening Olivia.

I sipped the drink as slowly as I could. I find it hard to make a glass of spirits last more than a few minutes, but as I patted my midriff, feeling the tightness of my waistband, I knew I had to cut down on the beer.

I stared at the amber liquid, swirling it around in the glass and frowning deeply, wishing the hands of the clock would move a bit quicker. Because I was stressed - it had been a long day - I wanted to leap up, go to the bar and get another large Bushmills, which I imagined downing hurriedly. Instead, I restrained the urge, and sipped minuscule amounts of whiskey as I watched the hands of the clock reach twenty-eight minutes past. I sighed and knocked back the thin layer of drink left. Any minute now Rick would arrive and hopefully give me some news that I could at least act on. It was feeling so helpless, unable to think of a scheme to combat the internet attacks that was so frustrating.

The last two minutes were the worst, my focus moving between clock and empty glass, feeling desperately in need of a good long pint.. As soon as Rick arrived, I promised myself, I could buy him a drink, and - to hell with it! - get myself a pint.

As the clock cleared nine-thirty, a jumble of chaotic thoughts bombarded my brain, so that I drifted into fantasies about all kinds of vengeance I might heap on this Eclipse scumbag. But it was pointless and hopeless, as it existed only in my imagination. Even the bastard's name was unreal, like something out of a comic. Except this Eclipse bastard sounded deadly serious in his intention to harm in the sickest way possible.

In my dark vision of revenge, I had drifted, and the hands of the clock had almost reached twenty-to-ten. Where the hell was Rick? Perhaps he was held up by a domestic problem. Maybe his wife had been delayed. That was it. She'd got home late and he couldn't leave his child on his own.

I went to the bar, glanced at the door, half-hoping he would walk in as I was getting a drink. But no one came through the door so, instead of a pint, I limited myself to a half. I returned to my corner seat and almost downed the half pint in one gulp. It was now quarter-to. I took out my mobile, scrolled to Rick's name in the phone book, keyed the send button and held the phone to my ear.

Nothing. Not a voice mail message. Nothing.

I began to panic. I had a bad feeling about this.

From my meeting with Rick yesterday lunchtime, I knew vaguely where his house was in relation to the pub. So I typed in his postcode on my smart phone map section and discovered the most direct route was across a small park. I decided I would hurry to meet him, and if I didn't bump into him on the way, then I could always call round. After all, his text message had said it was urgent.

I downed the rest of my half, said goodnight to the barmaid, and hurried out onto the main road. I crossed to the other side, turned right into a side street, and walked quickly towards Victoria Park, about 150 yards down on the left. What worried me most as I hurried breathlessly towards the park, was the fact that his mobile had registered nothing when I rang it. Maybe, I tried to convince myself, he forgot to charge it. Perhaps a pay-as-you-go which he'd forgotten to top up. Or just a bad signal.

I was clutching at straws. And then I heard it in the distance. Faint to begin with but soon getting closer and more urgent as the siren became more pronounced. Heading in this direction.

As I reached the park I heard a strangled scream and a babble of voices. Someone choking and retching, followed by the sound of fluid and more choking. I turned into the park, and I saw by the light from a streetlamp some people gathered round a body on the ground. In the bushes, a woman clutched her stomach and was sick. A man stood nearby, holding the lead of a small dog, incongruously wagging its tail as another man bent over the prostrate body, which lay across the path. I could see a dark pool by the figure's head, which I knew was blood, even though there was no colour in the dark pool, like a shot from an old black-and-white film.

As I edged closer, I saw the victim's military camouflage shorts, and then I inched even nearer, hardly daring to confirm my suspicions as I saw his blond hair. It was Rick. His throat had been slashed and he'd lost a lot of blood.

A man knelt at his side. 'Oh God!' he wept. 'There's no pulse that I can find. I think he's dead.'

Rick had been murdered. But why? Was it a random attack? A violent mugging? No, it couldn't be. Meeting me with information concerning Eclipse and then winding up dead was too much of a coincidence.

The siren wailed loudly as it reached the street near the park, then died rapidly, the flashing blue lights adding an eerie brilliance to the night, a scene that was reminiscent of so many accidents. Except this was no accident.

The kneeling man stood up. 'Over here!' he shouted. 'Over here! Quickly!' The dog barked but still wagged its tail. I moved closer to the body, just in case I was wrong, but it was Rick all right. There was no mistaking him by his teenager garb, and his blond tousled hair.

Two police officers, one male one female, strode hurriedly towards us.

'Someone's been stabbed,' the same man said, waving them over. 'Right here. In the park.'

Behind the police officers, I could see more people gathering, moving forward towards the crime scene tentatively, cautious but curious. Another distant siren fractured the evening's stillness as it drew nearer and I knew before long this crime scene would soon be awash with emergency services and forensic teams.

I made a split-second, impulsive decision, which I prayed I wouldn't live to regret. I quit the scene. I drew back from the small group of witnesses near the corpse. The police didn't notice me backing away, as they were now attending to the victim, bending down and checking to see if there was any sign of life. As I got to the end of the path leading from the park into the street, I lit a cigarette, to look as if this was my reason for moving away from the immediate scene; but the few people gradually moving toward the crime scene to satisfy their morbid curiosity hadn't noticed me. I walked quickly up the street toward the main road as another police car, siren wailing, came flashing round the corner. Head down, I hurried towards my car which I had parked on the opposite side of the main road, just around the corner from the pub.

As soon as I reached the car I didn't waste any time in leaving the district. I drove south towards the North Circular Road, trying not to go over the speed limit, the shock of Rick's death numbing me into submission. Proceed cautiously, said that voice in my head, even though my inclination was to distance myself from the horrendous crime as quickly as possible. I could feel tears pricking my eyes and wanted to turn the car around and return to the crime scene to help the police with their enquiries. But I didn't. That same warning voice urged me to keep going at a steady speed, telling me not to ignore my instinctive fear, the feeling that Rick's murder was not a random attack, and involved much more than one perverted sicko targeting schoolgirls in chat rooms. My instinct told me I was involved in something deadly and widespread, and I was determined I would fight back, even though Jiminy Cricket's bubble voice reprimanded me for not involving the police. My conscience screamed at me, telling me I still had time to change my mind, and I ought to turn around and arrive at the crime scene, pretending I had come from the pub where I was supposed to meet Rick.

Suddenly, I was dazzled by bright headlamps hurtling toward me, and I swerved left to give the vehicle plenty of room to pass. Flashing lights and the banshee wail of its siren, as the ambulance charged past me, north toward the terrible murder of the man who had gone out of his way to help me. I was instantly filled with remorse. Maybe I should have stayed at the crime scene and given the police the information I had concerning Rick and the internet troll. Why had I behaved with such recklessness? Was it ego? Working on Alice's case - a case the police failed to solve after eleven years - and coming up with a few answers myself had perhaps deluded me into thinking I could do better at investigating my daughter's troll. Who was I trying to kid? What did I know about computer hacking? Zilch. And even Rick, a computer expert, told me he was not a pro when it came to serious hacking. But expert or not, he rose to the challenge, went out of his way to help me, and for this he'd been brutally murdered. Unless, of course, it *was* just a coincidence, and it was a random, senseless knife crime, with no connection to the information he had regarding Eclipse.

I chuckled bitterly, and shook my head, as I waited at the red lights before turning east onto the North Circular. No. There was no way his murder was random. And it wasn't like he lived in a shitty area. Hard to imagine street gangs and knife crime where he lived. I shuddered as a vision of his corpse in that park flashed into my mind. During my time as a soldier, and later as a mercenary, I had seen violent death many times at close quarters, but nothing grieved me quite as much as finding that nice young man with his throat cut. A guy just trying to help. Not in it for financial gain. An ethical decision. For this he'd been slaughtered. And had it not been for me seeking his help, he might still be alive. But much as I regretted his death, it was not my fault. I kept telling myself, over and over like a chant - not my fault. Just trying to protect my daughter.

The lights changed green and I turned onto the dual carriageway, putting my foot down now. Distancing myself from the crime. Maybe I was being stupid, but it was too late now. No going back. I had to keep going. My main concern was to protect Olivia. And if it was the information Rick wanted to give me which caused his death, then I needed to see if I could get the same information from the American on the Isle of Sheppey as soon as possible. Information that caused the death of family man Rick, a young man I'd involved in my troubles.

'But why,' I protested loudly, and thumped the steering wheel, 'should I blame myself because of this evil bastard on the internet?'

Then it slapped me in the face. I'd missed what was obvious. There was no lone predator. There were others. And close by. No longer could I comfort myself with the notion that he or they were making futile threats from a country in Eastern Europe. It was now closer to home, and I was shit scared.

Highgate Tube station on the left. I'd almost gone too far to go back. Almost. But not quite. The sensible thing would have been to return to the crime scene and get some protection from the police.

Nah, I told Jiminy, *Call me pig-headed but the police got nowhere with the Bayne family case, so I was not going to risk the same thing with my own family.*

But as I drove home, questions fluttered in my head like confetti in a gale. What if they found Rick's mobile and read the text message he sent me about meeting him urgently in the pub? And when this hit tomorrow's news, how would Nicky react, especially if she found out I'd been on my way to meet him? And when I delved further into the identity of this Eclipse, would I be the next target?

Chapter 11

I arrived home around ten-fifteen. As soon as I walked in the front door I could sense the atmosphere. Houses are strange like that, almost as if the fabric of a building can absorb the moods of the occupants. And on this particular night, having witnessed the death of someone who was involved in our predicament, my emotions were brittle. I felt as if I were about to crack up. It was like entering a stranger's home, alien and unfamiliar, but I guess my sense of dread was heightened now that my adrenaline rush had left me feeling weak and exhausted.

I didn't call out that I was home, as I usually did, but walked quietly into the kitchen and dining room, which is where we all tend to live most of the time. A muted *News at Ten* was showing on the small TV set, and Michelle was sitting at the refectory table, staring at it lifelessly, a bottle and a glass of brandy in front of her. Which was worrying. The only alcoholic drink she touches is white wine.

She looked up at me as I entered and I could see she'd been crying. I guessed what had happened.

'Has that bastard targeted Olivia again?'

She let out a long sigh before she answered. 'It was another threat. Saying he's circulated her photo to men who are lined up to sexually abuse her in his dungeon.'

'Fuck! Where is Olivia now?'

'She's staying the night with Jackie's friend Claire. They both offered to look after her, and Claire's mother's going to drop her off at school tomorrow.'

'Well, that's something at least. Let's hope she stays away from the computer after reading that last message.'

'She didn't read the last message. I managed to persuade her not to use the computer until this thing is sorted, and I said I'd have a read of her emails if she didn't mind. She doesn't know about that last message. I deleted it right away. The same as she deleted all the others.'

I saw Michelle shiver as she thought about the message, reading it over again in her mind. I got another brandy glass from the cupboard, sank into a chair opposite her and poured myself a generous measure.

Michelle shot me one of those looks that I knew so well, challenging me to contradict her. 'I think we ought to call the police.'

'And what can they do? I mean, if this is some nutter in Poland...'

'And what if it's not? What if it's someone right here in London?'

I swallowed too large a measure of brandy and stopped myself from choking as it brought tears to my eyes. My voice was strained and hoarse when I spoke.

'This is happening more and more often. And the police can't seem to trace these bastards. Look at that case in the papers recently where a young girl committed suicide cos she was being bullied on the internet. They still haven't found the bastard responsible.'

Shaking her head intensely, Michelle said, 'All the more reason to involve the police. Because of that case in the papers, they'll have to take it seriously.'

I knew she was right, but I suspected this was something much bigger than internet bullying. And how the hell could I admit to having walked away from Rick's murder scene, knowing he might have had vital information to do with Olivia's internet abuser? I began to have serious regrets and doubts about my actions and realised I was sinking deeper and deeper into a dire situation, one which could only lead to more misery for my family. But I just needed a bit more time - time to find this Brad Shapiro bloke, the American on the Isle of Sheppey. Maybe I was clutching at straws, but I was hoping he might come up with some answers.

'Well?' Michelle demanded.

I realised she wanted me to make a snap decision, pick up the phone and call the police. But I wasn't ready for that yet, not with Rick's murder hanging over me. And then I had an idea, a way to put off involving the police for a while.

'You say Olivia deleted those threatening emails, and you deleted the last one...' I began.

Michelle interrupted me to say, 'Yeah, they were horrible. So I cleaned them out of the Trash folder as well.'

I was torn between relief and anger. 'How could you do such a stupid thing?'

'I was desperate. I wanted them gone. I was just trying to protect our daughter.'

I watched as tears ran down her cheeks. Not wanting to cause her any more distress, I placed a hand over hers and lowered my voice, injecting sympathy into my tone.

'I know you were, sweetheart. But now we've got nothing to show the police. No evidence. The crime scene's been wiped clean.'

She sniffed and brushed the tears away with the back of her hand, leaving dark smears from her eye-liner. 'They can do all kinds of things now. The police can investigate people's computer hard drives.'

'I'm sorry to say this, Michelle, but Olivia's been threatened. No crime has been committed. I'm just guessing, but I would have thought the technology needed to retrieve details from a hard drive is time consuming and costly, so I think the police might be reluctant to go down that route.'

'But I'm scared, Freddie. We've got to do something. We can't just sit here hoping this'll go away.' A sudden intake of breath as she remembered something. 'What about this American bloke, down the Isle of Sheppey? What did he say?'

The moment I'd been dreading. Confessing to her that I'd not been to see him yet. She stared at me, her eyes piercing, waiting for my explanation.

'I didn't get to see him.'

'What?'

'I left around half-five tonight and got as far as Southwark, then Rick sent me a text saying he needed to see me, and he might have got somewhere in identifying this troll. I arranged to meet him in a pub near where he lives, but he never showed up.'

'Why not?'

Avoiding her eyes, I stared into my brandy. 'I haven't a clue. I know he was waiting for his wife to come home, so maybe she was delayed. I tried to ring him but I never got a reply.'

I took a sip of brandy then renewed eye contact with her again.

'But this is important, Freddie,' she urged. 'It could be a matter of life and death for Christ's sake. You've got to get in touch with him right away. Ring him now. If he's got some idea, some clue who this bastard is, he ought to tell us.'

'You're right, sweetheart.' I took out my mobile and dialled Rick's number, knowing damn well there would be no reply. I waited. Listening. Michelle staring at me, her eyes glistening from her recent sobbing.

I shook my head and hung up. 'Nothing,' I said. 'No voice mail. No tone. Nothing.'

'Jesus Christ, Freddie! What are we going to do?'.

'First thing tomorrow morning,' I told her, 'I'll head for Sheppey and find this American geezer. He's the one, according to that ex-vicar, who can give us some answers. And then, if we find out who this bastard is, we can get the law onto him. And if they can't do anything, I'll make certain he won't be in a fit state to bother any children ever again.'

Michelle leaned forward, took my hand and squeezed. 'For once, Freddie, I'm with you one-hundred per cent.'

'Thanks, sweetheart. Try not to worry. If this Brad Shapiro's as good as they all reckon he is, we might be in with a chance to get this sorted.'

Michelle stared at the Courvoisier bottle and took her hand away from mine. I saw the way she longed to reach out for the bottle but held herself in check. Eventually, she accepted the urge to pour herself another, grabbed the bottle and unscrewed the top.

'Shit!' she exclaimed. 'I think I'm getting a taste for this stuff.'

Chapter 12

Wednesday 25 September 2013

As I spooned the last of my breakfast porridge into my mouth I began to feel queasy as the *Today* programme on Radio 4 neared news time. My stomach muscles rippled nervously as I waited for the pips to signal the start of the eight o'clock news, wondering if Rick's murder was the main story this morning.

Michelle was making another cafetiére of coffee and was distracted and distant, probably still worrying about the internet threats to Olivia. I had phoned Bill earlier and spoken to him, asked him to hold the fort while I drove down to Kent, and suggested he and Nicky might research anyone by the name of Peter Chapmays at the records office. He told me Nicky had checked her office emails, and there was one from Alice, saying she would like a meeting at our office at lunchtime. I told him I didn't think it would be a problem, as I hoped to be back from darkest Kent by then.

The *Today* programme broke off suddenly and I heard the BBC pips heralding the news. First the headlines prior to the details. Top story was about parliament voting against David Cameron's decision to give armed support to the rebels in Syria. Next item was about a vicious knifing in Finchley, a man murdered for the sixty pounds he had in his wallet.

I didn't hear the rest of the headlines, I was too absorbed with the brief report of Rick's murder, knowing there was more to come a few minutes later. As the newsreader gave a detailed report about the situation in Syria, I thought about Rick's murder. Whoever had slaughtered him wanted it to look like a violent robbery and had stolen his wallet. And probably took his mobile phone as well, which explained why I couldn't get a tone of any sort. The killer probably destroyed it along with the SIM card. Unless, of course, it was a genuine robbery, a random attack by someone desperate enough to kill for money. No. There was no way I could believe that. Meeting me to provide information about Eclipse, and being murdered before we met, was just too much of a coincidence.

I watched Michelle closely as she poured hot water into the cafetiére. She was still deep in thought, oblivious to the news bulletin. If she didn't react to the news about Rick when it came, I wondered what the best way to play it was. I had already told her I was going to meet him and he never showed up. She might then suggest I go to the police to tell them about our meeting, which was the last thing I wanted; at least not until I'd sorted out the business about protecting our daughter, using the help of Trev the Rev's ex-prison contact.

Suddenly, it was like a cold hand gripping my throat as the newsreader read the story of Rick's murder.

'In Finchley, a quiet suburb of London last night, a vicious knife attack was carried out resulting in murder. Police suspect the motive was robbery. The victim, Ricky Lee Bishop, thirty-three, was married...'

I gasped and exclaimed loudly, 'Jesus!' Which got Michelle's attention as she looked towards me open-mouthed.

'What's wrong?'

I raised a hand to silence her, making it obvious we needed to listen to the rest of the news report.

'...and his wife telephoned the police when he didn't come home,' the newsreader went on. 'She said he had gone to the local pub, a short walk from his home, as he often did to unwind of an evening. Mr Bishop was a computer programmer and worked from home. His wallet was missing, as was his mobile phone. His wife told the police that he didn't usually carry more than sixty pounds in his wallet. Mr Bishop, father of a four-year-old son, was only thirty-three. Both he and his wife were prominent members of the local Baptist church.'

Michelle looked at me and shrugged, indicating she didn't understand my concern with the news item. I realised she hadn't been listening to the start of the bulletin, and she didn't know Rick's surname was Bishop.

'That was him,' I said as the newsreader continued with the rest of the news. 'Rick. The bloke I was supposed to meet last night. No wonder he never showed up. He was robbed and killed on his way to meet me.'

Michelle gasped, and her eyes widened with horror. 'God! That's awful. Terrible.'

'Some evil bastard killed him for sixty fucking quid,' I ranted, piling it on, because I suspected I was the reason for his death. 'Sixty fucking quid. Can you believe it?'

Hands shaking, Michelle topped up our coffee mugs. 'His poor family. He had a young son they said. And his poor wife. Oh, God! How can people...?' She slumped into a seat and stared across the room, sinking into a weakened state.

I slurped the coffee too hurriedly and burnt my mouth. 'Shit!'

I startled Michelle out of her decline, and saw her mind latching on to questions, frowning as she concentrated on working something out.

'You don't suppose - ' she began.

'What?' I replied, uneasy about where this might lead.

'You arranged to meet him. You don't suppose it had something to do with what he was going to talk to you about.'

'Why would it?'

'Because it might have had something to do with this Eclipse.'

I laughed gravely. 'How could it? No one knew about our meeting. He sent me a text. I don't think anyone could have read the text he sent me.'

'This Eclipse, whoever it is, seems to be capable of invading anyone's space. Why not your mobile?'

'No, come off it, Michelle, you heard the news. He was robbed. The fact that he was meeting me just happens to be a coincidence. I hardly knew the guy.' Time to change the subject, I thought. 'It's this American bloke I need to speak to - urgently. My priority is to get this Eclipse bastard to leave Olivia alone. I won't be happy until that happens.'

I could see this had done the trick. Michelle glanced at the kitchen clock and said, 'Hurry up and finish your coffee. The sooner you get there to see if he can help, the happier I'll be. Fingers crossed he can do something to help.'

'Even if he can just find out who this bastard is,' I said, blowing on my coffee, 'that'll be good enough for me. And if he is in Poland, I shall get him, if I have to fly out there.' And as I said it, I had little idea how true those words were at the time. If I had know then... as they say.

Chapter 13

I drove south east and crossed the Thames at the Dartford Crossing. Most of the traffic was going into London and I made good time as far as the toll bridge. There was the usual crawl over the crossing, but nothing too daunting, and the drive down the M2 towards the Medway towns was steady and uneventful.

I'd switched my mobile to silent, and on the journey it vibrated several times indicating either a text message or a call which would go to voice mail. I ignored them, knowing one of them was probably Nicky ringing with news of Rick's murder, and I wondered how she was taking it. I decided I would speak to the American first, see what he could do to help, and then contact her.

I'd never been to the Isle of Sheppey before, although I'd been warned what to expect. But I wasn't prepared for the degree of neglect I saw as I crossed over the bridge onto the island. Boarded up shops and decaying buildings everywhere. It seemed to be an island that time had forgotten, and many houses and pubs had an austere 1950s look about them.

Back in the 1970s I was in the 9th Para Engineers, I prided myself on my map reading and stubbornly refuse to buy a satnav, in spite of my family moaning at me for being so obstinate. Maybe they had a point, I thought, swearing as I took a wrong turning towards Sheerness, the main town on the island, going left instead of right, following the coast around on the north western side. I passed a large dirty white building, featureless and sombre, with paint flaking and an old sign above padlocked double doors which read: SHEPPEY NITE CLUB. On waste ground next to the building was the skeleton of a rusting Ford Mondeo, long grass growing all around it, sprouting through the concrete cracks as nature attempted to reclaim the land. As a man who spends a great deal of time in clubs, because I supply bouncers to many West End night spots, the decaying club was like a hyena laugh as I thought about the rats and vermin which now occupied the forbidding empty space, dank, dirty and cold.

I drove through Sheerness town centre, glimpsing the usual fast food outlets and shops that sold nothing above a pound or 99p, before heading towards my destination. Brad Shapiro's address was equidistant between the main town and Minster and I wondered why the hell this American had chosen to live on the Isle of Sheppey after his release from prison. And if Trev the Rev was to be believed, the young man was a computing genius, yet he had decided to settle in what looked like one of the most down-at-heel areas in the United Kingdom. Maybe his prison sentence meant he was unable to secure gainful employment. Even so, I thought as I drove past another shuttered shop at the edge of a housing estate, with his skills surely he would have had better options than this.

Perhaps it was because houses were cheap in this area. And his was an unexceptional house, probably built around the 1930s, although there was a hint of art deco about it, in the rounded bay windows with metal frames. But that was where any style ended. It was a detached house, although the neighbouring houses were only separated by a small alley leading to a back garden on one side, and a gap of about a foot on the other. The house was two-storeys high and, although the outside plaster was painted in sunshine yellow, there was something dark and sinister about the building. Maybe it had something to do with the way it deliberately kept out natural light. Every window had black venetian blinds, all closed tight, keeping daylight from intruding. I suspected I would be meeting someone who valued complete privacy or anonymity.

There were two small front gardens, divided by a path, although the garden on the left had been concreted over, the wall removed, and the area was now a car parking space. A black Volvo estate was parked there, which I assumed must belong to Brad Shapiro. As I walked up the path past the Volvo, I saw the back seats were folded down to make maximum room at the back to carry equipment about, although the space was empty.

I stepped inside a wide porch with an arched roof and rang the doorbell. I heard it chime somewhere deep inside this brightly-coloured mausoleum. I waited, listening for footsteps along the hall. Nothing. Silence. No sign of life at the morgue. I rang again and waited, staring at the solid-looking oak door. I felt I was being watched. It was a strange feeling, like being put under a microscope. And my instinct told me I was right. Most people like to display their CCTV cameras as a deterrent to burglary; but the one I spotted was minuscule, concealed in the eye of a sun figure in a circular carving on the porch wall to my right. The camera was so small, unless you stared at it closely it could easily be missed..

I rang the bell again. Still there was no sound from inside the house. The ex-vicar had told me the American rarely went out, and even if he did, he didn't usually go very far. So I took out my notebook and scribbled on one of the sheets.

'Dear Brad,' I wrote. 'Trevor Reagan said I could call on you for advice. Having problems with a computer troll. Will call back in a half hour. Freddie Weston.'

I pushed the note through the letter box and walked back to the car, intending to find somewhere to have a coffee, and planning to return in a little while. As I got back in the car, and glanced towards the house, I saw the door was open, and a tall figure was standing in the doorway with my note in his hand. He must have watched me on the CCTV, decided not to answer, but when he saw me scribbling the note and posting it through the letter box, he must have read it and decided to answer.

This man was clearly a loner and guarded his privacy scrupulously.

I walked back up the front path. As I got closer I saw he was a man in his early-thirties, with jet black, medium-length hair, large brown eyes, a smooth, pale complexion. Thin-faced and good-looking, he reminded me of many gamblers I've known, starved of vitamin D because they rarely see daylight.

As I reached him, he gave me a wide grin and offered me his outstretched hand. 'Mr Weston? You don't mind if I call you

Freddie? And any friend of Trevor's is most welcome. Sorry to be so cautious and to have kept you waiting, but I expect Trevor has told you how we met.'

His accent was soft, not a harsh American voice, and his grip was firm, dry and reassuring as we shook hands. My first impression was that I liked this man and felt confident that he might be able to help.

'Yes, he did say something...' I began, but he interrupted me, stood aside and gestured for me to enter his mysterious stronghold.

'Please. Come in. Then you can tell me all about what troubles you. I expect it's my services as a geek you want.'

He chuckled warmly and closed the door behind me. A long hallway, dark and bare, with a staircase on the left, and devoid of personality. There were no pictures on walls which were papered in seventies woodchip and painted a standard magnolia, and the stairs and hall were uncarpeted. The hallway lacked any character, as if nobody lived here, and I guessed it hadn't changed since the day he moved in.

'I know what you're thinking,' Brad Shapiro said, amusement in his tone. 'How bare and lacking this hallway is. But I'm a practical person, and a hallway is merely a passage, a means of getting from A to B. But this here's my pride and joy. Observe.'

He ushered me into a darkened room. As I stepped forward, discreet wall lights came on, and I found myself standing inside what looked like a vast control room, a space station or a set created by a film studio. There were computers and monitors, cameras, laptops, screens showing the CCTV images of the exterior of the house, and a large flat-screen TV dominating almost an entire wall. This was gadget world gone berserk and I half expected the bass opening of the Bond theme to start pounding,. I felt as if I was cut off from reality, not just because of the state-of-the-art high-tech surroundings, but because no natural light bled through the blinds. It was like being sealed in a vacuum, and I wondered if the room was soundproofed. I listened carefully for any sounds from the outside world, a dog barking or a car passing, but there was no discernible sound.

Brad studied me, a gentle smile pulling at his mouth, almost as if he could read my thoughts. Just then I heard a child bawling in the street outside, followed by a mother yelling at it.

'Yes,' Brad chuckled, 'there is a real world outside, which intrudes from time to time. So you can rest easy.'

I let my breath out slowly, relieved I hadn't become trapped in a virtual world of machines. Even though this gleaming emporium of gizmos and gadgets looked hygienically flawless, I think I preferred the squalor of the disreputable world outside. This one was too make-believe for me.

'An impressive room,' I said. 'But each to his own. Call me old-fashioned but I think I prefer a bit of - shall we say normality?'

He laughed.

'But don't get me wrong,' I added apologetically, 'I guess this is your work station, and this is where you can catch me a troll.'

'Exactly. But you must tell me all about it.'

He saw me looking about for furniture to sit on, but there was only one high-backed black swivel office chair in front of a glistening silver workstation.

'So why don't we go into the kitchen and chill, have some coffee, and you can give me some details of this cancer on your computer?'

He ushered me along the bare hall to his kitchen at the far end. As I'd suspected, this was not going to be just any old cooking area. Pristine and shiny, it was a technological space for advanced gastronomy. Not a hint of wood to be seen anywhere. This was truly a space-age kitchen. But on the sparkling work surface was a tell-tale ready meal carton, and I suspected his eating habits were far less cultivated than his ultra-modern kitchen.

He gave me a friendly smile. 'How d'you like your coffee?'

I glanced at his expensive espresso machine. 'Strong and black, please.'

'Double espresso, do you?'

'Perfect.'

'Make yourself comfortable.'

He gestured towards a sky blue plastic table and four matching chairs that would have looked more at home in a trendy Hampstead playschool. He turned his back to me to make the coffee and I surveyed my surroundings. Apart from the empty ready-meal carton, everything was horribly clinical. Not a glimmer of untidiness or anything to upset the sterility of this kitchen that resembled an operating theatre. I wondered if he had some sort of Howard Hughes problem, fear of dirt and germs.

Still with his back to me, as water gurgled through the espresso, he said, 'I haven't got a fear of dirt like old Howard Hughes, you know.'

Uncanny. This man could read my thoughts. On the other hand, it was obvious to anyone visiting this house that his taste in immaculate modernism was extreme, and he probably felt a need to explain himself. The Howard Hughes comparison seemed pretty obvious, so I was not about to be spooked by it.

'I didn't think for one minute...' I began.

'I like order in my life. I'm a geek, you see. If my surroundings are uncluttered, my brain is organised and methodical, ready to solve some of the most challenging technologies. And it seems to work. I can usually solve most cyber problems. Which is why I'm way ahead of my game.'

Grinning, he carried two white china cups and saucers of thick black espresso over and sat opposite me, pushed one of them across, and looked me straight in the eye, almost as if he expected me to dispute his cyber superiority claim. I was reminded of my conversation with Trev the Rev when we discussed the geek's ego, and just to confirm how large it was he went on to tell me about how he would have liked to have been around during the war, stationed at Bletchley Park to work on the enigma code, hinting that he could have broken the code quicker than Turing and shortened the war by many more months.

I sipped my coffee, waiting for him to conclude this testimonial to his brainpower. Eventually, he grinned and shook his head. 'You must think me highly narcissistic and conceited, going on about myself like this. But I try not to hide my light under a bushel. I like to be realistic about my computing skills. What line of business are you in, Freddie?'

'I supply doormen to West End Clubs.'

'So I guess you must be quite handy with your fists.'

'It has been known.'

'Good. Now, please tell me about your daughter's problem with this troll.'

I gave him the details, told him about the troll's email address, and explained how much more threatening the emails were becoming. He frowned and stared at the table as he listened intently. When I finished, he looked up at me, his eyes moist, as if he was emotionally involved in Olivia's predicament.

'I think I can help you, Freddie.'

'How d'you know, Brad, even before you've - you've done whatever it is you've got to do?'

He smiled and tapped the side of his nose. 'Trade secrets, Freddie. But I guarantee I can stop this rat contacting your daughter again. And for this service, I charge three-hundred cash up front.'

Of course, I hadn't expected to use his services for free, but for three-hundred I wanted a result. The doubt must have showed in my expression because he held up his hands in surrender.

'Freddie, I promise you I will put an end to this monster once and for all. I'll even find his location for you. I suspect you're a man capable of dishing out a reprisal that will end this demon's career as a cyber paedo. First let me tell you a little true story. Ever heard of the artist James McNeil Whistler?'

I nodded.

'Well, Whistler painted a portrait for a client in just over an hour, and charged him forty guineas for it. When the client complained that it seemed an excessive sum for an hour's work, Whistler replied: "My dear, sir, you are paying for the knowledge of a lifetime".'

I shook my head. 'And the point of the story is - ?'

'You will now part with three-hundred, and I will go into the other room, and when I return in half an hour - or maybe a bit longer - I will have achieved the success you desire. Providing you can find something with which to amuse yourself during that time. Feel free to make more coffee.'

'My mobile's been alerting me to many calls or texts which need answering. But I didn't think you could get a result that quickly.'

'If it takes longer, I'll let you know. But I'm good. Believe me, I'm very, very good. Hour at the most.'

I took out my wallet, counted out fifteen twenties, and slid them across the table. After he had pocketed them, he grinned and said, 'Make yourself at home. I'll be as quick and as thorough as I can be.'

After he'd gone, I checked my mobile. There were two texts from Nicky, saying she had some very bad news and she needed to speak to me as soon as possible. There were also two alerts to my voice mail, and when I checked them one was from Nicky, again saying she needed to speak with me, and one was from Bill. I checked my watch. It was 10:15. I still had plenty of time to get back to London for our lunchtime meeting with Alice. I sent Bill a text, saying I wanted to speak to him privately and asked him to meet me for a coffee at Marine Ices near the Roundhouse prior to the meeting. I also sent Nicky a text, saying I would call her in about an hour's time.

I gazed around the soulless room, wondering how I could pass the next half hour or so. I decided another shot of espresso was not a good idea, so I checked thoroughly to see if there were any hidden CCTV cameras in the kitchen. I didn't think there were and, being a nosy bugger, I got up and thought I'd take a look inside some of the kitchen drawers. His house was so regimented and clinical, I wondered if he might suffer from OCD. I pulled open one of the drawers, which contained a tray of gleaming cutlery. The one beside it was filled with a disorderly array of kitchen utensils. Its untidiness dispelled my notion that he suffered from OCD, unless it was a question of out of sight out of mind.

The next drawer was more interesting. It was filled with official documents which proved irresistible to my enquiring mind. The document on the top of the pile was a folder from a firm of local estate agents. I glanced furtively over my shoulder and listened for the sound of a door opening and footsteps along the hall, just in case the American decided to return for any reason. Then I opened the folder.

To say it was a thunderbolt would be a gross exaggeration. But my mouth must have dropped open as I stared at the photograph.

It was a picture of the derelict night club I had driven past on my way into Sheerness, and it was being offered on a 75 year leasehold sale for £170,000. I rifled hurriedly through the other pages until I came to the deeds for the property. Brad Shapiro had purchased the scuzzy building - a cash sale for £155,000.

I shut the folder, placed it back neatly on top of the pile, and shut the drawer. I sat back at the table, wondering why this American had purchased a derelict night club. Maybe, I thought, he wanted to expand his virtual empire and create a space similar to the HQ of SMERSH. I could picture the scene as he sat in a swivel chair in front of a bank of monitors while stroking a Persian cat. But my imagination ran away with itself. The reason was probably far more mundane. Maybe he planned on reopening the premises as a night club. I almost laughed at the idea. A new night club opening on the Isle of Sheppey. From what I'd seen of the place, it wasn't going to happen. So perhaps, I guessed, he was thinking of broadening his computing business and needed bigger premises. Maybe he planned on recruiting staff. He was clearly talented and ambitious, so perhaps this was the first step in building a multinational company.

Whatever the reason, it had nothing to do with me. All I cared about was getting Eclipse to leave my daughter alone. And if he could manage that, as far as I was concerned he could use the premises to open a brothel.

I spent the next half hour checking with some of my club doormen, to see if there were any problems to sort out. Fingers crossed, everything seemed to be running smoothly, with the exception of one club where a doorman had broken someone's wrist in a fight. The punter, I was told, deserved it, having attacked a young girl, and it was unlikely he would press charges for assault. Jack, my Nigerian bouncer, who I have now put in charge of four West End clubs assured me that the incident would be sorted and there would be no repercussions.

Twenty minutes later, Brad Shapiro came back into the kitchen looking pleased with himself.

'A great result,' he said. 'Couldn't be better. Your daughter needn't even change her email address. You'll have no more trouble from this Eclipse moron. Guaranteed.'

I could feel the grin spreading across my face. 'That's fantastic, Brad. Let's hope whatever you did works.'

'Oh, it'll work all right. And you might like this.'

He gave me a little square of white paper on which was scribbled the name Alexei, with the address of an internet café in Krakow.

'Should you ever decide to go over there, you won't find him too difficult to locate. He operates from this internet café. I know Aleksy is quite a common name over there, but this one is the Russian spelling - Alexei. So you shouldn't find him too difficult to track down.'

'I hadn't planned on a trip to Poland, but I'll give it some thought. And now it's sorted, maybe I should just let it go.'

Brad shrugged. 'Whatever you decide. You never know. At least you have the information.'

'Yeah, thanks for that, Brad. Much appreciated.'

'I know I'm not cheap. But you get what you pay for in life.'

I saw his giant ego surfacing, the way he smirked cockily, his eyes full of executive arrogance. But what the hell! He had done me and my family a favour. And, giant ego or not, Brad was charming. I liked the guy.

He patted me on the shoulder, walked me to the door, and told me to drive carefully. I drove around the corner and parked the car. Then I called Nicky to hear her news about Rick, and gave what I thought was a convincing performance in pretending the first I knew of his death was on hearing about it on the news first thing this morning.

Chapter 14

Bill turned up at Marine Ices and slid into a seat opposite me. A cappuccino was on the table at his place which I had already ordered

'Thanks,' he said. 'But why here?'

I looked around the ice cream parlour, taking a deep breath to indulge in its milk and coffee aroma. 'They serve excellent ices, so I'm told.'

'I'll stick with the coffee for now. So what's the big secret? We have an office just round the corner.'

'I'm not sure I want Nicky to know about Rick's death.'

'She already knows. She's very upset. Course, she didn't know him *that* well - '

'You know what it said on the news about his murder being a violent robbery?'

'Yeah. Bastards killed him for a few lousy quid.' Bill's eyes narrowed shrewdly and I saw the beginnings of a knowing smile. 'But you're going to tell me something different.'

I nodded and told him in detail the events of the previous night. When I'd finished he stared at me silently for a while.

'Well?' I prompted. 'What do you think?'

'Same as you. That was no robbery. Too much of a coincidence.'

'That's why I wanted to meet you on your own. I don't want Nicky to find out. She's a bright woman and she'll come to the same conclusion as you did. That it was no robbery and it was made to look like one.'

'And you're worried that if you tell Nicky what happened, she'll insist on the police being brought in.'

'Exactly.'

At the table next to ours sat an elderly couple, too focused on consuming chocolate ice cream to converse. I saw Bill glance in their direction before he leant forward and lowered his voice.

'So why didn't you involve the police, Freddie? They might have been able to help catch the bastard who's targeted Olivia?'

'I don't know. It was impulsive. My instinct told me I was involved in something much bigger than internet threats.'

'All the more reason to involve the police.'

'I'm not so sure. Don't forget: Brad Shapiro, this American on the Isle of Sheppey, has got form. If the police took him in for questioning, things might have been different.'

'In what way?'

I went on to tell Bill about my meeting with Shapiro and the way things had worked out to my family's benefit, which was more important to me than anything else.

At the end of it, Bill shook his head and said, 'This is like a tower block stairwell: it stinks, mate. If Rick's murder wasn't because of a robbery, we are looking at a killer silencing him to stop you from finding out about this Eclipse.'

'Which I have done.'

'So why wouldn't he have killed the American?'

'Maybe the killer doesn't know about him. As Rick himself said, he wasn't exactly a professional hacker. He might not have been as skilful as Shapiro.'

'But are you sure this Shapiro geezer's managed to put a stop to this Eclipse?'

'No, not entirely. After I'd left his place I phoned Nicky, then I sent a text to Michelle telling her I hoped it was sorted. I haven't heard back from her yet.'

Bill screwed up his face as if he was in pain, and I saw his hands curling into fists.

'Christ! There's something still not right about this.'

'You don't have to state the obvious, mate.'

'I mean, if Rick's murder wasn't a robbery, is his killer just going to accept defeat? If you have managed to silence this Eclipse, is he just going to give up and go away. Assuming, of course, this internet monster is the puppet master.'

I sipped my coffee, which by now was stone cold. 'Look, all I'm trying to do is protect my family,' I protested as I slammed the cup into the saucer, startling the couple next to us. 'I had to get to this Shapiro bloke before the police did, and maybe he's done the trick. Maybe I was wrong to just walk away from Rick's murder, but I think Shapiro might have helped. I don't know. It's just a feeling I get. He's arrogant, I'll give you that. But I got the impression he knows what he's about.'

'Let's hope you're right.'

'And what about this meeting with Alice?' I said, glancing at my watch. 'Since last night we've got nothing much to report, have we?'

'That's where you're wrong, mate. We've got a new lead.'

I looked at him, waiting for the details, but he shook his head.

'I'll let Nicky tell you herself. It was mainly her legwork - ' he mimed a telephone at his ear - 'which got a result. And she's been so upset over Rick's murder, she deserves a pat on the back.'

I eyed him knowingly. 'You sure there's not more to it than that?'

'How d'you mean?'

I sat back and chuckled. He knew what I meant.

'Come off it, Freddie. A boss pulling an employee is not a good move.'

Chapter 15

When we got back to the office, Nicky, who was sitting behind her desk, got up quickly, rushed forward and flung her arms around me. I heard her sniffle and felt a tear on my cheek. She moved back, wiped the tear away, and offered me a brave smile.

'Oh, Freddie, I'm sorry. I'm finding the news hard to take in. I keep thinking about Rick and the way he was killed. It was senseless. And for what? Some evil bastard slit his throat for the pathetic amount he had in his wallet. Poor Rick. The bastards. The evil bastards. I hope they catch whoever did it and he rots in jail for the rest of his life.'

I caught Bill's eye and guessed he was thinking about my aborted meeting with Rick and the way I'd left the crime scene.

'Did you know Rick had a four-year-old son?'

'Yeah, he mentioned it when I went round on Monday.'

'His poor wife. It must be terrible for her.'

'Did you know her?'

'We never met. I didn't know Rick socially, only from a work situation. Once the dust settles - if it ever does - I'll go and buy a card and send it from all of us.'

'I think the firm could afford a ginormous bunch of flowers.'

She shook her head. 'They'll be inundated with flowers. A card signed by us would be more personal.'

'Card it is then.'

'Right,' she said. 'I'll sort it.'

The tragedy compartmentalised, I could see it was now down to the business in hand. Nicky turned with a display of efficiency, went back around her desk and fetched a giant notebook and an A4 brown envelope.

'I don't know if Bill told you, but we've made some progress with this Peter Chapmays character. Shall we go into your office and catch up?'

We went inside and I made myself comfortable behind the desk while Bill and Nicky sat in front.

'Alice'll be here in less than half an hour,' Bill said, glancing at his watch. 'We need to zap through this as quickly as we can.'

'Before we start,' I said, 'Can I ask you something? Does Alice know I've spent the morning on personal stuff? I mean, we agreed to work exclusively on her case. I wouldn't want her to think I was moonlighting.'

Bill tugged his chin thoughtfully. 'I think you should be open about it. I'm sure she'll understand.'

'You're right. Especially - touch wood - if Shapiro has managed to kick this Polish or Russian bloke into touch.'

Nicky raised her eyebrows enquiringly as she looked at me.

'When I met this American on the Isle of Sheppey this morning,' I explained, 'he said the troll was based in Krakow - even gave me his first name - and thinks it's the last my daughter will hear from him.'

'That's great news. But I thought you were seeing this American last night.'

'Something came up the last minute.'

'To do with your bouncers business?'

I avoided eye contact with Bill as I lied. 'That's right.'

She nodded and flipped over the cover of her notepad. 'Now about this suspected hitman, Peter Chapmays. I thought I'd try the records office, to see if this man exists. The only vague description we have is from the phone call to the Carlisle hotel. The receptionist thought he was about 40, which means he could have been born anywhere between 1970 and 1976. If it's a false ID, and an unusual name at that, I thought I would make a start on Births, Deaths and Marriages around 1972, assuming he might be about forty. And this is where I got really lucky. There was one Peter Chapmays born on December 12 1972 and he died three months after his second birthday in February 1975.'

'So he's stolen a dead child's ID.'

'Which isn't uncommon in that shifty world of spooks and undercover officers,' Bill said. 'But there's more. Much more. Sorry. Carry on, Nicky.'

Nicky turned over a page in her notebook. 'Trawling through court records we discovered a Peter Chapmays was a member of Free the People Now, a bunch of anarchists, and in 1999 he was arrested along with others in the group for planning an anti-capitalist demonstration in Canary Wharf.'

I flashed Nicky a great big smile. 'This is great stuff, Nicky. Thanks for your brilliant work. Go to the top of the class.'

'Thank you, kind sir. But there's more. And I think Bill deserves some credit too.'

Bill waved it away with a flippant hand gesture, leaving Nicky to continue.

'Because the planning of this demonstration, which was to be a peaceful one, was concocted at a large-scale party which was raided by the police, the judge exonerated them, saying there were no charges to answer to. As the demonstrators appear to have won on this occasion, they didn't mind being photographed, posing on the courtroom steps. The quality's not that good, but you might find it interesting.'

She took the picture out of the envelope, stretched across and handed it to me. It was a grainy colour press photograph of six of the demonstrators on the courtroom steps, posing and giving thumbs up and victory signs. They were all casually dressed, jeans, T-shirts, colourful hair for two of the women, and the four men all had long hair.

'Notice something about one of the men?' Bill asked.

'Yes,' I replied. 'He seems reluctant to show his face. He's got an arm around one of the women and is turned towards her, almost burying his face in her neck.' I looked at Bill questioningly. 'Is that our man d'you think?'

'Well, the odds are good. One in four.'

'He seems at ease with this woman. A girlfriend you think?'

'We think so,' Nicky said. 'But we have all their names, so I guess the electoral roll's the next step.'

Just then the entrance door buzzed in the outer office. Alice was ten minutes early. Nicky got up and went to let her in.

While we waited for her to enter, Bill stared at me with a fixed expression, his eyes keen and penetrating, a look I knew so well from our distant past when we were mercenaries.

'What's up?' I asked.

'Thinking about Rick's murder, that's all.'

'You think I should have called the police, don't you?'

He shrugged just as Alice entered. She was wearing tight-fitting black denims, black trainers and a dark blue V-neck sweatshirt over a white T-shirt, with a brown leather handbag at her side, strapped diagonally across her body.

'Don't get up,' she said as Bill and I half rose.

She and Nicky sat down, and without any preamble Alice asked us what had been happening. Bill told her about how we knew Peter Chapmays was a child who died aged two back in 1975, and how we thought his identity had been stolen by the hitman. I then handed her the photograph and Bill explained about the plans for an anti-capitalist demonstration by the anarchists, and their subsequent courtroom appearance, and how one of the accused was Peter Chapmays.

Frowning and squinting at the photograph, Alice asked Bill, 'Which one do you think is him?'

'It's probably the one who's slightly in profile.'

'Deliberately trying to hide his face?'

'It looks like it.'

'I don't understand. This man belongs to an anarchist group, demonstrating against capitalism, yet he might be a cold-blooded hitman. It doesn't make sense.'

Bill smiled thinly. 'It does if you think of him as an impostor. The party where they planned the demonstration was raided by the cops. So this Chapmays might have been working undercover.'

'Undercover? Who the hell would he have worked undercover for?'

'He might have worked for the Special Demonstration Squad, a part of the Met's Special Branch. I think, though, the SDS was disbanded about five or six years ago, and was reformed as the National Public Order Intelligence Unit.'

Alice looked horrified. 'Are you telling me the man who murdered my family was a policeman?'

'"Was" might be the key word here. He may have turned; become what they call a rogue cop who was then recruited by someone else.'

She held the photograph up. 'But we're not absolutely sure this is the man.'

'We're pretty sure it's one of them,' I said. 'And it's doubtful the others have got false IDs, so we may be able to track down the whereabouts of the Chapmays through one of them.'

Alice was silent as she looked at each of us in turn. 'To think the police came up with zero in eleven years, but you've uncovered this man's identity...'

'False identity,' I reminded her.

'Whatever. You've at least got something to go on and it's only taken you less than three days. So what happens now?'

'Next step will be to find some of these activists.' I looked at Bill. 'We ought to start with the two women, in case one of them was his girlfriend.' Bill nodded in agreement. 'They shouldn't be too difficult to trace.'

'Well done! You obviously had a busy morning uncovering this information.' She flashed me provocative look. 'So what was your role in all this, Freddie?'

'Sorry?'

'When I called in mid morning and asked to speak to you, they said you weren't here.'

She had injected half a million into our firm, and I couldn't blame her for wanting her money's worth. He who pays the piper, and all that. I decided it was time to come clean.

'I had to visit the Isle of Sheppey in Kent.'

'I don't know it.'

I laughed. 'No, and you don't want to.'

'Get to the point, Freddie.'

That was when I told her all about Olivia and the internet threats. When I ended our tale of horror, she gave me an understanding smile, serious and sympathetic..

'Well, of course, Freddie, family always come first. And you think this American guy has resolved the problem?'

I shrugged. 'I hope so. I'll soon find out.'

'I hope for your daughter's sake he's managed it. If this man is based in Poland I suppose there's not much the police can do.'

'I've got his real first name, and the name and address of the internet café he uses in Krakow. If he threatens my daughter one more time I'll go over there and make sure he'll never interfere with a child again. Eclipse! It'll be a total eclipse!

Permanent!'

Alice's face hardened as she stared at me, her eyes frosty. The room became still, and Bill and Nicky froze, suddenly aware of the change in temperature.

'Look, don't worry about our investigation into your family's killer,' I started to explain, but Alice raised a hand and interrupted me.

'Why did you use that word?'

'What word? I'm not with you.'

'Eclipse.'

'Because that's the email name the bastard's using. Why?'

The blood seemed to have drained from Alice's face as she almost whispered, 'Because it's just come back to me... the name... the one I heard my father use... when I was eight. Several times he referred to someone as Eclipse. I'd forgotten until you mentioned it just now.'

They say when you're close to death your whole life flashes before you. It was like that now, only this was a flashback of more recent events racing through my brain. To steady myself, I leant forward on my elbows, staring at the desktop, then ran the fingers of both hands through my hair. When I came to and looked up, the three of them were staring at me expectantly, waiting for my response.

'First of all,' I asked Alice, 'can you remember how long ago you decided to use our agency?'

'It was nearly three weeks ago. Before your business got started. Why?'

'Because that's around the time my daughter's intrusive internet problems started happening.'

'Are you saying the two are connected?'

'It's starting to look that way. And there's something I need to tell all of you. Well, Bill already knows - I told him half an hour ago.' I looked towards Nicky, afraid of how she might react to my confession. 'Last night, on my way to Sheppey, I'd only got as far as Southwark when I got a text from Rick saying he had urgent information about the internet troll, and asking me to meet him at his local pub. He never showed up. He was murdered. Possibly because of investigating this Eclipse on the internet.'

'But... but on the news,' Nicky began falteringly. 'It said he... he... the police think he was robbed.'

'That's what his killer wants them to believe.'

'So when did you first hear about his murder?'

'I *heard* about it on the news. But I already guessed he was dead.' I saw Nicky about to say something and I continued before she got the chance. 'When he didn't show up at the pub, I tried to ring him but there was no response. So I decided to walk to his place across the park. When I got there, the police were at the scene, and I heard a bystander say a man had been knifed.'

Not an outright lie, just economical with the truth. And I knew what Nicky's next question would be.

'Shouldn't you have said something to the police?'

'I suppose I panicked. Acted impulsively. I thought if Rick had been killed by someone acting on behalf of this Eclipse, it involved something much bigger than an internet troll hounding my daughter.'

'All the more reason to involve the police, I would have thought.'

'Maybe. But, I'm sorry, my first priority is my daughter's safety. And knowing how useless the police have been investigating Alice's family's murder - '

Nicky stood up. 'I'm sorry, Freddie. This isn't right. I don't think I want to get involved. Someone I know has been murdered and we're talking about concealing evidence from the police. Jesus Christ! This is serious. We could all end up in jail.'

'Hang on, Nicky,' I protested. 'Let's just think this through for a minute - '

'No, you hang on. Think of the affect this murder has had on his wife. She thinks he was killed for a paltry sum of money. If he was killed because he'd unwittingly got information about - I don't know - organised crime of some sort, then his wife should know about it.'

'It won't bring him back to life,' Bill said quietly and matter-of-factly.

'That's not the point, Bill, and you know it.'

Alice looked up at Nicky, her eyes moist and pleading. 'Please, Nicky, sit down and let's talk this through. If when we've thrashed it out we decide to bring the police into it, we can. But first let's talk about it. Please, Nicky. I've lived with this nightmare for eleven years, ever since that school trip when they told me my family had been wiped out. And now it looks as if my father was involved in something really nasty. He must have known this Eclipse, the man who targets young children. I can't believe my father... who... who loved us very much... He liked children, for God's sake. I know I said he spent a great deal of time on the computer, but he also spent a lot of time with us. He was a wonderful father. I can't believe he...' Her lips quivered and her face crumpled as she bent over, her hands covering her eyes as she sobbed.

Nicky leant over and cradled her, smoothing her hair, while her muffled sobs sounded like animal growls of pain.

'It's OK, Alice. I'm sure your father wasn't involved in hurting children. There's probably a reason he contacted this Eclipse; something to do with his computer games, maybe.'

Alice must have known how feeble that sounded, because she wriggled free of Nicky's embrace, wiped her eyes and said to Bill and me, 'I'm your client. If you're still up for it, I'd like you to find the man who killed my family, and the man who was murdered last night, and bring him to justice. And I want to learn the truth about my father. Whatever he was involved in, I want to know what it was. Only then can I...'

She broke off, and I thought she was going to cave in again. Instead, she shivered, and I saw the terrific effort it took her to cope with the news that her father may have been involved in something shockingly corrupt. Maybe it was because she had become hardened over the years by the tragic murder in Scotland, but she recovered rapidly and I could see she wanted to get on with a discussion about the investigation.

'We need to talk this through,' she said, looking at Nicky. 'Before we decide on calling the police.'

I suppressed a smile, guessing she had no intention of involving them. It was said to placate Nicky, who stood next to her, looking awkward and uncomfortable. I got the impression Nicky was upset because the solace she offered the tearful young woman had been rebuffed.

'Please, Nicky,' Alice pleaded, 'sit down so we can talk this through.'

'Sure.' Nicky slid quietly into her seat.

'There's something I'd like to know,' I said to Alice. 'What made you pick our agency in the first instance? There are plenty of far more successful and well-established enquiry agencies in London.'

'Well, I'll be honest with you. There was one other I decided to go with before I found your agency on the internet. This would have been about a month ago. I knew I had to pick my investigator carefully. And I thought I'd found him. He was very much a one-man band. He seemed tough and bright, and told me he was ex military, and later joined the police force and fast-tracked to detective in the Metropolitan Police at Scotland Yard.'

'Did he tell you why he left the police?'

She shook her head. 'I didn't think to ask.'

'So why didn't it work out with this investigator? I mean, why did you drop him?'

'I didn't. He dropped me.'

I exchanged a look with Bill, who was frowning hard, and I knew he had smelt the proverbial. 'Didn't that strike you as odd?' he asked.

'He told me it was personal. He was closing his business and going home to Peterborough.'

Nicky, presumably having resigned herself to continuing with our investigation, grabbed a notepad and pen and began scribbling furiously. 'What was this investigator's name?'

Alice hesitated before answering. 'His name was Jack Dawe.'

Bill and I looked at each other and stifled a laugh.

'Yes, I know it sounds - well, a bit unusual. He said his name was John but he'd been called Jack in the army and the name stuck.'

'Have you got a number for Mr Jack Dawe?' I asked.

She rummaged through the clutter of her shoulder handbag and handed me a business card. They all watched and waited as I dialled the man's number. As soon as it clicked into the final digit, I held the phone up so they could all hear the discontinued tone.

'So he was telling you the truth about going out of business.' I put the phone down. 'But the question is, was it personal or was it something far more sinister?'

'At the time I didn't question it. But in view of what's happened since - '

'Is there a mobile number on the card?' Bill asked, but the question was redundant because I had already started dialling. The call was answered after the third ring.

'Hello? Who's this?'

The voice was cloaked in secrecy, guarded and suspicious.

'Mr Dawe?' I said. 'Mr Jack Dawe?'

'Who wants him?'

'My name is Freddie Weston of Weston and Turner. We're a firm of private investigators and we currently represent Alice Bayne. I believe a month ago you agreed to carry out investigations on her behalf, and then you backed out for some reason. I wonder if you could tell me what those reasons were.'

'It was personal.'

'Could you be more specific?' Long pause. 'Hello? You still there?'

A hissing noise. I wasn't sure if it was him or the phone line. I strained to hear his words. 'Do yourself a favour. Leave well alone.'

Although it was difficult to hear him clearly, I could still detect fear and urgency in his voice.

'I'm not sure I follow you.'

'Forget it. And that's all I've got to say. Don't call this number again.'

The line went dead. I knew if I redialled it would probably switch to voice mail. Alice stared at me, eyebrows raised.

'He hung up. Having first warned me off the case. Told me to drop it.'

Bill pointed a finger expressively. 'Which means someone has got to him.'

'Exactly. Why would a self-employed bloke suddenly go AWOL and abandon his business? An ex copper at that. And it looks as if this Peter Chapmays could have been an ex undercover copper.' I stared pointedly at Nicky. 'Now can you see why going to the police is not an option?'

She wriggled uncomfortably. 'Surely you don't think...'

'I don't know what to think,' I cut in. 'But I know one thing. This Peter Chapmays is definitely the killer.'

'So what are you going to do?'

'Find him, of course.'

Nicky spluttered. 'What? I can't believe this is happening. The man's dangerous. A cold-blooded assassin, and you think you can just - what happens if he finds out you're looking for him?'

'I'll cross that bridge when I come to it.'

'Huh! That bridge could collapse while you're only halfway across it.'

I didn't say anything. But I had to admit, she had a point.

Chapter 16

Having discovered from the electoral roll the whereabouts of the two anarchist women, Bill and I set off in the late afternoon. We had decided that, instead of conducting our investigations separately, it would be safer if we worked together.

I let Bill drive while I contacted Michelle to see if Olivia had been hounded by Eclipse again. So far so good. It looked as if whatever technological wonders Brad Shapiro had performed, it was working.

Although we knew the names of the protesters from their court appearance, we had no way of knowing which of the two women was which. The first one we decided to visit was Sandra Beeston, who lived at Upper Norwood in south London.

We parked a 100 yards from the housing estate where she lived. As we walked away from the car I noticed Bill limping more than usual.

'Ankle playing you up?' I asked.

'Yeah, a sure sign it's going to rain,' he grinned. 'It's like a barometer. The pins in the ankle fear the rust.'

As we neared the housing association flat on the ground floor of a respectable-looking block, and walked up to the double-glazed glass front door, covered on the inside by a net curtain. I heard Bill chuckle.

'What's so funny?'

'It's comforting to know our anarchists are well provided for these days.'

We rang the bell and waited. Presently the door was answered by a woman with blue and red streaks in her hair. At a rough guess I would have given her age as early thirties, which made her quite young back when she was involved in planning the Canary Wharf demonstration, and I wondered if her anarchy was a thing of the past and was she now a respectable citizen in a more humdrum situation. Apart from the brightly-coloured hair, the clothes she wore didn't seem to suggest she was an activist. Far from it. She wore a dress that could have been from Laura Ashley, but may have been purchased from a charity shop. In fact, if I'd been asked to describe her in a sentence, it would be camp village maiden!

But she wasn't the woman who Chapmays had his arm around. I clocked the wedding ring on her finger.

'Mrs Beeston?' I enquired.

Suspicion grew quickly like a an invisible and protective wall between her and us. She stepped back a pace and I could see she was about to slam the door shut; so I put my hand on the glass to prevent it from closing.

'We'd just like a quick word about someone you appeared in court with back in 1999, after the party to plan the Canary Wharf demonstration.'

'What business is that of yours?'

I handed her one of our business cards. 'We're not police. This is not official. We'd just like some information.'

She stared at the card, then looked up and said, 'Private detectives are even worse than the police. You bastards work as agent provocateurs, working against socially responsible and decent citizens who are trying to unite the country against tyranny. And you got the name wrong. Beeston was my maiden name.'

'So what's your married name?' Bill asked, smiling brightly.

She stared at my partner and shivered, almost as if he had made a lewd suggestion.

'If you don't know, why should I tell you?'

'We only want to ask you about Peter Chapmays,' I said.

Her eyes flickered briefly at the name, and then she composed herself and her face became an expressionless mask.

'He joined Free the People Now in 1997, and we're trying to locate him. Would you happen to know where he is?'

'I haven't a clue. And even if I knew, I wouldn't tell you.'

'You might if you knew how he betrayed you. Chapmays was an undercover cop. Didn't you ever wonder why your party was raided prior to the demonstration at Canary Wharf?'

'If that was true, it was a stupid thing the police did.'

'Because you all got off scot-free? But that doesn't alter the fact that someone betrayed you, and it looks like it might have been Chapmays.'

'So what? It was a long time ago, and Peter's vanished off the scene. Disappeared. Leaving poor Chrissie...' She stopped speaking as she realised she had said too much.

Bill pounced. 'Christine Bailey was his girlfriend, wasn't she?'

She stepped back, then pushed her body against the glass. 'Piss off!' The door slammed shut.

Bill shrugged. 'Well, at least we know she was the girlfriend. Next stop Christine Bailey.'

***

Described in the newspaper court report back in 1999 as a primary schoolteacher, Christine Bailey lived in her own house - a modest Victorian terrace house - in Neasdon. It was much nearer our office than Sandra Beeston's flat, so we felt we'd had a wasted journey to Upper Norwood, but we had no way of knowing which woman was Chapmays' girlfriend. The drive from south London to Neasdon had taken us forever and it was almost five-thirty. But if Christine Bailey still worked as a teacher, at least she would be home by now. After Bill rang the bell, the door was opened by a surly teenage boy.

'Is your mother home?' he asked.

The boy nodded, staring at us with a mixture of suspicion and hostility, but made no effort to summon his mother to the door. I wondered if he was in trouble with the police.

'Who is it, Dan?' a female voice called from the back of the house.

'There's two blokes to see you.'

'What?'

Provoked by his mother's response, the boy shouted angrily over his shoulder, 'I dunno. Two blokes.'

We waited, staring at the boy while he stared back at us. The face-off didn't last long because he soon lost the battle of wills and stared at his feet, clearing his throat nervously. I noticed he wore a Queen's Park Rangers supporters' shirt, with the 'Air Asia' sponsorship logo on the front, and not a school uniform, so I guessed he must have changed once he got home. His mother, wearing a flowery apron, appeared from a door at the end of the hall. Her mouth fell open as she approached us.

'Blokes to see you,' the boy said to his mother, then made his getaway, taking three steps at a time up the stairs.

'Yes? Can I help you?' the woman said, her tone cold and defensive. Her hair had changed from her photograph, and was now cut short and had been dyed a uniform black. Apart from the apron, she dressed in the style of rock chick: a pencil skirt with a slit up the side, high heels, and a glittery T-shirt.

'Would you happen to know where we can find Peter Chapmays?' Bill asked.

Christine Bailey looked as if she'd been kicked in the stomach. Her mouth opened and closed before she found the courage to speak. 'What did you say?'

'We're looking for your boyfriend, Peter Chapmays.'

'Who are you? What do you want?'

I handed her a card, and she accepted it with a trembling hand. 'A client of ours is trying to trace the whereabouts of Peter Chapmays,' I said. 'Have you any idea where we might find him?'

She stared into the distance wistfully, and for a minute I thought she was going to break down. She shuddered, and I could see thoughts racing through her head. Using a displacement activity to control herself, she fumbled with the back of her apron, untying it. Then she stood aside and eased the door open wide.

'I think you'd better come in.'

She took us through to the small kitchen at the back. It looked as if it had been recently refurbished with brand new units and a built-in hob. A chilli con carne was bubbling in a large pot. From upstairs I heard a bass and drum beat, not so loud as to be intrusive, but clearly putting up a defence against our invasion of his home.

'You'd better sit down,' Christine Bailey said, and glanced at the ceiling. 'If Dan comes downstairs, I don't want him to hear whatever it is you've got to say. Is that clear?'

I nodded. She sat down by a weathered pine table and we sat opposite her.

'So what do you want Peter for?'

I cleared my throat softly before replying. 'A client of ours is looking for him. I'm afraid I can't tell you any more than that. We're bound by client confidentiality.'

'Do you happen to know where he is?' Bill asked.

'Last I heard, he was in South Africa.'

I exchanged a brief look with Bill and waited for her to elaborate.

'We met in 1997, and started going out together.'

'How did you meet?'

'He was introduced to me at a meeting of Free the People Now. We were interested in the same things: saving the planet, giving ordinary people more control, and trying to get the powers-that-be to see sense. We started going out together. Then it became more serious.'

She stopped, and withdrew to her memories, clearly thinking about her relationship with Chapmays.

'Go on,' I prompted gently.

'We started living together. Of course, because of his activism and commitments, Peter was away a great deal of the time we were together.'

I bet he was, I thought, as I tried to imagine the double life he led.

Christine Bailey dropped her head and patted her stomach. 'Then I became pregnant.' She glanced up at the ceiling again. 'Dan is Peter's son.'

After this revelation, she stared at us both, as if challenging us to disbelieve her.

Bill said, 'And did he vanish off the scene once you became pregnant?'

She shook her head emphatically. 'No, it wasn't like that. For the first couple of years, Peter was a devoted and loving parent.'

'So what happened?'

'Dan would have been almost two. And Peter was showing symptoms of a nervous breakdown. He used to burst into tears, almost for no reason. He told me he was scared for his life, saying government killers were out to get him. Then he suddenly disappeared at the start of the new millennium. The end of January.'

'How did you know he'd gone to South Africa?' I asked.

'He wrote to me. He said he was sorry but he had to get away from Britain. He said we could go and join him when the time was right.'

'And when did he get in touch, asking you to join him?'

'I never heard from him again. He vanished from my life completely.' Her eyes darted sideways to avoid our probing stares.

'Not even a letter or a phone call?'

Still she avoided eye contact with us as she answered my question. 'Nothing at all. I don't know what happened to him. Dan keeps asking about his father and I told him his dad had a nervous breakdown. What else could I say?'

'It must have been difficult for the boy,' I said, and she looked at me once more. 'Do you still have the original letter he sent from South Africa?'

'I tore it up.'

'Why did you do that?'

'I suppose I was angry at the time. Now I wish I'd kept it.

'And it was definitely posted in South Africa?'

Her mouth fell open before she replied. 'Of course. Where else could it have been posted? The stamp and postmark were South African.'

'Have you any idea where in South Africa he might be?' Bill asked.

'None at all.'

'For all you know, he might have returned to this country.'

'Why would he do that and not contact me?'

Bill shrugged. 'So you've really no idea where he is.'

Her eyes flared with sudden anger. 'I've just bloody-well told you I haven't a clue where he is, and he's never been in touch since that original letter. What is it you find so hard to understand about that?'

Bill held his hands up in surrender. 'Sorry. Just trying to understand about your boyfriend, the father of your son, disappearing like that. You must admit, it does seem - well - a bit strange.'

'Oh, tell me about it,' she replied bitterly. 'Why are you looking for him anyway? Surely I have a right to know.'

'We just want to ask him a few questions about some of his anarchist friends,' I lied.

She laughed humourlessly. 'You don't think he'd tell you, do you? Split on his friends. I don't think so.'

'Well, we're sorry to have troubled you.' As I stood up, I noticed her fiddling with our business card on the table. 'I don't expect you'll need the card now. Shall I take it?'

She held on to it. 'You never know. If Peter *should* get in touch, I'll know where to contact you.'

Strange, I thought, why would she offer to do that?

We thanked her, and she walked us to the door and shook hands with us, almost as if we were old friends parting. As we drove away I asked Bill if he noticed the way she had avoided looking at us when we asked her if she had heard from Peter Chapmays.

'Notice?' he chuckled. 'Not a very convincing liar, if you ask me.'

'So you think he's been in touch with her since his defection to South Africa?

'Maybe. That's if he ever went to South Africa.'

'You think she lied about that?'

As I turned the corner out of the narrow street, from the corner of my eye I saw Bill shake his head.

'Not necessarily. Just because she received a letter from South Africa, written by him, doesn't mean he went there.'

'He could have got someone to post it for him, you mean?'

'It's easily done.'

'Did you notice how she hung onto our business card when I offered to take it off her?'

Bill laughed solemnly. 'It was so fucking obvious, mate, it was like a flashing Coca Cola sign in the Sahara desert. I think he contacts her from time to time. But I don't suppose she knows what he does for a living now. She probably still thinks of him as a white-hearted activist out to save the world, and being persecuted by the government.'

'If she has our card,' I said, 'and he contacts her...'

'I'm way ahead of you, pardner,' Bill broke in. 'If she tells him about our visit, I think we might get a visit. So I think we'd better be prepared. You still got that shooter I leant you?'

'That little Glock 26? I'd forgotten all about it. It's still hidden under my floorboards at home.'

'Well, I'd get it out if I were you... said the bishop to the bishop.'

'Don't you mean actress to the bishop?'

'I know what I mean, mate.'

Chapter 17

By the time we got back to the office, Nicky had gone home. We decided our best bet would be to trace the whereabouts of Jack Dawe, the private investigator who had abandoned Alice's commission and escaped back home to Peterborough. That's if Peterborough was his home.

It struck us both as odd that a person running a successful business - because if Alice had researched him, he must have had a reasonable reputation - would suddenly disappear, almost as if he feared for his life. But then, out there was a killer who had slaughtered Alice's family, and more recently Ricky Bishop, just because he found out who this Eclipse was. And Brad Shapiro had confirmed Eclipse's identity, who was a man named Alexei based in Krakow. So it seemed Chapmays was working for Eclipse in this country, stopping anyone from getting at the truth.

'Alice's old man must have been heavily involved with some really vicious bastards,' Bill observed as he turned the computer on. 'It has to be Mafia, or organised crime on a large scale.'

'That's why we need to find out who threatened this investigator. And whoever it was had enough of a reputation to scare him off.'

Bill stared at the computer screen, his eyes fierce and penetrating. 'You don't think we might be getting in too deep?' He glanced across the desk in my direction. 'This is more dangerous than anything we've ever done.'

I laughed the fear away. 'What about our time in Angola? It's how you ended up with pins holding your ankle together.'

'A Jeep hitting an IED's nothing compared to this... this weird and freaky hostility. It's enough to send shivers down the old cliché.'

'You're not getting second thoughts about this, are you?'

Bill didn't reply, concentrating on the screen. 'Here we are. That's useful. There are only two people named Dawe in Peterborough.'

'There may be some who are ex-directory,' I pointed out.

'There may be one or two shut Dawes, but let's walk through the open Dawes first.'

I groaned, but couldn't resist adding, 'And then you can see if there are any Jars in the area.'

'I'm going to hate myself for asking - ' Bill grinned.

'When is a Dawe not a Dawe?' I explained. 'When it's a Jar.'

'Steed threatens steed, and fire answers fire,' Bill quoted. 'And groan answers groan.'

It had always been like that in the past. Whenever we got into a tight spot we'd go into terrible gags mode. It relieved the tension.

He picked up the desk phone. 'Shall I be mother?'

'Shame Nicky's not here. She's excellent at performing.'

'Don't you mean lying?' He dialled the number and waited for about four rings. 'Hello, Mr Dawe? My name is Bill Walters. This may seem a bit strange, but I'm trying to trace an old mate of mine from our army days - we were great buddies back in the nineties - and I just wondered if this might be your son or brother, because I know John - who we used to call Jack, comes from Peterborough.' Bill paused as he listened carefully. 'Ah, well, that does tend to alter things more than slightly. Sorry to have troubled you. Thank you for your time and good luck with your wedding.'

He hung up and explained, 'Geezer in his early twenties, getting married next week, and no relation to our Dawe.'

'Here,' I said, stretching across the desk and grabbing the phone. 'I can't let you do all the work. You'll only sulk.' I read the other number from the monitor and dialled it. I waited for a long while, and was about to hang up when it was answered. I heard a television playing in the background.

'Hello?' Who is it?' The voice was cracked with age, and the rising inflection made him sound startled, as if he never received phone calls.

'You don't know me, Mr Dawe...' I began, but he cut in.

'Is this one of those sales calls, because if it is...'

It was my turn to interrupt. 'Not at all, Mr Dawe. I'm a friend of your son.' I paused, hoping he had a son. 'I know his name's John, but in the army we always called him Jack. I've lost his address, and I promised I'd look him up. I live in London but I happen to be in Peterborough tomorrow, so I thought it was good opportunity to sink a few beers with him.'

A brief pause while he digested the information. Then: 'Well, I'm not so sure about this. John asked me not to give out his address if anyone got in touch.'

Bingo! It looked like I'd hit on the right one. I gave Bill a thumbs up sign as I spoke to the father.

'I quite understand. I've got his phone number, only he doesn't seem to be answering.'

'He don't want anyone calling him.'

'But I only spoke to him at his office in London about six weeks ago. And he definitely wanted me to look him up. He gave me his address, I scribbled it on a bit of paper but I'm afraid I've lost it. He'll be really annoyed if he knows I was in Peterborough and didn't call to see him.'

He dropped his voice, speaking conspiratorially, a losing battle to compete with the blaring television.

'Sorry,' I said. 'I can't hear you, Mr Dawe.'

'Hang on a minute.'

I waited while he went and turned the volume down. When he came back, he said, 'That's better. Now where were we?'

'You were about to let me have John's address.'

'You got a pen and paper?'

'Fire away.'

'But I think there's something I've got to tell you. John's been suffering from depression lately. He hardly goes out.'

'I think as one of his closest mates when we were in the army... if I can't cheer him up no one can.'

Reluctantly, as if he was still unsure of whether he was doing the right thing, Dawe's father said, 'Well, if you're sure it's all right.'

'Positive,' I assured him. 'Now where is it he lives?' He gave me the address and I scribbled it on a notepad. 'Oh, I think it would be nice if you didn't warn him I was turning up tomorrow.'

Suspicion crept into his voice. 'Why's that then?'

'It'll be a nice surprise. I can picture his face when he opens the door.' I clocked Bill's sardonic expression, and gave him a cocky grin as I ended the conversation. 'I wouldn't want you to spoil the surprise. He'll be over the moon when he sees me. I'll really cheer him up. So thanks for your help, Mr Dawe.'

'Your welcome, son. But I didn't catch your name.'

I hung up.

'Nice one, Freddie. So it's off to Peterborough first thing tomorrow.'

I sighed. 'As long as it's not a wasted journey. Even if and when we confront Mr Jack Dawe, he might be so shit-scared we might not get anything out of him.'

'There are ways and means.'

'You mean, we might have to lean on him a little? Poor bastard. If there was any justice in the world, we should leave him alone. Let him sink into obscurity.'

I saw Bill's lips tighten in that determined expression I knew from old.

'No way. If he has any information to stop this cold-blooded killer from murdering any more people, he ought to share it with us.'

Chapter 18

Bill smiled across the table at Michelle. 'I always said Freddie would make someone a lovely wife.'

'Don't tell him what a good cook he is. It'll only go to his head.'

I had made grilled sirloin steaks, with Gratin Daupinoise potatoes and walnut and chicory salad with goat's cheese 'Just something I rustled up on the spur of the moment,' I said with pretend modesty.

'Yeah, yeah, yeah.' Bill laughed. 'Don't give me that bo... rubbish.'

Olivia sniggered. 'Were you about to say "bollocks", Bill?'

'Olivia!' I rebuked her, half-jokingly. 'It's OK for the grown-ups to say bollocks, but not school kids.'

'Oh, that's mild, Dad, compared to half the things you hear at school.'

'OK, sweetheart. Let's not go there.'

I grinned contentedly, looking around our kitchen-cum-dining room, an area in which I love to spend time with family and friends. I love cooking, which has become a passion of mine. It was a shame Jackie, who was now eighteen, was out on a date with her boyfriend, because then the family would have been complete.

Just before leaving the office, I suggested to Bill that it would be better if he came and spent the night at our place, because Wanstead's not far from the M11, so if we made an early start, we could be in Peterborough by ten. He agreed, and on our way to my place we called at his flat in Shepherd's Bush so that he could pick up a few things and an overnight bag.

'So what's this case you're working on?' Michelle asked Bill, the question I'd been dreading, but one which I knew was inevitable.

Playing for time, Bill chewed his steak slowly, then said, 'I expect Freddie's told you about our rich female client.'

'Freddie tells me nothing. That's why I'm asking you, Bill.'

I could see Bill struggling to provide an answer, wondering what I'd already told Michelle and how much of our investigation he ought to mention, seeing as how dangerous it had become. I think Michelle must have noticed his discomfort, because she leant forward and began to interrogate him.

'Don't tell me it's something dangerous, Bill. *Is* it something dangerous?'

Time for me to get him off the hook.

I chuckled loudly, opting for the double-bluff. 'Yeah, this trip to Peterborough tomorrow's to see if we can expose a ruthless hitman who'll stop at nothing to eliminate innocent people on behalf of the head of a mysterious criminal gang.'

It sounded like a joke but at least I hadn't lied.

'Freddie! Be serious.'

I winked at Olivia. 'I am being serious.'

'At least Dad's sorted out that awful internet monster.'

'Yeah,' I said. 'So far so good. No more nasty messages from that evil bastard - who, this American discovered, works from an internet café in Krakow.'

I could have hugged Olivia for getting us off the subject of our investigation.

'I wonder how this American was able to trace him?' Michelle queried. 'And to the exact spot. It seems a bit - well, a bit fantastic.'

I shrugged. 'No more fantastic than the way this weirdo was able to pick on Olivia in the first place. Computer geeks! Jesus! They're everywhere. At least now it's Whitehat, one - Blackhat, nil.'

I could see by Michelle's quizzical frown that she was about to ask me what the hell I was talking about, so I explained about the good and bad computer geeks. She shook her head as if she couldn't quite believe it.

'It all sounds like a stupid game.'

'A sick, stupid game,' I said. 'But at least it's over now.' I tapped our old pine refectory table. 'Touch wood.'

I was relieved at the way the discussion about Olivia's nightmare having been resolved, moved the focus from our current investigation; although I was horribly conscious of the daunting fear that the internet persecutor was in some way connected to Alice's father and the way he and his family were murdered. I knew that sooner or later I would have to take a trip to Krakow and try to put an end to this internet monster. I felt as if I was locked in some nightmarish computer game that was shockingly real and threatening, a game that could end with tragic consequences.

As if she could sense my troubled thoughts, Michelle asked me what was wrong.

I gave her a reassuring half-smile. 'Just thinking about how awful it must have been for Olivia,' I sighed. 'And glad it's been resolved.'

Bill came to the rescue. 'Like we resolved that film director's problem back in the eighties. Blowing up half the studio.'

I laughed. 'At least he got the shot he wanted.'

Between us we told Michelle and Olivia the story of how we had done some part time work at a small film studio in Battersea, and how a special effects man couldn't deliver anything but a damp squib. Then, because we were used to handling explosives in our army days, we improvised and blew the joint apart.

For the rest of the evening, we entertained Michelle and Olivia with funny stories from our good old days, some of which may not have been so funny at the time but I've rarely known an episode which didn't look better in retrospect.

Bill looked relaxed and unstressed for the first time in days, and I guessed he enjoyed being in a family environment. His melancholic existence, living in a euphemistically named studio flat in Shepherd's Bush at the age of fifty-five, with no family to turn to, he seemed to accept as his destiny. So it was a nice change for him to unwind in a family atmosphere. Three bottles of wine and several glasses of brandy later, I felt a brotherly warmth towards him, even though we were both starting to speak in tongues and knew it was time we hit the sack. The time had flown and suddenly it was half past midnight and I wanted to set off by sparrow fart.

I showed Bill to the spare room, then tiptoed quietly across the landing. Michelle had gone to bed at eleven, not long after Olivia, and I slid quietly into bed beside her. I listened for a while to her breathing, with the tiniest rumbling of a subtle snore, which was comforting in its normality.

Chapter 19

Disorientating voices coming from the radio alarm startled me awake at 6:30.

After I showered and dressed, I tapped quietly on Bill's door, but his room was empty. I came downstairs and found him sitting at the kitchen table nursing a mug of instant.

'Bloody hell!' I said. 'You too lazy to make a cafetiére of proper coffee?'

'Do it yourself, you snobby git!'

I switched the kettle back on. 'Catch me drinking that shit. You want some toast?'

'Just one slice.'

'It might be a long day. One slice ain't enough for a growing boy.'

He patted his stomach and growled, 'Growing in the wrong direction.'

I slid two pieces of sliced wholemeal into the toaster. 'I'll join you in one slice. Let's stop off on the journey and have a traditional English somewhere. It'll break up the journey.'

'Yeah, sounds like a winning plan.' He stared at me for a moment. 'You look like shit, Freddie. You did all the driving yesterday. I'm still on your insurance from that caper on the River Thames last year. Why not let me drive?'

'It's OK, mate.'

'No, Freddie, I insist. At least let me do the journey up there. I'm one half of the partnership, remember.'

I gave him my car keys. 'Go on then. You've talked me into it.

We had our toast and marmalade, washed down with fresh coffee. By now it was 7:15. I put our plates and mugs in the dishwasher, and we were just about to leave when Michelle appeared in her bathrobe.

'I just came down to say cheerio to Bill. It was lovely seeing you again, darling. Don't leave it so long next time. You know we love having you.'

'I really enjoyed last night,' Bill responded as they hugged and kissed. 'Great evening.'

Michelle tightened her bathrobe as she walked to the kitchen door. 'Right, I'd better go up and shower, then wake Olivia up in time for school.'

We followed her out, Bill carrying his overnight bag, and left by the front door. I hadn't bothered to put the car in the garage the night before and left it parked in the street. As we stepped out into the east-facing front garden, we blinked at the brightness of the low sun rising over the rooftops into a clear sky.

'Looks like it's going to be a nice day,' I said.

About to cross in front of the car to the driver's side, Bill stopped and clicked his fingers. 'I think you might have forgotten something, Freddie.'

'What?'

'Two old geezers like us, up against a ruthless assassin at least twenty years younger... we may need that Glock of mine.'

'Michelle should be in the shower by now,' I said. 'I'll go back and get it.'

'And I'll get this old crock heated up.'

I turned the front door key quietly and let myself in. I couldn't hear anything from upstairs, so I walked stealthily into the living room, over to the far corner by the drinks cabinet. I lifted a small occasional table and moved it to one side. Concealed under the floorboards in this area was the gun and the box of ammo. I started to kneel down to lift the carpet carefully -

Suddenly, an unholy blast and crashing sound as I lost my balance and was thrown sideways. At first I didn't know what the terrifying noise was. The whole building shook, and the walls of our house shuddered as it bore the blast of the nearby explosion. Glass smashed and splintered in the living room windows and

I covered my eyes. The numbness from the shock to my brain suddenly cleared and I knew exactly what had happened.

'Bill!' I screamed. I picked myself up and ran to the front door. As I opened it I had to cover my face with my arm to protect myself. The crackling of the flames, and the protesting sound of metal grinding was like a fierce pressure squeezing my body in a vice. Although the car must have been at least ten or more yards from the house, the intense heat from the burning vehicle seemed to scorch my arm, and I coughed and spluttered as I inhaled the acrid smoke and petrol fumes. I took my arm away, and forced myself to look at the wreck as my eyes smarted from the fumes and vapour.

I blinked the fog from my eyes and watched what remained of the burning vehicle, knowing Bill was certainly dead. There was no way anyone could have survived such a blast. My only comfort was in knowing it would have been instantaneous. He wouldn't have felt a thing. No last minute prayers; no life flashing before him. Nothing. At the turn of the ignition he ceased to exist.

I stared dumbly at the wreck, guessing that the car bomb was meant for me. For us both, probably. And then my shoulders began to shake and tremors of shock vibrated in every nerve ending. I began to weep, heavy choking sobs, as I shuddered uncontrollably. Time slowed down and I can vaguely remember a woman's cry. Was it Michelle? Or was it someone in the street? It seemed distant and unreal and I couldn't seem to focus on anything but a bizarre thought that my lovely Jaguar had been destroyed, followed by a surge of guilt that my brain was capable of such selfishness.

'Freddie! What's happened?'

Michelle rushed to my side and threw her arms around my waist

'Car bomb,' I cried. 'Probably meant for me.'

'Dad! Dad! Are you all right?' I heard Olivia cry from the bottom of the stairs.

'He's fine. Your Dad's OK,' Michelle shouted back. 'But stay back, Olivia. D'you hear me? Stay back.'

I stared at the wreck, and saw in my mind the charred corpse of my friend, but I knew the image was false. I took a deep, shuddering breath, and let it out again.

'Someone's going to pay for this,' I sobbed. 'I'll find the bastard, and he'll pay - by Christ, he'll pay.

I felt Michelle's arms stiffen before she took them away. Then she stood in front of me, blotting out the appalling destruction in the street.

'What the fuck are you involved in, Freddie? You can't do this to your family. You hear me? Whatever it is you're involved in, you've got to stop it. Stop it right now.'

I pushed her to one side and waved a hand at the smouldering wreck. 'You see that. That's one of my best mates in there. So don't start with the accusations, darling. All right?'

Her lips tightened into a narrow loathing as she stared at me, her bitterness growing like a tumour. I suddenly felt a deep loneliness. What if this destroyed my family? What if Michelle left me? How could I cope? These questions raced through my head as I stared at her, seeing nothing but hatred in her eyes. Hatred for what I had become. A vigilante. Someone who confuses justice with revenge.

I heard the familiar and distant wail of sirens. The sounds which had haunted me only two days ago as Rick lay bleeding in a park with his throat slit. And now Bill, an ex-soldier who had come through a tour of duty in Northern Ireland, and then a spell as a mercenary in Angola and the middle east, who had come through them all relatively unscathed, had met his end in an ordinary suburban street in Wanstead.

'Whether you like it or not, Freddie,' Michelle hissed, 'the police are now involved. So you're going to have to tell them everything... everything you know.'

Chapter 20

Michelle started to show the two police constables, one male and one female, into the living room. As I followed them in, my eyes focused on the occasional table which I had moved away from the wall and I suddenly felt very nervous. A firearm hidden beneath the floorboards was not something I wanted anyone to find, especially Michelle. I had already made up my mind who to blame for the car bomb, and I needed Bill's gun to protect myself, because knowing what I knew about Chapmays, there was no way I was going to involve the police, in spite of what Michelle had said..

'All this broken glass,' I protested. 'We can't sit in here. Why don't we go out the back to the kitchen?'

Through the broken window I saw the fire services using fire extinguishers on what was left of my car, while more police officers cordoned off a large area of the street, for by now crowds had gathered to watch the scene unfold..

Michelle, who had abandoned her shower during the explosion, and was clad in nothing but her bathrobe, looked down at her bare feet and the fragments of splintered glass on the carpet.

'Yes,' agreed the female PC. 'You haven't got your shoes on. We need to get you away from this broken glass.' She sounded like a teacher reprimanding a misbehaving child.

As we walked through to the kitchen, I made a mental note to excuse myself at some stage, so that I could move the occasional table back into place.

'I'm Constable Fowler,' the female PC said. 'And this is Constable Evans.'

She stood opposite us by the refectory table and gestured for us to be seated. She pulled a chair away from the table, causing Michelle to wince at the scraping noise. Her male colleague remained standing, awkward and ill-at-ease, as if he was a rookie and this was his first day on the job. I noticed how his eyes darted to Michelle's legs as she sat down, her bathrobe opening slightly and revealingly. Staring at him as she tucked it back in place, he blushed and looked away.

PC Fowler sat opposite me at the table and took out a pen and notebook, while her colleague stood stiffly at attention.

'Now then...' the female PC began, but was interrupted by Olivia entering. She had thrown on a pair of old jeans, trainers and a *Billy Elliot* T-shirt. She hurried over to Michelle and sat on her lap.

'Mum, what's going on? What's happening? Where's Bill?'

I felt tears welling up again as I watched Michelle stroking her hair and cuddling her.

'Who's Bill?' the female constable asked.

'My friend and business partner,' I said. My voice sounded peculiar, as if I was listening to someone else talking.

'And where is your friend?'

My mouth felt dry and I swallowed before answering. 'He was in the car when it blew up.'

Olivia moaned loudly, 'Oh, no! Not Bill!' She clung tightly to Michelle, buried her head in her neck and sobbed.

PC Fowler stared at me. 'What happened to the car? Do you know how the fire started, sir?'

'It didn't catch fire,' Michelle shouted angrily. 'It was an explosion. A car bomb. Bill was murdered. Someone planted a bomb in my husband's car.'

***

Half an hour later Michelle was dressed in jeans and a denim shirt, and the interview was now being conducted by a Detective Inspector Carton and a Detective Sergeant Myers in the living room.

After the uniformed constables discovered it was a car bomb, and not a mechanical fault which caused fire and an explosion, we became part of a major crime scene. As they took action, summoning the CID and a SOCO team to the area, Michelle managed to run upstairs to get dressed hurriedly, while I swept the glass up in the living room and moved the table back in place.

Our living room is luxuriously large, and we have space enough for two three-seater settees in an L-shape. DI Carton and DS Myers sat on one settee, and Michelle and I sat on the other, with Olivia sandwiched between us.

DI Carton looked like a humble and overweight pen-pusher with receding hair, but his eyes looked as shrewd and focused as a bird of prey. His sergeant was dapper, slim and expensively attired in a three-piece suit, with meticulous hair cut short. Neither of them looked like a soft touch.

'Mr Weston,' Carton began, 'have you any reason to suspect anyone of wanting to kill you and your partner?'

'Yes, I have.'

He raised his eyebrows, affecting surprise. 'Really. Now before I ask you for the name or names of any persons you suspect of planting this bomb that killed your business partner and not you - '

He paused, and I could see where this was heading. He would want to know why I hadn't been in the car with Bill when it exploded.

'Why would someone want to kill you or your partner?'

'Revenge,' I replied.

'Which implies you have done someone a disservice of some sort.'

'You could say that.'

'Would you like to elaborate?'

'Have you heard of a villain called Mark Lennox?'

'Yes, but he's never been part of our manor, and I believe he's getting on in years. Please continue.'

'Forty-seven years ago my father committed suicide, and I always suspected Lennox had something to do with it. Then last year my mother found a letter in her loft proving my dad was being blackmailed by Lennox.'

Myers, who was taking notes, stopped writing to ask, 'What did he blackmail your father about?'

'It transpired that my father was gay.'

I heard Michelle's intake of breath.

'Surely,' Myers continued, 'that was not a strong reason for blackmail.'

'It was illegal back then. The law wasn't changed until the late sixties. So I guess he was scared of the disgrace - scared of ending up in prison for being homosexual.'

Carton's eyes were like piercing laser beams. 'Did you know your father was gay?' He shook his head slightly, as if he knew in advance what my answer would be.

'No, none of the family knew.'

'So how did you find out?'

'Through my friend Bill. He snatched Lennox one night, and got him to confess. He must have leant on him a bit too heavily, because Lennox ended up with a stroke and is now in a home somewhere with senile dementia.'

Carton put fingers to his lips briefly, parodying bewilderment. 'Let me get this straight. Your friend, Bill Turner, snatches a villain on your behalf, and tortures or frightens him into confessing about blackmailing your father? So what part did you play in this?'

'Nothing. Bill owed me a favour from our army days.'

Sorry, Bill. I know if it had been the other way round you'd have done the same thing, my old mate.

'So are you trying to tell us that a senile old villain puts a price on your head?'

'It was probably someone in his firm. Like I said: revenge.'

Carton looked towards Michelle. 'Did you know about this, Mrs Weston?'

'I hadn't a clue. I mean, I knew for years Freddie suspected Lennox of having something to do with his father's suicide. But I didn't think, after more than forty years, Freddie would be so stupid as to...' She stopped, wondering if she'd said too much.

'Do what, Mrs Weston? Were you going to say he wouldn't be so stupid as to snatch Lennox with the aid of his friend? I don't think it's something a person could do on their own, do you?'

Carton switched his focus to me. 'I'm right, aren't I, Mr Weston? If what you're telling me is true about this gangster, you'd have wanted to interrogate him yourself. Isn't that right?'

I shrugged. 'I left it to Bill to interrogate him. Interrogation was his speciality. If you don't believe me, check his military record.'

'The Jaguar was your car I believe.'

The sudden change of tack. I had to admit, I hadn't seen it coming, but I could guess where it was leading.

'Yeah, it was my car, but Bill was included on my insurance and he offered to drive as we were going to meet someone in Peterborough.'

'Are you sure it wasn't the other way round? *You* asked *him* to drive.'

'No, he offered. So I took him up on it.'

'Mrs Weston?' Carton threw the question at Michelle, eyeing her acutely.

'I've no idea. They were down to breakfast before I appeared. I only came down to say goodbye to Bill.'

Silence. Her words triggering a raw iciness from the recent death.

Carton cleared his throat before continuing. 'What business were you and Mr Turner in?'

'A private enquiry agency.'

'As in private detectives you mean?' Surprise in his rising inflexion, making it sound ridiculous.

'If you like.'

Now Sergeant Myers decided it was time to go for the jugular. He leaned forward on the edge of the settee and locked eyes with me. 'Let's get back to the business of the car. Even if, as you say, he offered to drive, how is it you didn't get in the passenger seat at the same time?'

'I'd forgotten something and had to come back to get it.'

'What did you forget?'

'The address of the bloke we were going to visit in Peterborough. I'd left it on the work surface in the kitchen.'

I didn't think Michelle would remember if she had or hadn't seen a scrap of paper in the kitchen when she came down to see Bill off, so I felt the lie was beyond challenge.

Carton resumed the questioning. 'That seems suspiciously convenient.'

'Convenient. What's that supposed to mean?'

'It means, coming back into the house because you had forgotten something was a convenient way to stay alive if you knew a bomb was going to go off.'

My eyes burned with anger and I felt a constriction in my chest. 'Are you suggesting I had something to do with Bill's death? Jesus Christ! We were close pals. Years ago, when we were in the services, we looked out for one another. There was no way... now way I would have done anything to harm Bill.'

Carton stared at me deadpan and his voice didn't waver as he spoke. 'I'm sure you appreciate that in a serious murder like this we have to investigate every angle, including your relationship with your business partner.'

It crossed my mind to ask him if there were ever any non serious murders, but I buried the inappropriate thought.

'Mrs Weston,' he said, 'your husband's friend and business partner spent the night here. What sort of evening did you have?'

'We had fun. Freddie cooked us a lovely dinner, and he and Bill told us loads of funny stories from the past. It was just a nice relaxing evening, especially now that this evil internet troll seems to have stopped pestering Olivia.'

'Oh?' Carton stared at our daughter. 'What was all that about?'

Olivia's voice was hushed and timid when she replied, and we strained to hear her. 'A few weeks ago I talked to someone in a chat room, who sounded OK. But whoever it was sent nasty emails to my friends. And then it got...much worse.'

'In what way?'

'He said he was going to come and get me, and lock me up in a room like some girl in Austria.'

'Did this person have a name?'

'He called himself Eclipse.'

Carton threw his next question in my direction. 'Do you think this internet creature had something to do with the explosion?'

'It's possible. But I doubt it. Especially as I managed to get someone to put a stop to the internet attacks.'

'How did you manage that?'

'I was put in contact with a computer expert in Kent - a brilliant hacker I'd heard about through our office manager. I don't know what he did - I'm not *that* computer literate - but whatever it was, it seems to have done the trick. Thank God!' I smiled at Olivia and patted her leg.

I knew I had to keep Rick's name out of this. If, like me, they suspected it wasn't a brutal robbery, but because it might have had something to do with Eclipse and Peter Chapmays, their investigation would certainly put the kibosh on our own. And it was still at the forefront of my mind that the killer may have been an undercover cop; and then there were Ed Warren's observations about the mysterious visit to Bayne's firm from what looked like a high-ranking police officer. So there was no way I was going to trust any of them. And now that Bill had been murdered, I was even more determined to continue with my own investigations.

Maybe it was telepathy as these thoughts raced through my brain because the sergeant stared at me through narrowed eyes as he asked, 'So what were you and your partner investigating at the moment?'

I could feel Michelle looking at me intently as I replied.

'A young woman who asked us to search for what became of her father.'

'What's her name?' the sergeant asked, his pen poised ready.

I hesitated as I tried to recall her married name. I knew if I said Alice Bayne it might stir media memories of the shooting in Scotland. Fortunately, her married name surfaced after only a short pause. 'Mrs Egerton. Alice Egerton.'

I hoped my hesitation merely showed a reluctance to divulge our client's name for reasons of confidentiality.

'And are you confident this investigation had nothing to do with the car bomb?' Carton asked.

I chuckled to show how ridiculous that idea was. 'Absolutely. Why would an investigation into what became of a young woman's father have anything to do with this terrible tragedy?'

'So you think this Lennox's firm might have been responsible.'

'The only explanation I can think of.'

'I noticed you have a garage. Why did you decide to leave the car in the street.'

'Well, for a start, Michelle's car is in there, and we planned to leave for Peterborough much earlier than her running Olivia to school.'

'Did you hear anything suspicious in the night?'

'I slept like a log. I expect Bill did too. We'd both had a fair bit to drink.'

'Planning to drive only six hours later.'

I glared at Carton. 'So what if Bill's alcohol level was slightly over the limit? It's not going to make much difference now, is it?'

It was hard to know what Carton thought as he stared impassively at me. It was Michelle who broke the silence.

'So what happens now?'

'We'll need you and your husband to come along to the police station to make official statements, independently of one another. It'll be very thorough, and I should warn you it may take some time. Meanwhile, the wreck of the car will be taken away and examined carefully by our forensic team. And I think we may be able to dodge any media frenzy by avoiding any mention of car bombs, which will help with our investigations. Our uniformed officers are already under strict instructions not to speak to or leak this to the press.'

Although I was still numb from the terrible loss of my close mate, I was relieved the police decided to keep the details of the explosion from the press.

My next move was to try and excuse myself, use the loo and text Nicky and Alice to let them know what happened.

Then, as soon as the dust settled, I planned to meet with Jack Dawe in Peterborough and find out who had warned him off Alice's investigation.

Chapter 21

Tuesday 1 October 2013

Alice sat in the office with Nicky and me, and a heavy silence descended as we thought about Bill's funeral at Mortlake crematorium scheduled for twelve noon on Thursday. Macabre thoughts taunted me as I pictured the coffin at the service, knowing I'd be wondering just how much of Bill had been pieced together inside it.

Because of his murder, Alice kept blaming herself for involving us. I didn't doubt she was sincere, but I suspected she kept repeating it so that I could reassure her. So I told her what she wanted to hear.

'Don't be so hard on yourself, Alice. Bill was an old soldier. He knew the score. He took loads of risks in his lifetime, so maybe there comes a day of reckoning. You must have noticed him limping now and again. That was a souvenir from Angola, from the time his Jeep hit an IED.'

'That was years ago, though,' Nicky said. 'When you and he were much younger.'

To lighten the situation, I said, 'I'm not expecting my free bus pass for a while yet.'

Nicky smiled to humour me. Then Alice stood up, walked a few paces, and I saw she was thoughtful and restless, wanting action instead of the three of us sitting around feeling morbid and sorry for ourselves.

'It's obvious,' she began as her thoughts took shape, 'that with poor Bill gone, it would be difficult, if not impossible, for Freddie to work alone. So I've got a suggestion to make. Why don't I take Bill's place? Officially join the company as a partner?'

A gob-smacked pause from both Nicky and myself. Ignoring the way we stared at her with expressions of incredulity, Alice sat down again and looked at each of us in turn.

'And why not? I regularly run half marathons, I'm proficient in martial arts, and I have personal reasons for bringing down the bastards behind these murders.'

I suppressed a smile as I shook my head. 'Alice, we are not talking about martial arts in a sports hall where the competitors don't have guns or knives or bombs; we are talking about a serious life-threatening conspiracy here.'

'And I know, come hell or high water, I've got to do something about it. Put an end to whoever is responsible before it ruins anyone else's life. So how about it, Freddie?'

I hesitated, and she leapt up again.

'That's settled then. Thank you for the gracious way you've invited me on board.'

A grin spread across my face as I rose to face her. 'I warn you, Alice. It could be bloody dangerous.'

'That's choice coming from an old geezer like you. And what about you, Nicky? You still think we ought to involve the police?'

I could see Nicky wrestling with her conscience as she got slowly to her feet, frowning hard as she struggled to verbalise her doubts. 'I just think... I think we need to consider what we're getting into.'

'We've already done that,' I said. 'We've talked ourselves hoarse. The car bomb that killed Bill...'

Nicky raised a hand. 'I know. I know. We don't need to go through that again.'

She was talking about the fact that none of the national papers reported anything about a car bomb or a person being killed. The only mention of the incident was in my local rag, a report of a car catching fire and exploding. Either the police wanted it kept quiet while they carried out their investigations or there was something far more sinister going on. And Bill's life seemed to have been air-brushed out of existence.

'Listen to me, Nicky,' Alice said. 'You're our office manager. There's no need for you to get involved in anything other than - well, organising the office and gathering information. If it comes to the crunch, you don't know much about the investigation. Freddie and I will back you up. So how about it? Are you staying to see this through or not?'

A tentative smile from Nicky. 'Well, I know I shouldn't say this, Alice, seeing as this is all about you losing your family, but most of my other jobs have been dull compared to this one. Even the acting ones. This investigation is a lot more exciting, and if I'm honest, I'm starting to enjoy it.'

Alice hugged her briefly then checked her watch. 'Great, Nicky. Thanks for your support. Right! We've wasted enough time in the office. We need to head for Peterborough, talk to this ex-detective and find out who scared him away. Shall we go in my Saab or your hired car, Freddie?'

'Hired car. Less distinctive.' I offered her my hand. 'Welcome to the company, Weston and Bayne.'

'Let's stick to Weston and Turner, as a tribute to Bill.'

Chapter 22

We made Peterborough in just over two hours in the Renault Scenic rental car. Alice complained that we should have gone in her Saab seeing as she had a satnav which might have made finding Jack Dawe's address easier. I protested that we had my computer map which I'd printed off Streetmap UK and confessed to her my fear of losing my map-reading skills.

'I think you've already lost it,' she said. 'We just turned left there when we should have gone right.'

'You were holding the map round the wrong way.'

She giggled. 'And I think you're talking bollocks.'

'No change there then.'

I turned the car round in the narrow street, and we went back past the T-junction where I had gone left instead of right. We took the next right into a no-through street of cramped, brick, two-up two-down terrace houses and cruised slowly, Alice reading off the numbers until we came to the dead end right outside the house belonging to the ex-investigator.

'That might be useful,' I observed. 'As it's at the end of the terrace, it's got a back entrance.'

'Surely you wouldn't consider breaking and entering, would you?'

She said it so sincerely I thought she was serious until I noticed the slight smile on her face.

'First of all,' I said as I parked the car, 'let's see if he's home.'

When we knocked, the bang sounded alarmingly loud in the quiet street. We waited, staring at the drab and greying net curtain in the front room window. I bent over and peered through the letter box, but all I could see was a gloomy hallway, a door on the right near the stairs, and a door at the end, presumably leading to the kitchen. I knocked again, lightly this time, because there was no way he wouldn't have heard my first knock, and I didn't want to alert the street to our presence.

Alice shivered. 'It doesn't look like anyone's home. And it's ominously quiet.'

'Ain't nobody here but us chickens,' I sang softly.

'What?'

'Heard it on *The Muppet Show*.'

'I almost regret asking.'

'With my daughter when she was nine or ten.'

I saw the wistful look in Alice's eyes, and I knew the allusion to my harmonious family life had aroused in her a memory of her tragic circumstances, reminding her of what might have been.

'Come on,' I said. 'Let's take a look round the back.'

Halfway down the narrow side entrance was a tall gate. I tried the latch, expecting it to be bolted on the other side, but it opened, creaking on rusty hinges. We passed a back window which looked out onto the alley, which was also masked by a net curtain so dirty it was almost opaque. The back garden was mostly overgrown grass and there was a small shed at the end. As we came around the side, we saw there were two doors, one was the back entrance and the other looked like a door to an old outside privy. I rapped on the back door with my knuckles, just in case Dawe was home and asleep after a night of binge drinking. After all, his father had told me he was depressed. Depressed and scared, so who could blame him if he drank himself legless in the local pub.

Alice suggested we try the back door. I expected it to be locked but it opened, leading us into a small scullery-kitchen, containing a manky gas cooker next to an old fashioned white sink, piled high with dirty crockery, next to a wooden draining board. We had gone back in time. The house was circa 1930s and didn't look as if it had been improved in any way since then. I wondered why the back door had been left unlocked, and saw there was an ordinary key in the lock, not a Yale type, so leaving via the back door would mean taking the key from the inside, and locking it from the outside before leaving. Either Jack Dawe was still here, or he had gone out the back door, leaving it open. Which was not what a frightened man would do.

We crept quietly up a step and into the next room, which had a hideous green-tiled fireplace with a two-bar electric fire in the grate, in front of which sat an old easy chair with wooden arms, the varnish faded, and the stuffing of the cushions frayed and torn. A hideously-patterned square Formica table stood by the window, and the matching chairs had tubular yellow metal frames and padded plastic seats, most of which were split.

'Surely he can't have lived here,' Alice whispered. 'I got the impression he was a bit of a high-flyer.'

'Not any more.'

'But this house, it's - ' She struggled to find the right words.

'Maybe he inherited it from his granny or someone. And now he needs it as a safe house. Come on, let's take a look around.'

There was hardly any room to move in the front room, it was crammed with junk like a second-hand shop, bursting at the seams with heavy oak furniture, ugly and cumbersome items, wartime utility mainly, with no sense of style. Stuff that had no value, except maybe if you were looking for properties for a wartime film set. It smelt damp and musty in there, and the threadbare carpet looked as if it was caked with dust.

I looked at Alice, pulled a face, then pointed upwards. Stairs creaking loudly, we climbed the short staircase to the landing. There was a bathroom just as you reached the top, the door was open revealing a chipped-enamel bath, with maroon-coloured stains, over which stood a monstrous gas heater. There were two rooms up there, and I chose the one at the front of the house, which was probably the master bedroom. As soon as I walked in and smelt the sickly odour of putrefying flesh, I knew what I would find.

His body was sprawled across the filthy bed, his head lolling at an angle, covered in a plastic bag tied tightly around the neck by a belt. I saw Alice falter and put a hand to her mouth as she gagged. The fetid room was dark, the heavy curtains closed, the only light coming from a six inch gap in the middle, throwing a sliver of light across the body. The face inside the bag was grim, bloated and hideous, a mask of horror. He wore a short sleeved shirt, and I forced myself to step closer to peer at the putrefying flesh of his arm. It didn't look as if rigor mortis was long gone, and the decomposition was fairly recent, otherwise the stench would have been far worse. I'm no expert in these matters, but I knew enough to guess that he death occurred maybe two days ago. Bedclothes were strewn all over the floor and there was an upturned bedside table and lamp on the floor.

Alice looked as if she was about to pass out, so I opted to speak to her, forcing her to reply. 'If you were a copper, what would you make of this?'

She swallowed hard before answering. 'The belt around his neck looks very tight. The way the buckle's been slotted neatly into a notch. I wouldn't think that would have been easy to do - not as you find it harder to breathe. But then I can only guess. How can anyone know what it's like?'

'What else can you see?'

'Why are the bedclothes strewn everywhere? If he killed himself he would have just laid down on the bed and done it, wouldn't he?'

'Of course. But it looks as if there was a struggle.'

'But why wouldn't... I mean, if it wasn't suicide, why would the killer leave everything looking as if there was a struggle?'

I shrugged. 'Maybe he wasn't trying to make it look like a suicide. Perhaps he didn't care what the crime scene looks like. The walls in these houses must be quite thin, so he decides to use what he thinks is a quiet method of killing.'

'But Jack Dawe made it hard for him. Put up a fight.'

'Yes, and from what you told me, he was ex-army, so he must have been reasonably tough, even if he was out of condition. But we can only guess about what happened. The only ones who'll get nearer the truth will be crime scene officers and forensics.' I took a deep breath and almost gagged on the pungent stink of decaying flesh. 'Come on, let's get out of here. There's nothing we can do now.'

As we walked on to the landing I patted all my pockets. 'Why is it you can never find a hankie or tissue when it's needed.'

She took a packet of handy tissues out of her handbag and gave them to me. 'Will these do?'

'Thanks. It's to wipe prints off the door handles.'

'Yes, I think I could have worked that out for myself.'

Chapter 23

On the drive out of Peterborough I saw Alice shifting awkwardly in her seat, rolling her shoulders to ease the tension.

'How d'you feel?' I asked her.

'Dirty. I need a good long soak in the bath. That smell seems to stay with you.'

I smiled grimly. 'It's hard to shake off.'

'Not your first experience of corpses, I take it.'

'No. Although it's been a while.'

'This murdering bastard's got to be stopped, Freddie. He's already tried to kill you with the car bomb. He couldn't have known Bill was going to drive, and you were going to go back to collect the gun. In order to plant the bomb, he must have followed you both home. Either that, or he knows where you live. But how could he know you would try to find Jack Dawe? The only ones who knew about that were you, Bill, Nicky and me.'

'Unless he happened to ring up Dawe's father, same as we did, and found out someone phoned to get his son's address. So, not taking any chances, and guessing we'd go up there to speak with Jack Dawe, he decides to stop us by planting the car bomb. Then, when he finds out I'm still alive, he goes up to Peterborough to silence Dawe. It looks now as if he's getting careless and taking risks. Because he knows we're on to him and getting closer.'

'But how could he possibly know that?'

'There is one person who thinks the sun shines out of his arse. And probably doesn't have a clue about the sort of man he is.'

'You mean that schoolteacher?'

'That's the one. Christine Bailey. When Bill and I went to visit her, there was something not quite right.' Suddenly the thought hit me, and I thumped the steering wheel. 'Shit! Why didn't I think of it? She's got my business card. OK, so it's not got my home address on it, but it has the office website, email address and mobile. If he works for this Eclipse bastard, who can access our texts and calls - '

'But if she still sees her old boyfriend, why would she give him your details?'

'If he was an undercover cop originally, and infiltrated the anarchist group, he's probably brilliant at deception and a very convincing liar. Plus they've got a young son, and that can often create a strong bond, even though he may disappear for months on end.'

'But he disappeared out of her life nearly fourteen years ago.'

'Still, he may have been in touch with her during those years. He might even have provided money for the son.'

I noticed the tension in Alice's hands as she squeezed them tightly in her lap.

'A ruthless, cold blooded killer like that looking after his family. That doesn't make any sense.'

'Like a lot of bad guys, he leads a double-life. And don't forget, Hitler was loved by millions of Germans, was kind to animals and a vegetarian.'

'I take your point. But his son would have been about three or four when he shot my little brother. You would have thought being a father himself, he'd have had some compassion, sense of decency and moral standards.'

'Try telling that to the Taliban who shot a fifteen-year-old Pakistani girl.'

Alice sighed loudly. 'What a shit-awful world we live in.'

'It's been like it for thousands of years. Nothing's changed.'

Because I'd been used to the automatic transmission on my Jaguar, and I wasn't concentrating as I changed gears coming on to the A1, there was a terrible grinding noise as I tried to slam the gear stick into third, forgetting to put my foot on the clutch.

'Must change my underwear when I get home,' I chuckled.

Ignoring my bad joke, Alice said, 'So what happens now?'.

'I need to have another word with this Christine Bailey.'

'I think *we* need to have a word with her. Woman to woman might work better.'

'I think you're right,' I agreed. 'But the biggest problem's going to be getting her on her own. She won't talk to us in front of her son, and she teaches during the day. We'll have to do a bit of surveillance. Find out when the son goes out on a regular basis. But that could take a bit of time.'

'Meanwhile, there's a killer still out there who...'

'That may not be a problem,' I interrupted to set her mind at ease. 'With Jack Dawe dead, he knows we'll find it tricky to get any more info. And I don't think he's going to want to take any more risks.'

'I hope you're right, Freddie.'

'So do I.'

A long and thoughtful silence before she spoke. 'About Jack Dawe's murder: you don't think we ought to - ' She didn't finish the sentence but I knew what she was driving at.

'Inform the police, you mean?'

'We could do it anonymously. At least then his father will find out what happened to his son. It's better that he knows.'

'Whether he finds out now or in weeks or months is still going to be a shock. I don't think we ought to risk it. We were never in Peterborough and we never found his body. It's better that way. So let's drop it, shall we?'

'If you say so. Changing the subject: how are things at home now?'

'Lousy. I get the silent moody from Michelle. She knows I'm caught up in something dodgy and wants me to drop it.'

'What did you tell her about the investigation?'

'Not much. I didn't lie as such. I said you wanted me to find out what happened to your father, which in a way is true.'

'What about the explosion?'

'She thinks the car bomb was something to do with that villain's mob I took revenge on last year.'

'The one who was responsible for your father's suicide?'

I nodded, and went on to tell her the full story. When I finished, she was silent for a while.

'Well?' I prompted.

'Sounds to me like you got lucky, what with him having a stroke followed by senile dementia. It could so easily have gone the other way, and Michelle will know that.'

'Which is why I'm getting the passive-aggressive treatment. It could be worse. If I hadn't sorted out this internet freak that attacked my daughter, I think my marriage would be over by now. As it is, I'm on two yellow cards.'

Chapter 24

Thursday 3 October 2013

The only close family of Bill's was an older brother living in Aberdeen, who he had never really got along with. When I phoned and told him of his younger brother's death, he grumbled about how difficult the journey would be to attend the funeral, so would I understand if he gave it a miss. It was no skin off my nose, I told him, and as Bill was dead he wouldn't be aware of his brother's absence. It was a short conversation, lasting less than two minutes.

But I did get in touch with some of our old ex-army pals, and they showed up for the funeral, as did Bill's ex-wife from a childless marriage of twenty years ago. Her name was Diana and she made the effort to come down from Sunderland where she lived with her second husband and two children. Although I had never met her until this day, I remembered Bill telling me how much she loved him, would always love him, but said she couldn't possibly stay with him when she discovered he was a mercenary. He said it was something to do with her socialist-pacifist upbringing, and she regretted their parting but it was inevitable considering he made his living from someone else's death.

While we hung around in the reception area outside the chapel of rest, waiting to be ushered inside for the short and ill-attended funeral, the polite conversation was strained. Michelle was watchful and suspicious, her eyes sweeping over Nicky and Alice, as if she was assessing their candidacy for attending the funeral of someone they had only known for such a short time. When I introduced her to Alice, she nodded curtly.

'You can't have known Bill for very long. Less than a week, was it?'

'That's right. But I liked him and thought I would come and pay my respects.'

Michelle nodded. A throat clearing strained silence in the waiting room as everyone was stuck for something to say. I was glad Michelle and I had persuaded Jackie and Olivia not to miss another day at college and school instead of travelling across London to attend Bill's funeral, a service that would be over in a flash.

A short, slim, attractive woman sidled into our group. She wore a tight black dress, black high-heel shoes, a black fedora worn at a jaunty angle, and a red ribbon around her slender neck, with a medallion of some sort attached to it. The shade of the ribbon matched her lipstick. She looked stylish, as if she might once have been a model. She introduced herself.

'I'm Diana. You must be Freddie. When Bill and I were married, he talked about you a lot.'

'We go back a long way,' I replied, wondering if anyone noticed my use of the present tense. 'You've come all the way from Sunderland, I believe. That's quite a journey.'

'Well, I know we were married for only three years but we parted as friends. There were no recriminations.'

She spoke with a curiously attractive Geordie dialect, her statements sounding like questions.

'As you've come all that way, no doubt you'll join us in the pub afterwards.'

She shook her head emphatically. 'No, I'm sorry, but I think I'll have to catch the train back before the rush hour.'

'It's a long way to come for a very short service,' I persisted. 'The proper send off for someone like Bill would be in the boozer.'

'Reminiscing about your days in the army?' She glanced at the huddle of old ex-soldiers and spoke with a trace of bitterness. 'If you don't mind, I'll give that one a miss.'

I didn't know what to say and was relieved when an usher asked us to enter the chapel for the service. I'd arranged for the Dire Straits recording of 'Brothers in Arms' to play softly while we waited for the service to begin. It's quite a lengthy song, so I arranged for a fade out just before the chaplain was due to speak. As the song played I caught the eye of Bill's ex-wife and she shook her head slightly, probably disapproving of the music choice.

As I was the closest friend of Bill, I had given the chaplain a few details about his background and what little I knew about his childhood for the eulogy, but kept off the subject of his mercenary exploits, although I let it be known that he was a good soldier in the 9ᵗʰ Para Engineers. The chaplain read from the outline I'd given him, talking about the diversity of Bill's skills, and spoke about how he was also a trained and brilliant paramedic. Then he went on to read about Bill's love of Shakespeare. I don't think my old pal ever went to the theatre; he just enjoyed reading Shakespeare, mainly the histories, dipping into passages and memorising quotes, especially relevant passages to do with soldiering, *Henry V* being one of his favourites. The chaplain paused prior to his conclusion, looking around at the middle-aged ex-military men, before ending the tribute with the quotation 'we few, we happy few, we band of brothers.' We all bowed our heads for 'The Lord's Prayer', followed by a mumbled 'Amen', and then the coffin began its journey to the furnace as my appropriately chosen 'Brothers in Arms' faded up.

In spite of Michelle's disapproval of the way I had brought Bill's misfortune to our doorstep, as we watched the coffin disappearing through the gap in the curtains, she took my hand and squeezed it. The sympathy and understanding was brief and of the moment, and I knew it wouldn't last.

There were a few sniffles, especially from Bill's ex-wife, and I noticed one of Bill's old comrades wiping a tear from his eye. It was over in a trice and we shuffled out into the warm autumn sun.

I saw Diana taking a mobile and a business card out of her handbag and I guessed she was about to ring for a taxi. 'How are you getting to Kew Gardens station?' I asked her.

'The same way as I got here. By cab.'

'I'll give you a lift, Diana.'

'That's OK. I don't want to keep you from your booze-up.'

I wanted to tell her that according to the online details of the crematorium it was only a ten minute walk to the station, but her high heels looked precarious and weren't designed for anything more distant than crossing a wine bar.

Michelle placed a hand on Diana's to stop her dialling. 'I'll run you Diana. Freddie can get a lift with one of his old comrades. Kew Gardens station's not far.' Michelle saw Diana about to protest, and added, 'I insist. It's no trouble at all.'

'Thank you.'

I shook hands with her, thanked he for coming, and watched as Michelle walked her to the car, thinking how sad it was that she had made the hefty journey for such a brief farewell. I wondered if it was closure and she could now get on with life and no longer indulge in thoughts of how things might have been had Bill not been a mercenary. I also wondered what her husband and children had been told was the reason for this trip. Then I freed it from my mind. What did it matter? I was never going to know.

Alice gave Nicky and me a lift to the pub, The Botanist Brewery on Kew Green. I had reserved an area for us, and put in an order for a the first round of drinks. I decided to put off ordering any food until Michelle turned up, but when my mobile bleeped, I saw that it was a text message from her, saying she didn't feel like drinking, had gone home, and would I mind using public transport to get back.

Bad enough that I felt guilty and responsible for Bill's death, without Michelle rubbing my nose in it. And as if to compound the way I was being swallowed up by the insatiable monster of death and gloom, Jeremy Wallbank, an old comrade from the 9th Para regiment, cornered me, demanding to know the truth about how Bill died. He clearly didn't believe my story about the faulty vehicle catching fire.

'Knowing Bill,' he said, 'he'd have been out of the driving seat in a flash. The car wouldn't have exploded immediately. That was a fucking car bomb, Freddie, and don't try to tell me any different. What the fuck's going on?'

His voice had risen, and I noticed one of the bar staff staring at us, a worried look on his face. He knew we would spend lavishly, but equally he didn't want customers in attendance who might lower the tone of the place.

'Please, Jem, keep your voice down. I can't tell you at this stage. It's too dangerous. I don't want it to get out.'

'Don't want what to get out? That's not good enough, Freddie. I want to know what really happened to Bill. And what the police are doing about it? Don't give me any more of your bullshit, Freddie. I'm not fucking stupid. I want t know what happened to our old mate.'

Jimmy Gresham, a corporal from our time in Northern Ireland in the mid-seventies, attracted by the intensity of his harangue, stood at his side, nodding fervently. He was soon joined by the four others: Clive 'Squirrel' Nutkin, Jack Bradley, Ken 'Gunner' Thomson and Dick Russell. Their eyes bored into me as I was forced into the focus of their enclosing circle. Surrounded. Clearing my throat nervously, I racked my brains for something I could tell them that wouldn't compromise our investigation, upsetting my client.

But it was Alice who came to my rescue.

'I'll tell you what's going on,' she said, as she pushed her way into the circle and stood next to me.

Some of them exchanged puzzled looks as she paused, and I could see her working out just how much of the story to give them.

'Before I married, my name was Alice Bayne. If some of you cast your minds back, you might remember me from the media.' She stared at them, waiting for one of them to recognise her.

Dick Russell was the first. 'Jesus!' he gasped. 'You're the young girl whose family was wiped out in Scotland.'

Some of them exchanged looks and muttered that they remembered the dreadful incident.

'Well,' Alice went on, 'for eleven years the police got nowhere. So I came to meet Freddie and Bill to see if they were prepared to take the case on. Then, when they agreed to represent me, they did something the police were unable to do: they discovered the false identity of the killer, who it turns out is or was an undercover cop.' She paused, looking at each of them in turn, waiting for a response. It was Jem who provided it.

'Is that why the police have kept the car bomb incident quiet?' She shrugged. 'It could be. But we don't really know.'

'So what happens now?' Jimmy Gresham asked.

'The killer's been getting careless,' I said. 'I think he's running scared. So we think we have a plan to flush him out.'

The circle of six ex-soldiers stared at me with mixed expressions of admiration and envy. They had all settled for a safe but humdrum existence and clearly missed the danger and excitement of their younger days.

I smiled at Alice, grateful for her assistance in getting me off the hook with my old army pals and giving them as much information as she dared.

'Is there anything we can do to assist in tracking down this bastard?' Jem said.

I stifled a smile as I looked at the old soldier, who was now at least six stone overweight, and hadn't aged well, looking more like a man of seventy than someone in his mid-fifties.

'Thanks, Jem, but all we ask is total silence. And I promise I'll give you the full story after it's all over.'

An uncomfortable silence. I could tell they were all thinking that we might end up the same way as Bill, and often it's the bad guys who triumph.

It was Nicky who broke the spell of doom. 'Shall we order some food now?'

Chapter 25

Saturday 5 October 2013

Alice and I sat in her car. We'd been there for half an hour, parked diagonally opposite Christine Bailey's house. I checked up on the QPR fixture for today, and discovered they were playing at home against Barnsley. Our only hope was that Bailey's son was an avid and regular supporter. If he was, at his young age, and probably with money being tight, he was more likely to attend a home game.

At 11:45 a young lad wearing a QPR strip arrived at the house and we watched him knock. Presently, as if he'd been expected at that time, Bailey's son came lumbering out of the house, slamming the door, and the two lads hurried along the street towards the main road.

'Let's give it fifteen minutes,' I suggested to Alice, 'just in case he might have forgotten something and comes back for it.'

We waited ten minutes and then decided to tackle Christine Bailey, just in case she left to go shopping now her son had left the house. We crossed the street and I rapped on the door, standing to one side to let Alice be the first to confront Bailey. I intended leaving most of the talking to my new partner as I knew she would appeal to the woman's sense of justice; although I realised it still might be tricky, seeing as Chapmays was the father of her son, and she might flinch at the idea of betraying him, even though he had betrayed her political group to the police.

The door opened cautiously, as if she'd been anticipating trouble since Bill and I paid her a visit just over a week ago. Her mouth opened in confusion when she saw Alice, and when her eyes flitted to me she began to shut the door. So I put one foot in and flung my shoulder against it. The frame flew out of her hand and slammed into the wall.

'Hey!' she yelled. 'What the hell's going on?'

'We just want to talk to you,' Alice said.

'Get out! I've got nothing to say to you.'

'That's too bad. Because we're going to talk to you whether you like it or not. We can do it out here on the doorstep, in front of all the neighbours, or you can invite us in and we can sit down and have a civilized discussion.'

Her eyes widened and radiated fear.

'What about?'

'I think you know bloody well why we've come here. It's about your boyfriend.'

She shrank into herself as she stared at me. 'I've already told this man here, I don't know where he is.'

'You lied to him,' Alice hissed. 'And you lied to his partner, who is now dead. Killed in a car bomb. So you'd better start talking to us. Do I make myself clear?'

I thought the woman was about to start bawling, but in a moment she composed herself and stood aside. 'You'd better come in then. But I don't see what else I can tell you.'

She closed the front door and took us through to the back room. We sat at the table and she remained standing, her arms folded across her chest.

'I'm not going to offer you anything to drink,' she said, 'because you won't be staying long enough. I've got nothing else to say. I haven't seen Peter for years.'

Alice raised her eyebrows in mock surprise. 'No? Then how is it he knew of the whereabouts of Freddie Weston here and his partner?'

'I really have no idea what you're talking about.'

'I'm talking about Peter Chapmays killing this man's partner.'

Bailey snorted scornfully. 'I don't believe you. And I don't believe Peter would do such a thing.'

'No? He's the only one right now who has a motive for killing Bill Turner, this man's partner, in a car bomb that was intended for both of them.'

'This is... this is absurd. Why would Peter want to kill this man's partner? What possible reason would he have? It's so ridiculous...'

Alice raised a hand to stop her. 'It's not so ridiculous, and you damn well know it. Your boyfriend was an undercover cop who betrayed you then disappeared for years on end. And since then he's become a cold-blooded hired killer.'

'Hired killer!' Bailey shrieked. 'What fucking planet are you living on?'

Alice shook her head in desperation, knowing this was going to be difficult persuading this woman that her boyfriend was a hitman.

I decided it was time to step in and give her the full details of the Bayne family massacre. 'Let me introduce you to Alice Bayne. You might remember her from headline stories eleven years ago when her family was murdered up in Scotland. Her mother, father and little brother were shot, and the gunman showed no mercy whatsoever.'

I paused, giving her time to digest the information as she stared at Alice. Then I went on to explain about the way we had stumbled on the name of Peter Chapmays, pinpointing him as the man who purchased the car tracker; and the newspaper picture from the anarchists' court acquittal confirming his false identity as Chapmays. I ended the account by telling her of the way he had stolen a dead toddler's identity. After I finished her face was ashen and I could see she was deeply affected.

'There m-must be s-some mistake,' she stammered. 'Peter would never harm anyone. He was against capitalism and all that it stood for. And now you're trying to tell me he killed people for money. I don't believe you.'

Alice stared at her; her eyes cold as steel. 'It's true. And you know it's true. Deep down you know damn well it's true. I've lost my entire family because of your fucking boyfriend.'

Bailey laughed in desperation. 'But this is absurd. Who or why would someone pay him to kill your family?'

Alice looked at me, knowing this was a tricky one to answer, and Bailey leapt on it.

'You see! You haven't got a fucking clue, have you? It's ridiculous. You can't think of a single reason why someone would hire him to kill...'

'We may not be able to prove it right now,' Alice interrupted. 'But we can guess at the reason. We think he was involved in organised crime. So was my father. But the only person who can tell us why my family was slaughtered is your boyfriend. Which is why we need to speak to him.'

'What makes you think I know where he is?'

'Oh, come on, Christine!' I shouted as I got up out of the chair, causing her to flinch. 'After I left you my business card, someone found out where I lived, and my partner was murdered.'

Her head drooped, her shoulders shook, and we heard the bubbling of tears. I looked at Alice and nodded, giving her the signal to take over. She stood up and went to Bailey, tentatively sliding an arm across her shoulder.

'I know how hard this must be,' Alice said, her voice soft and sympathetic. 'It must be difficult to accept. But deep down you must know, having had to listen to Peter's lies in the past, that there was something not quite right. You must know that. You're not stupid, Christine. Think back to the way he suddenly disappeared out of your life. You must have found that odd. Suspicious.'

'But what about Dan? Our son,' Bailey sobbed and moaned as her body shook. 'If he found out his father...God! I can't believe this is happening. His father a... a killer. Oh, God! No! Please! Say it's not true.'

'Sorry, Christine, the man who left you so suddenly almost fourteen years ago was not who he pretended to be, and since then he got in with the wrong people and he's become a ruthless killer. The man doesn't possess a conscience, Christine. My little brother was only ten when he shot him in cold blood.'

An animal cry of pain came from deep inside Bailey's chest. 'Oh, no, my Dan! What can I tell Dan about his father?'

Over Bailey's head Alice threw me a look. It was confident and manipulative, and I could see she was capable of moulding Bailey so that she might inform on her boyfriend.

'I know all this has come as a dreadful shock, Christine.'

Christine sniffed nosily and wiped her nose on the sleeve of her sweater.

'Christine, listen to me,' Alice said. 'We may still be wrong about Peter. Perhaps he wasn't the one who... But there's only one way to find out, and that's for us to confront him. I don't mean you, Christine. I mean me and Freddie. Give him a chance to explain himself. It's the only way.'

Bailey looked up through misted eyes, her voice chocking with emotion. 'You think there might be some mistake? You think he could be innocent?'

'That's for us to find out.' Alice grabbed Bailey tightly be the shoulders and stared into her eyes. 'Look at me, Christine. Whatever you do, you mustn't tell him about our visit. He'll only lie to you again. The only way is for you to... Do you have a mobile phone?'

Bailey nodded.

'If he visits you, you must send us a text to let us know he's here. Can you do that without him knowing?'

'I think so.'

'It's very important, Christine.'

'What will you do to him?'

'Follow him. Go to his place and talk to him. Find out the truth.'

'But what if...?' Bailey stopped, unable to say what was on her mind.

'What if he's guilty, you mean? Let's deal with that when the time comes. What sort of car does he drive?'

Bailey shook her head, more in confusion than a refusal to answer. 'I think it was... it was a black BMW.'

'What sort of model is it?'

'How the hell do I know?'

'OK. It doesn't matter. When he came here to see you, how much time did he spend with you?'

Bailey broke away from Alice and held the edge of the table for support. She looked weak and distraught, her make-up smeared, her hair dishevelled, and there was a trail of snot on one of her sleeves. Her body shook as she lowered herself into a chair.

'Christine,' Alice continued, 'how much time does he spend here when he visits?'

Bailey looked up, her eyes pleading. 'I wasn't lying when I said he never visits. What I meant was, he's only been about twice this year. And before that it was just once in about five years. He's like a stranger. And the effect this has on Dan is terrible. It would be better if he didn't come at all.'

'So is he likely to come back again soon?'

Bailey nodded. 'He promised he would. He said very soon. Within a week, he said.'

'As soon as he does, Christine, send us that text. When he was here the last time, how long was he here for?

'Most of the afternoon and evening - about six or seven hours. He spent a lot of the time in Dan's room, trying to bond with him. Oh God! What's going to happen if he goes to prison. What will Dan do then?'

'At least you'd know where you could find him,' I said, keeping any emotion out of my voice. 'Dan would be able to visit and talk to his father regularly. It might be better than seeing him only two or three times in five years.'

'And how will he feel if he finds out it was me who was responsible for putting him away?'

Alice stood over Bailey, her nostrils flaring and her eyes filled with cold determination. I knew she was about to state the hard reality of the circumstances, giving the woman no choice but to play along with what we suggested. 'Whatever happens, Christine, your boyfriend cannot continue working for whoever it is he works for. He can't be allowed to continue murdering innocent people. And let me make it quite clear what the consequences will be if you should warn him about our visit. There'll be even more unnecessary bloodshed, and it's a risk we're not prepared to take. Do I make myself clear?'

Bailey's head sunk onto her chest. 'Yes,' she mumbled.

'Sorry, Christine: I didn't catch that.'

Bailey raised her head and nodded, staring zombie-like at Alice through clouded eyes. 'Yes. All right. I'll do it. I'll do it.'

'Thank you, Christine. It's the best way. It's the *only* way, believe me. Now we'll leave you to think about what we've said.'

We started to leave, but I turned back at the door for a final word. 'A word of warning, Christine. When Chapmays turns up, he mustn't suspect anything. You've got to act normal and not make him suspicious. If you can't handle it from the pressure, make out you're coming down with the flu or something. But he mustn't suspect anything. Otherwise you could be in danger. Remember, this man is ruthless, and killed Alice's ten-year-old brother rather than leave a witness behind. So if he thinks you're about to shop him - '

I left the unfinished sentence hanging ominously, hoping it would serve as a warning in case she decided to confront Chapmays and confide in him. It was a terrible risk we were taking, but it was the only way we could think of to smoke the bastard out.

As soon as we had left the house, and Alice was behind the wheel of her Saab, she turned to me and asked, 'Will she play ball and warn us when he comes round, d'you think?'

I stared thoughtfully through the windscreen, watching an old lady shuffling painfully along the street, supported by a triangular pulpit frame on wheels. Eventually, I turned to Alice and said, 'Christine Bailey will sit there for hours now, in a state of shock. She'll weep and moan, feeling sorry for herself and her son, but as we've planted the seeds of doubt about his past, the way it was obvious he was not who he pretended to be, she'll soon realise she has no option but to go along with what we've suggested.'

'I hope you're right.'

'She's a primary schoolteacher, don't forget. And what we told her about Chapmays showing no mercy when he killed your kid brother, must effect her. It must do.'

'Meanwhile, we'll just have to sit tight and wait for her to contact us.'

I glanced at my watch. 'Time for me to get home and face the music. If this investigation gets any worse, I think Michelle will freak out. I could find myself being taken to the cleaners via the divorce courts.'

'Oh, Freddie, I'm sorry. This is all my fault.'

'Or even worse, sleeping in the spare room.' I grinned to let her know I was joking. Well, perhaps half joking, because I had yet to get home to face the music.

Chapter 26

A week went by and we heard nothing from Christine Bailey. Because it looked as if Chapmays was trying to bond with his son, Nicky suggested he might visit on a Saturday, and perhaps take him to a football match. So the three of us arranged to come into the office for at least half the day. But it was almost midday and it looked as if it was going to be an unproductive Saturday, and Michelle wasn't too pleased when I told her I needed to go to the office to sort out one or two problems. She gave me a cold stare, shrugged, and took refuge in the garden, a trait she had inherited from her father whose obsessive gardening was a means of escape from her mother's equally obsessive dusting and cleaning.

The three of us sat in the inner office, me behind the desk, and Nicky and Alice on chairs in front of it. Because of Alice's huge financial input in the business, I suggested she should take pole position behind the desk, but she waved it aside. I didn't think it was gender bias, with her doing it out of deference to me as the male instigator of the business; I just didn't think she cared about anything to do with status and her only concern was the job in hand.

We spent most of the morning going through everything we had learnt about the case so far, right from day one when Alice came to assign us to the investigation. It was her idea that in order to protect ourselves from any legal ramifications in the future, we ought to have a written record of everything we had discovered up until now. Rather than waste our week waiting for Bailey to call, we spent most of the time writing up accurate records of the case. Nicky wrote it all down, first in shorthand, then in longhand before transferring it onto the computer, printed out copies for each of us to look through, and then made two USB pen drive copies, which Alice and I could store in a safe place away from the office. I stuck mine in a pocket, next to my passport, which I had taken to carrying around in case I needed to make a trip to Krakow the last minute, although I didn't fancy my chances going up against some evil arsehole in another country, and for the moment I decided the best bet would be to see if we could nail Chapmays.

I began to wonder if we would hear from Christine Bailey soon? I kept asking myself the same questions over and over. If she was telling the truth about Chapmays' visits, how infrequent they were, would we still be sitting here twiddling our thumbs months from now? I was well aware that without his old girlfriend's help, we were stuck. We had very little chance of finding him. We didn't know his true identity, and he was clearly careful about remaining anonymous and hidden.

While the evenings during the past week had not been exactly welcoming and friendly with Michelle still upset about Bill and the way I had lied to her about interrogating Lennox , she did at least concede that Olivia had been free of internet attacks for nearly two weeks now. But I still had to be ultra careful about everything I said, because every time I opened my mouth Michelle questioned and contradicted me as if she was a prosecuting counsellor. 'You don't know how close I came to starting divorce proceedings, Mr Weston,' she snapped at me at one stage. When she said it I stifled a smile because I knew that with those words at least my marriage was safe. But only for the time being; because if Michelle discovered the case we were working on was somehow connected to the pervert violating Olivia on the internet, then things could only go from bad to very much worse. If that happened, I had two chances of repairing my marriage - slim and none.

Alice caught me looking at my mobile on the desktop, willing it to buzz, and she smiled. 'What is it they say about a watched kettle?'

I sighed. 'I know. But this is frustrating. I mean, where do we go from here? With Jack Dawe out of the way, Chapmays knows the only way we can find him would be through Christine Bailey, the way *he* found *us*. He probably feels a bit more secure now. The media didn't report a car bombing, so he thinks his ex-girlfriend will be in the dark about that.'

Nicky, reading through the transcript she had typed, looked up. 'But he might not have rung Jack Dawe's father and found out he'd given you his address. Maybe he's smart enough to guess at what your next move will be. Which means he might guess about Christine Bailey, and you paying her another visit.'

'If that's the case,' Alice said, 'he'll do one of two things. Either he'll try to kill Freddie, having failed the first time; or he'll stay away from Christine Bailey, disappear from her life again.'

I drummed my fingers on the desk thoughtfully. 'But all evil bastards, psychopaths and mass murderers relate to someone. Christine Bailey said he was a devoted father when his boy was a toddler. And it sounds like he's trying to bond with the lad. We are in the same boat as her, inasmuch as we haven't a clue about his true identity. So it could well be that he might look on her place as a bolthole, somewhere he can lead a normal family life in his Peter Chapmays disguise.'

Alice was about to say something but we all froze as my mobile began buzzing and spinning clockwise on the smooth wooden surface of the desk. I snatched it up, clicked on text, and saw that it was a number unlisted in my mobile phonebook.

I scrolled to the message.

'It's from her,' I said, and read it aloud. '"He's here now. Upstairs with Dan. C Bailey".'

I grabbed my leather coat from the back of the chair and slid my arms into the sleeves. I felt a metal lump bumping against my thigh and tapped the left side of my coat that concealed the gun in my inside pocket. 'Come on!' I said. 'We don't know how long he's going to be there.'

'Please be careful,' Nicky said, throwing her arms around Alice. 'Have you got the tracker?'

'It's in my glove compartment,' Alice replied.

Then we were on our way.

***

Alice parked the Saab on the opposite side of the street to Christine Bailey's house, a good hundred yards away from it. There was only one black BMW in the street, parked a little way beyond her house. To fit the tracker might prove awkward if the son's bedroom was in the front and he or his father happened to look out of the window just as one of us attached it beneath his rear bumper. As if Alice could read my mind, she said, 'I'm just guessing but usually the master bedroom's the one at the front of the house. So let's hope it's Christine Bailey who uses it.'

I looked at my watch. It was just after four-thirty. At the moment it was fairly quiet but we needed to move fast, before the street became busy with people arriving home from the shops.

Alice leaned across, opened the glove compartment and removed the tracker. 'I'll do it,' she said. 'I'm wearing my track suit and I'll sprint along until I get to his car - I'll just look at someone out jogging, then - if the coast is clear - I'll attach the tracker and keep on jogging to the end of the street.'

'I'll slip into the driving seat,' I said, 'and keep an eye on the house. If I see anyone looking out of the window, I'll give one warning blast on the horn and you can continue jogging along the street. Then you can jog back along the opposite side, and try again when the coast is clear. Hopefully that won't be necessary. As soon as I see you've attached the tracker, I'll drive to the end of the street, pick you up, then we can wait there until Chapmays leaves.'

I heard Alice taking a deep breath. 'OK, here we go.' She slid out of the driving seat, carrying the small black tracker as unobtrusively as possible under her left hand as she began to sprint at a steady pace along the pavement. I slid quickly into the driving seat, keeping a watch on Bailey's house in case someone came to the upstairs window.

I watched as Alice neared the BMW, but just then - Shit! - a woman carrying a shopping bag came out of the front gate of the house right opposite the car and nearly collided with Alice. I gritted my teeth and watched as Alice nodded to the woman, and then carried on jogging to the end of the street. The woman walked slowly in the same direction, heading for the main road and shops.

I saw Alice crossing the road, and watched as she jogged back on the opposite side in my direction. She got to just in front of the Saab, gave me a quick look and mouthed 'Shit!' then crossed the street again and headed back towards the BMW. I stared at the upstairs window of Bailey's house as she sprinted up behind the BMW. There was no one looking out of the window. I saw Alice glancing quickly around to make certain she wasn't being watched, and then she stooped and attached the tracker to the rear underside of Chapmays' car. It was done. I started the engine, put it into drive, and cruised slowly to the end of the street. I found a parking space near the main road and pulled over, then shifted into the passenger seat as Alice slid back into the driving seat.

She blew her breath out with relief. 'Glad that's done. Now we can follow him at a safe distance. Let's hope we haven't got long to wait.'

'That's the least of our problems, Alice. We haven't worked out what happens when we find out where he lives.'

'We've got the bastard. It's as simple as that.'

My turn to blow out my breath. I realised I was perspiring, took a handkerchief out of my pocket and dabbed at my forehead. Alice made a joke of it.

'A handkerchief! Where was your hankie when we were in Peterborough and you needed to wipe off the prints?'

'It's a learning curve,' I replied. I wiped my forehead, blew out my breath again, and tucked the hankie back in my pocket. 'Christ! It's hot.'

'If you don't mind me saying, Freddie, wearing a heavy leather coat seems a bit extreme in this warm autumn weather. Or is it nerves that's bothering you?'

I gave her a cheeky grin, heralding what I was about to reveal, opened my coat and pointed to the large pocket on the left. 'Good for pickpockets this coat. Also a handy size for concealing a small firearm.' I tugged the gun a little way out of the pocket, showing her the butt.

'You're armed!'

'You're observant,' I joked, letting the gun slip back inside the pocket.

'Have you got a licence for that thing?'

'Don't be silly. I haven't used a gun since I was in the military back when dinosaurs ruled the world.'

Hands like talons, Alice gripped the steering wheel nervously. 'Freddie, listen, ever since my family was killed, I have a revulsion for anything to do with guns.'

'Sure you do, Alice. And that's understandable. But if we track this evil bastard to where he lives, what do you plan to do? Call the police?'

'I'm sure I can handle it myself.'

I gave her an ironic chuckle. 'If you mean what I think you mean, you can forget the martial arts and the Bruce Lee scenario.' I patted the left side of my coat. 'This firearm's a Glock 26 - nicknamed a "Baby Glock" because of it's handy size. It has a magazine of ten rounds and a bullet from it will travel at roughly 1,400 feet per second. So if you fired at someone standing just twelve feet away from you, it would... well, you work out the maths.'

'I hear what you're saying, Freddie, but...'

'No, let me finish. There's only one way of dealing with someone like a professional hitman, and that's hit them before they hit you. Chapmays killed your kid brother, showing no pity whatsoever. He crossed the line eleven years ago, which means he won't care or have any conscience about how far he goes or what he does now. That's why we need to protect ourselves - fight fire with fire. So far we're playing him at his own game. Using the same method to track him as he used to track your family.'

Alice shuddered. 'I know you're right, Freddie. It's just that I don't want to resort to becoming as bad as him. I would still like to retain some moral standards.'

I patted the bulge in my coat again. 'This is a precaution. I'll use it if I have to, but if possible I'd like him alive and in one piece, so we can get a confession out of him and find out who's behind it all. He's the instrument. Someone else gives the orders and he jumps. And they're as guilty of your family's murder as he is.'

'What I don't understand is, how come he's not done anything to try to stop me getting at the truth for the past eleven years, but since I decided to employ private investigators, he's been murdering some of those involved?

'Presumably you left it in the hands of the police most of that time, and they got nowhere with the investigation. He must have known that. So what was the last contact you had with the police and what did you tell them?'

An intake of breath as Alice came to a realisation. 'Shit! It was an argument I had with the Detective Chief Inspector Moss at Surrey Police, after I'd made an initial contact with Jack Dawe. I told him I planned using the private investigator and was confident he might succeed where the police had failed. I said it not so much as a threat but for two reasons. One, I hoped it might galvanise him into continuing with a case which he no longer considered a priority and two, to get him to realise that if I threw enough money at the investigation then I might make some headway. It's amazing how money will open doors when dealing with certain people. You don't suppose Moss is corrupt, do you? He might have contacted Chapmays, who was once an undercover cop.'

I shrugged. 'It might be Moss. On the other hand, it could be one of dozens of coppers - all it takes is one or two corrupt ones - passing the information to Chapmays. And let's face it, gossip soon goes around in a workplace or pub. It could be anyone.'

She was silent as she mulled this over. In the silence, my stomach rumbled loudly. Alice laughed and it broke the tension.

'When was the last time you ate anything, Freddie?'

'I don't know. It's so long ago, I can't remember.'

'We don't know how long he's going to stay with his son. Why don't you pop along to the main road and get us a McDonald's or something?'

I pulled a face.

'Beggars can't be choosers.'

I thought how incongruous this was, seeing as how the firm had half a million in the kitty; but I knew she was referring to the choice of takeaways available in the area.

'OK,' I offered. 'I'll pop out and get us something. I don't suppose it matters if Chapmays leaves the house in the meantime. We can track him wherever he goes. On the other hand, I don't want to be too far behind him. Ring me on my mobile if you see him leaving and I'll hurry back.'

***

At five-fifteen, after we'd eaten sandwiches which I bought in a small supermarket, I saw Alice adjust her mirror and peer intently at the reflection.

'Don't turn round and look,' she warned me. 'I think this is him leaving now. Yes, definitely. He's getting into the BMW.'

While I slid right down in the seat, Alice picked up a brochure, buried her head in it and pretended to be reading. I felt the vibration in Alice's car as he zoomed past us, and saw Alice's eyes following it along the street.

'OK, Freddie, you can sit up now. He's turned into the main road.'

'Let's give him three or four minutes start,' I suggested. 'Just in case he's caught up in traffic or stops at slow-changing lights.'

We gave him five minutes, then Alice started the car and we followed. I took the live tracker out of the glove compartment, which worked pretty much like a satnav, and was easier than staring at the screen of a smart phone.

We followed him towards central London, but when he branched left for Shepherd's Bush, I felt a lump in my throat. It was where Bill had lived, in a small studio flat off Goldhawk Road.

'What's wrong?' Alice asked, sensing my sudden slump.

'That's where Bill used to live. I'm still finding it hard to get over his death.'

'You know, you mustn't blame yourself, Freddie. It was as much Bill's decision as yours to take on this investigation.'

Difficult to say no, I thought, with someone handing us half a million for the job.

'Yeah, you're right,' I said. 'Bill took risks most of his life. Some like you wouldn't believe.' I chuckled as one of the memories flitted through my brain. Then changed the subject. 'You think this bastard lives somewhere well-protected? Block of serviced flats, maybe, with CCTV cameras on every corner?'

'If he does, we'll have problems. But we'll just have to work something out. At least we've got him in our sights and pretty soon we'll know where he lives. Maybe we'll get his real identity. So if he is well-protected, we won't have to move right away. We can keep him under surveillance until we come up with a plan.'

I almost smiled as I listened to her. 'Alice, do you mind if I ask you something, and I hope you don't take it the wrong way?'

'Go on.'

'Since you're now my partner in the company, and we seem to be getting somewhere with the investigation, you seem to be - well, more relaxed. Almost as if...' I hesitated, reluctant to reveal what I thought.

Alice smiled. 'I seem to be enjoying it. Is that what you were going to say, Freddie?'

'Well...' I began awkwardly.

'No, you're probably right. It's become my *raison d'être,* and I think I'm becoming addicted to the adrenaline rush. But I still want to nail this bastard for what he's done, not only to my family but to Ricky Bishop, Bill and Jack Dawe. None of them deserved to die.'

'And we're still no nearer to knowing the reason why.'

We were both silent for a moment, lost in our separate thoughts, but probably thinking along the same lines, wondering about Alice's father and his possible involvement in organised crime.

We headed south of the Thames, crossing over Putney Bridge, not that far behind Chapmays. From there we followed his trail to Mitcham, along Purley Way near Croydon, until we reached the M25. From there the tracking took us west, until we reached Junction 5, which was where we went a bit wrong. The traffic was heavy and we were in the middle lane. Here the road diverged and, before we knew it, we missed pulling out into the third lane which would take is to the A21. Instead, we were heading south on the M25. I grabbed a book of maps from the glove compartment and turned to the relevant page, while Alice fumed and cursed.

'Panic not,' I assured her. 'It's not far to Junction 4 and we can take that exit and double back. It shouldn't take long.'

It took us less than ten minutes to get to the next junction, then back on the M25 in the other direction until we reached the A21. From there the tracker took us through Sevenoaks. On the other side of the town, just past a pub called the White Hart, we took a narrow road called Letter Box Lane, and we hadn't gone very far along it when the tracker indicated that we were very close to our destination.

As it was now just gone seven the light was fading rapidly. Alice switched the headlights on, keeping them on dipped. Soon it would be dark and there were no street lights here. High and dense rhododendron bushes concealed houses from the road, and there were other tracks or driveways leading to the houses beyond the protective shrubbery. Behind us a car's headlights lit up, and flashed twice as it slowed to pass us in the narrow lane. Alice eased the car forward slowly, getting as close to the edge of the lane as she dared, in case we got stuck in a rut. Less than a few yards ahead was a track, and a signpost with the name of the house on it: 'SHANNON' And beneath it the word 'PRIVATE'.

Another car passed us, and the trees lit up like ghostly figures. It looked as if this lane could be quite busy and I worried about our leaving the car parked in this dark corner blocking half the road.

'We can't leave the car here to do a recce,' I told Alice. 'Not unless you leave the parking lights on. Even then it might be a bit dodgy. It's ridiculously narrow here.'

Alice nodded towards the signpost. 'And you're sure this is it?'

'Unless the tracker's lying, we've arrived. It's just down that driveway.'

'I don't suppose he'll be going out again, do you?'

'Why? What's on your mind?'

'Why don't I switch the headlights off, turn into his drive, then we can explore quietly on foot.'

Alice gripped the steering wheel tightly, so I placed a hand over hers and said, 'Listen, Alice, let's not take risks at this stage.

We know where to find him. We could always come back mob-handed.'

'Who have you got in mind?'

Another impatient flash of lights as a car overtook ours.

'I don't really know. Our old comrades from Bill's funeral offered to help.'

Alice sniggered. 'You're not serious, are you? Two of them looked as if they were ready to go into sheltered accommodation.'

'Just a thought. Admittedly not one of my best.'

Alice's breath shuddered as she exhaled slowly. I could tell she was wound up like a spring, ready to snap. She was so close to her family's killer, and I knew she didn't want to just turn around and go home. I couldn't blame her. I'd have been exactly the same in her position.

Then, before I had a chance to stop her, she thrust the car into drive, switched the headlights off and drove into the gap in the shrubbery and on to the pitted track. I felt the bumps as we bounced over potholes. It was unnerving. I couldn't see anything other than dark shadows and I doubted whether Alice could see much either, although she was much younger than me. My side of the car made a loud crackling and scraping noise as it came in contact with shrubs and branches. She jammed on the brakes and cut the engine hurriedly. We had only gone forward on to the track about the length of the car, but at least we were off the road. We sat quietly for a moment, tense and listening. The only sounds we could hear were the occasional cars passing in the road.

'At least we're off the road,' she whispered. 'You got a torch?'

'I've got a small penlight. But I don't think we'll need it. It's not pitch dark yet, and our eyes will soon get used to it. Besides, if he happens to look out of a window and sees a torchlight in the trees, we might as well have phoned ahead to let him know we were coming.'

I tried to open my door but it jammed against the foliage. 'I'll have to get out your side, Alice.'

'OK. Here we go.'

As she opened the door, the roof light came on. 'Damn!' She tapped the manual button and extinguished it quickly. 'I should have realised. Right. Let's go.'

I followed her out and clicked the door shut quietly. We walked carefully along the dark drive which curved around with dense trees on either side, our feet crunching on loose stones, but at least the ground was firm and hard as we'd had no rain for a while. Before we reached the end of the curve, and not realising just how short the drive was, we rounded a corner and saw we were almost at the front of the house. We stopped, but too late. Two bright halogen lights lit up the whole area.

Stupidly, we froze, caught like escaping prisoners in a searchlight. If anyone in the house happened to be looking out, they would see our figures, paralysed for a moment from the sudden shock.

'Quick!' I grabbed Alice's hand and pulled her off the drive and into the cover of the trees. We fought our way through the dense shrubbery, branches scratching and tearing, unable to see where we were going. 'Duck down and stay still!' I hissed. As we were now out of range of the halogen sensors, after three or four minutes we were plunged into blackness as the lights cut out.

'Sometimes animals, a fox or something, can set those things off,' I whispered. 'If he hasn't seen us he might ignore it. Or with any luck he might have been at the back of the house and not seen the lights come on.'

We stayed still for a moment, listening for anything like a door opening, footsteps nearby, anything to indicate he might have been alerted to our presence. I couldn't hear anything, other than Alice's shallow breaths.

'What about my car?'

'If he hasn't seen those halogen lights then he won't bother to look.'

'What do we do now?'

'It's obvious we can't get close to the house without being seen,' I said. 'So we might have to go back to the car and come back tomorrow, when we won't have to cope with finding our way around in the dark.'

'There must be a way of getting to the side or back of the house at night without alerting him.'

'What we need to do,' I whispered, 'is find some sort of map of the area. Wouldn't a Land Registry website give us the information we require? Then we can come back tomorrow night. Come on. I don't think we've been rumbled. Let's get back to the car.'

We rose and moved through the trees, pushing branches aside, following the driveway until we were certain we were out of sight of the house and safe from setting off the halogen lights again. We scrambled through the last of the prickly branches and stumbled onto the drive. I could just make out the shape of the car and I was relieved I no longer had to confront Chapmays who had more of a killer instinct than me or Alice. I heard a scuffling sound, and my flesh was pinched through the thick leather of my coat as Alice grabbed my arm to stop herself from falling.

'Sorry, Freddie. Maybe this wasn't such a good idea to come unprepared. At least we've got a vague idea of the terrain now. We'll do some research and come back and get the bastard.'

She spat out the last sentence with anger, and I was aware that it was disillusionment at the failure of our mission. So near yet so far. She held on to my arm as far as the car. 'Do you want me to drive?' I offered.

'No thanks, Freddie. I'll drive. It'll take my mind off the abortive mission.'

'Not abortive, sweetheart. At least we know where he lives now.'

I opened the car door and slid over to the passenger seat. Alice settled herself in and I heard her breathing freely, probably relieved we no longer had to take Chapmays on while we weren't properly prepared.

As she slid the key in the ignition, I patted her leg. 'Don't worry, Alice. We'll be back tomorrow night and we'll have the bastard. But next time we'll come prepared.'

A sudden jolt as if someone had punched me in the chest, and I heard Alice stifle a cry. The voice from the back seat said, 'You're here now, so I've saved you another journey. No, don't turn round unless you want me to blast a hole in both your heads.'

Chapter 27

Having seen the lights come on, he must have left by the back door and cut across the land through the trees on the opposite side of the drive.

'I don't know how you found me,' he said. 'Which is very unfortunate - for you that is.'

His voice was an expressionless monotone and I detected a slight northern tang. I wanted to reply, but my mind was paralysed by fear. Chapmays I suspected was a psychopath, a man with no conscience; a man whose only motivation in life was serving his own selfish needs and desires. He would have no hesitation in killing both of us.

Time had suddenly slowed down. I tried to measure our chances, hoping an adrenaline kick from the fear would help bail us out of this treacherous situation, but my brain struggled to function. Beside me, I couldn't hear or feel any movement from Alice, who was still as a rock. I couldn't even hear her breathing, so quiet was it in the tomblike confines of the car.

'Now then,' Chapmays said, 'this is what will happen. You will both get out of the car on the driver's side. You will then walk forward at least three paces to the front of the car. Is that clear?'

I knew he was taking no chances. He was not going to risk my smashing the car door into him as he climbed out. This would give him room to manoeuvre.

'Cat got your tongues?' he rasped, and jabbed me hard on the back of the head, the metal of the gun sending shivers of hot and cold pain up and down my nervous system. 'OK, out you get. Now!'

Alice pushed open the door and stepped out into the darkness. I followed her across and we moved forward until we stood about six feet in front of the car.

'Hold it right there,' Chapmays commanded as he followed us out.

We stopped, waiting for the next instruction. I guessed he would take us further on to his property, just in case a cyclist or a dog walker happened to be passing in the road. 'OK. Now walk slowly along the drive towards the house.'

We did as he instructed and, as we turned the corner to his house, the halogen lights came on again, flooding the area with the circular drive in front of the house where his BMW was parked.

The house, I briefly noted, was white, with large sash windows, and looked as if it was early 20th century, but then I've never been strong on architecture, especially when I have a gun pointing at my back. There were three stone steps leading up to a front door, the top half of which was criss-crossed with panes of glass in four panels.

'Open the door and walk inside,' he told us.

I pushed open the door, which opened to the right, instinctively holding it for Alice to enter before me, and we found ourselves in a large hall with a black and white chequered floor. I let the door swing behind me, but Chapmays crossed his left hand over his right to stop it, making sure he still had a tight grip on his gun. A quick glance back and I saw the barrel had a silencer attached.

On a hall table I saw a pile of unopened letters, the top one being a bill for water rates. I squinted and strained, cursing the deterioration of my sight, and my need to wear off-the-peg reading glasses. I caught Alice staring at it as well, and I hoped her young eyes were capable of reading the name on it.

'Into the room on your right,' Chapmays said.

We entered a large living room. The beige carpet was soft and springy, and the furniture was chintzy, the image of a man who fancies himself as worthy of living in the stockbroker belt. On a glass coffee table lay a lightweight, sandwich-thin laptop. I stared at this for a moment, and it seemed to be sending me a message of hope, as I began to rack my brains for a way of saving us from this cold lunatic's sentence of death.

Chapmays kept his distance, making certain he had a clear shot if either of us tried to grab him. He was smart enough to know that anyone whose life is in danger will resort to any means to survive. I didn't think he would give us an opportunity. But I suspected he wanted information. He would want to know how we managed to track him down. And once he had this information, I guessed he would have no further use for us.

'Sit down over there.' He nodded towards a large four-seater settee.

Alice sat at one end and I sat at the other. I saw him smile thinly at this, knowing we had deliberately widened the gap between us.

'I see what you're doing but it won't work. You'd both be dead in an instant. So don't even think about it.'

It was the first time we'd had a good look at this man. He was nondescript, like the character from soap opera about the civil service. Average height, brown hair with a side parting, cut to medium length. Everything about him was ordinary, except for his thin, swan-like neck with an extremely prominent Adam's-apple.

I perched on the edge of the settee, leaning slightly forward, letting my coat flop open. If only I could find a way of getting to my gun, but the chances looked remote. He'd shoot me clean through the head before I'd got it out of my pocket, let alone clicked the safety off. And he probably guessed I was carrying a pistol, but he was probably too scared of getting up close to search me.

'There's something I need to know,' he began, pointing his silenced revolver at each of us in turn. 'How did you manage to track me down?'

I cleared my throat before replying. 'It's a long story, Mr Chapmays.'

'Or is it Mr Keene?' Alice said. He looked surprised at that, and she added, 'Yes, I read your mail in the hallway. And I presume the initial P stands for Peter, the same as in Chapmays.'

'Of course. It's safer to use the same first name. Now, I think I asked you a question. How did you find me?'

'Through your girlfriend, Christine Bailey, of course,' I replied. 'She's betrayed you, Peter. She sent us a text telling us you were round at her place, then we came over and stuck a tracker on your car, the same as you did eleven years ago to Alice's family. Ironic, isn't it, don't you think?'

He flushed. 'The two-faced cow. The lying fucking bitch.' His insipid voice now had an edge to it.

'Whoa!' I exclaimed. 'Who was it who betrayed her and her friends to the police in the nineties? And who's been masquerading as a dead toddler for all these years?'

'Enough!' he snapped. 'I did what I had to do because it's a case of survival. The fittest survives. Plain and simple.'

'And does your survival mean killing innocent children?' Alice's voice trembled as she said it.

He paused while he thought about this. Then, he spoke in the prissy tone of a bureaucrat justifying his actions. 'I'm not a cruel man. I take no pleasure from the pain of others. When I put bullets through your family's heads, they would have died instantly. There was no pain involved.'

Tearfully, Alice said, 'But why my brother? He had his whole life before him.'

He shrugged. 'It was regrettable, but necessary. Survival, you see. I couldn't leave a witness behind. Nor will I.'

He glared at her, angry now, possibly blaming her for Bailey's betrayal of him. He was smart enough to know that another woman could have talked his girlfriend into it. I realised how close we were to death, and I had to use our one chance of survival.

'A good thing we've taken out an insurance against anything that might happen to us, accident, murder suicide or disappearance.'

He chuckled humourlessly. 'Oh, please! What can you possibly...?'

'A transcript,' I cut in. 'We have all the details of our investigation on our office computer, from day one when we discovered Peter Chapmays bought a tracker from that firm near

Guildford, right up to today. We spent most of the week writing it. And we have several USB pen drives. One which has been deposited with Alice's solicitors. So if anything should happen to us - '

'I think you're lying.'

I patted my coat pocket on the right, thanking God I had brought the flash drive with me, never imagining it might come in useful in this way.

'I've got a flash drive with me. If you'll allow me to get it out...' I nodded at his laptop. 'You can boot it up and take a look if you don't believe me.'

He aimed the gun at my forehead. 'OK. Take it out very slowly and chuck it over here.'

I fumbled for the little plastic pen drive, brought it out and threw it across the carpet. With his gun trained on me, he bent over, picked it up and moved to the coffee table, which was only about a yard from where Alice sat, and I could see what was running through her head. It was a slim chance. But at least it was a chance.

He kept his eye on us as he knelt down, felt for the laptop catch and opened the lid, then found the switch at the back of the keyboard and clicked it on. His gun was aimed at Alice, and I wondered if he knew she had trained in martial arts. Or maybe he had decided that she being younger could move quicker then me. Which was probably true.

He waited a moment for the familiar Windows tune to declare it open, then took the top of the pen drive off with his teeth, found a USB port at the back and slid the drive inside. His eyes dropped to the keyboard but only for the briefest moment, alternating between operating the laptop and keeping a watchful eye on us. Once the document was open he scanned it hastily, in between looking up and observing our movements. I knew we would have to make a move at some point because there was no way he would let us live, given that he had already eliminated every one who got closer to discovering his identity or that of Eclipse. And still we were no nearer to knowing who he was protecting or working for, unless it was the Russian in Krakow that Shapiro had told me about.

'This is all very interesting. Anyone reading it would have no difficulty in finding out about Peter Chapmays, a child who died back in the seventies. But your evidence only goes as far as tracing this non-existent person to Christine Bailey. There is nothing here that I can see about the real Peter Keene.'

He yanked the pen disk out of the USB port, threw it sideways across the room, and, without bothering to close the programme, slammed the lid of the laptop down.

I pointed the finger of my right hand at him, hoping I could use misdirection so my left hand could edge a little closer to my gun pocket. 'You're forgetting something, before you were recruited by whoever you're working for now, you were an undercover cop, probably employed in your real name, and your handlers in the Special Demonstration Squad will not only know your real identity, but they may have helped provide you with false documents in the name of Peter Chapmays.'

'Crap! The trail from my false ID will lead nowhere, except back to a dead child in 1975.'

By the shifty way his eyes moved from mine to the laptop I saw that he was lying. It was only a second of lost concentration, because I had unseated him briefly with my guess about his identity. And in that one fearful second I knew I had to make a move, hoping that if I went for my gun, Chapmays would aim at me, giving Alice a chance to go for him. It was a huge risk, but I had no other option.

I reached into the pocket as I stood up, tugging the gun out by the butt with my left hand. I saw Chapmays raise his silenced revolver, as I brought my right hand across to aim with both hands, but first having to click off the safety. I knew there wouldn't be time as he could get in the first accurate shot. But from my left I saw something flying through the air. I hadn't seen Alice get up from the settee, which she had managed in one fluid movement, flying across the room towards Chapmays on the other side of the coffee table. I saw him swing the revolver in her direction, but too late. She sailed through the air and one of her legs caught him on the side of the head and one on the shoulder. His revolver went bouncing across the carpet towards the door. But Alice, drop kicking him with both legs, landed badly on a corner of the coffee table and I heard her gasp with pain as the sharp wooden edge caught her in the ribs as she turned. I had the gun in both hands now and my thumb fumbled for the safety. Chapmays raised himself from the floor and reached for the laptop. I now had the safety off and raised both hands taking aim, but Chapmays was quicker with the laptop, which came spinning through the air. Instinctively I turned my head away but the laptop struck me on the side of the head and I fell back, my vision impaired by the blow, and the pain unbelievably intense, like a steel hammer pounding my skull. As I tried to get up from the sofa, I felt strong hands like talons, twisting and tugging the gun out of my hand as Chapmays took it away from me. There was nothing I could do to stop the maniac from putting a bullet in my head.

Through half-closed eyes, flooded with tears of pain, I saw his finger tighten on the trigger, and I knew this was it. But just then he vanished from sight and I heard a terrific screech of anger or pain, followed by more crashes. I blinked the tears from my eyes and summoned up the effort to raise myself from the sofa, and what I saw gave me hope. In the marble fireplace, Chapmays lay with his head against the fender, and Alice stood over him. She bent over and picked up my gun, just as he attempted to reach for it, where it had clattered onto the tiled surround. She was smart enough to take several paces backwards, away from him, the Glock aimed at his prostrate body.

My head pounding, I hobbled over to the door and picked up his revolver, stopping to pick up the flash drive which I put back in my pocket. Alice, I noticed, shook almost uncontrollably and had difficulty holding the gun steady. But it didn't matter now. I had Chapmays' revolver trained on him.

To calm Alice, I said, 'I've changed my mind about guns and martial arts. Whatever it is you did when I was looking death in the face is something I wish I had on camera.'

Ignoring my comment, Alice stared at Chapmays with loathing. Her shaking I guessed might have been to do with trying to retain her self control and not shoot the bastard out of revenge for what he had done to her family, more than the struggle to overpower the assassin.

'Get up!' she commanded.

He got into a crouching position, and for one moment I thought he was going to make a desperate bid to hurl himself at Alice. But I was wrong. As he tried to stand up straight, wheezing and panting, I could see he was far from tough. A man who was fearless only when he had a gun in his hand.

Alice stood facing him, the Glock aimed at his head. 'You'll go to prison for the rest of your life, you cold-blooded bastard. But first of all you need to tell us who it is you're working for. Who ordered you to kill my family?'

He smiled but his eyes registered nothing but a cold indifference to life. 'Go fuck yourself!'

'Do yourself a favour, Peter,' I said. 'Think of Dan, your son. You need to square things with him before you go down. Don't let him think you've got no human qualities, that you're just a scumbag who has no scruples whatsoever.'

He ignored me and stared at Alice. His smile widened, goading her with his indifference. 'At least I've still got a healthy son, who has all his life before him. Whereas you, you pathetic little bitch, have nobody. I made sure of that when I killed your family, including your little brother. You should have seen the look on his face when he knew in that brief moment he was about to die.'

An icicle of fear sliced into my nervous system as I realised what he was up to.

'And I enjoyed the power I had. If I'm honest, I have to admit I enjoyed shooting that little bastard, your pathetic little brother. You should have seen the hole I made in his head.'

Alice's face was a mask of darkness.

'No, Alice!' I screamed. 'Don't do it.'

My last few words were blurred by the loud crack from my pistol. Chapmays fell back into the fireplace, a large red hole in his head where the bullet had entered.

Chapter 28

Alice was in a traumatised state as she stared at his body, the horror of what she had done consuming her like flames in a burning building. She held the gun in front of her in the firing position, unable to rouse herself from a frozen attitude of disgust and despair. Then she moved slightly, staring at the gun as if it was contaminated, and I thought for a moment she was going to vomit. She turned the gun towards herself as if she couldn't believe it had gone off in her hand and it was all a terrible mistake. She was stunned and confused, her eyes glistening with tears of distress. I was afraid she might accidentally pull the trigger and injure herself, so I darted forward, my mind racing as I tried to think of a way to deal with the situation.

'Alice! Put the gun on the coffee table in front of you.'

Deeply shocked and turned to stone, she didn't seem to hear what I said. 'Alice!' I repeated. 'Listen to me...' I walked to the right of her, took her arm and gently lowered the gun. 'Drop it on to the coffee table. It's all over. There was nothing you could have done. He was never going to jail. He forced you to assist in his suicide. You have to believe that.'

She unlocked her fingers and let the gun drop on to the coffee table. A good sign. She could still function, even though her trance-like state meant she was still traumatised by the killing. She turned to look at me, fighting back tears.

'Oh, God!' she whispered, awed by the terrible magnitude of the killing of another human being, however much that person deserved to die. 'I killed him. It means I'm as bad as he is. I've descended to his level.'

I gripped her shoulders, staring at her with a fierce candour. 'No! You mustn't believe that, Alice. It was self defence.'

'He was unarmed when I shot him.'

I was relieved to notice she had overcome the burden of tears, and I thought she might be open to what was running through my mind. First, I had to reassure her that what she had done was an accident, brought on by the evil psychopath's gloating over her family's murder.

'And your family was unarmed when he shot them. So was Rick and Bill, and the detective up in Peterborough, and Christ knows how many others he may have killed in the eleven years since he killed your family. You mustn't even think of blaming yourself for his death. He was a monster, who at least had the decency to fall on his sword at the end. Although decency is the wrong word. Don't you understand, Alice? He forced you to pull that trigger. If he'd been arrested, he would have found some way of ending it. They would eventually have discovered him hanging in his cell.'

'Except now, with him dead, we won't know who ordered him to kill my family.'

She was starting to think rationally, which was a good sign. She looked into my eyes, and I saw a sudden determination in her expression as her lips clenched tight before she spoke. 'I know what we must do, Freddie. Give me your hankie.'

I frowned. 'What for?'

'Please, Freddie, we might not have much time.'

I stepped back, fumbled in my pocket, and gave her my handkerchief. Then she bent over, picked up the Glock, switched the safety on and wiped it thoroughly.

'What the hell are you doing?'

She gave me back the hankie, held the gun in her hand, switched the safety off and put it back on the table. 'Now there's only my prints on it.'

'I don't understand what you're up to, Alice.'

She turned and gave me her most determined look. 'You were never here, Freddie. I tracked him alone from Christine Bailey's, and when I confronted him about the murder of my family, he threatened me with his gun but I shot him first. This will give you time to get to Krakow and find this Russian who seems to be behind all these killings. But you'll need to leave right away, because once they arrest me, and read all the notes we made, they'll want to question you as well.'

I had to admit, her thinking was sound, and I was impressed by the way she had recovered and taken charge of the situation.

'I think we can do better than him threatening you,' I said, and went and stood near Chapmays' corpse, carefully avoiding treading in a pool of blood trickling across the tiles. 'Stand to one side, Alice. This was more than a threat he made. It was self-defence, but he missed.'

I raised the revolver and fired. A loud pop and a lump of plaster fell from the wall where the bullet had lodged itself. I wiped my prints off the gun and stuck it in Chapmays' dead hand. 'I presume you're going to call the police?'

Alice nodded. 'After you've gone.'

'They'll see that bruise coming up on the side of your head, and they'll see there's been a struggle in here. So you need to be vague about what actually happened. In a desperate situation, you wouldn't remember exactly what happened; every single detail. There was a fight and...' I stopped as I thought of something and clicked my fingers.

'What is it?'

'They'll want to know where you got the gun from, Alice. It's illegal, so what you have to say is that it belonged to Bill, and before he was killed by the car bomb he gave it to you for protection against Peter Chapmays. And because Chapmays was responsible for all those murders, no one can blame you for wanting to protect yourself. Especially as you suspected you were next on his hit list.'

'You need to get going, Freddie. And there's no way you can take my car, otherwise they'll wonder how I got here. How long do you need before I call the police?'

'It's probably a fifteen minute walk to that pub on the main road, where I can phone for a cab to take me to the station.'

'I'll give it half an hour to be on the safe side. And you need to phone Nicky tell her you didn't go to Christine Bailey's house today. When the police eventually get round to questioning you,

you can tell them you were on your way to the airport by then. Good luck, Freddie. And don't take any unnecessary risks in Krakow. Anything you discover about Eclipse, go to the British Consulate and tell them what's going on. Now's the time to blow this thing wide open.'

I threw my arms round her, holding her close for a moment, and felt her heart beating strenuously in her breast. 'Sure you'll be all right for half an hour, sitting here with a corpse for company?'

She smiled bravely. 'I think I can manage. I don't believe in ghosts.'

I left without looking back, selfishly relieved she had decided not to involve me in the death of her family's killer. But I was aware that with Chapmays dead we had only dealt with one element of the tangled web. Admittedly putting an end to the paid assassin was a huge relief, but he'd been acting under orders from the mysterious Eclipse, so there was another major obstacle to overcome. And now it was up to me to track down this conspirator and discover what Alice's father's crime was that had him and his family murdered in such a brutal fashion.

Chapter 29

Sunday 13 October 2013

When I stirred bells were ringing in my head and Quasimodo was banging them with a steel hammer. I was disorientated and my head ached and throbbed with a dull pain. I blinked open my eyes, focusing on a white door I didn't recognise, and a wall with a flat screen TV. The clanging in my head shifted to the acoustic sound of bells and traffic noise, and I groaned as I realised where I was. A hotel in Krakow, and it was Sunday morning, a day when Catholic Poles flock in their thousands to their devotions. The bells I could hear came from a church close to my hotel.

And then it all came back to me. The fight in the house near Sevenoaks and the shooting of Peter Chapmays, then my escape to Poland to search for Alexei the Russian conspirator going by the online name of Eclipse.

After I had left Alice the previous evening, I used my pen torch to stagger up the lane, facing any oncoming traffic until I reached the main road. The pub was nearer to the turn off than I thought, so it didn't take me long to stride it out to the welcoming lights and the crowded Saturday night bar and restaurant. Although I needed to order a taxi quickly, to get out of the district before the police arrived, I was desperately in need of alcohol, so first of all I bought myself a large brandy. I saw the barman staring at me suspiciously, so I went into the Gents and looked in the mirror. There was no bloody gash or bruise from the laptop Chapmays had used as a Frisbee, because my hair where it had hit the side of my head had offered me a little protection, but the swelling was enormous, giving my head a terrible lopsided appearance.

But there was nothing I could do about that I decided. I checked flights to Krakow on my smart phone and found one leaving Gatwick airport at nine-thirty. I called a taxi and asked him to take me to Gatwick where I arrived just after eight. Once I'd booked a flight and gone through security, I telephoned Nicky and told her what had happened. At first she was silent, probably worried about becoming involved in yet another killing, but when I impressed on her the need to stick to the story Alice and I had agreed on, and said the police would now be informed of everything that had happened, giving them the transcript of our investigation as evidence, she became understanding and supportive, telling me to watch my step in Poland.

The next phone call I made was trickier. When I told Michelle I was on my way to Poland to go after this Eclipse, she yelled at me that he had stopped pestering Olivia, so what was the point of my journey, unless it was to stir up trouble. I said my flight was booked and they would be calling us through to the boarding gate soon, and was about to give another excuse about my mission when she hung up.

Somehow I didn't think bringing her back Duty Free perfume on my return would help to revamp our matrimonial partnership.

I swung my legs out of bed and groaned. My head still ached, even though I had taken painkillers as I waited at Gatwick, where I had also shopped for a small holdall, shirts, socks, underwear and shaving gear. I switched the kettle on and checked the time. It was almost eleven. The hotel staff had left me undisturbed, probably after being instructed by reception that I had arrived by taxi in the wee small hours.

I made myself an instant coffee, winced at the bitter taste, then washed down another couple of painkillers. The nearby bells were suddenly silenced, and I heard shouts and cries from the street, the revving of cars and the clatter of trams. After I was shaved, showered and dressed, the headache became calmer, a tender discomfort, rather like a toothache that subsides then resurfaces intermittently. I could just about cope with that, I thought.

At Gatwick departure lounge, I had bought a small guide book, containing maps of every district in Krakow. I flicked through a few pages to get my bearings and found I was very close to the

Old Town, so I walked along the crowded streets until I came to the Rynek, the main square. By now I was starving hungry, so I chose one of the many cafés in the square, facing the Cloth Hall, a fine Renaissance building as described in my guidebook. It was still quite warm and, as I was wearing my leather coat, I sat outside and watched tourists ambling about and photographing the sights and monuments, until a waiter came and took my order. I chose Polish sausages, sauerkraut and bread with a half litre of Tyskie beer to wash it down.

After I'd eaten I began to feel a bit more human and wondered if it was time to go and find the internet café the Russian frequented. To say I felt nervous and vulnerable would be an understatement. I'd never been to Krakow before, but Bill and I had been to Warsaw back in the early eighties, when we worked freelance and were commissioned by a bank executive whose Polish wife decamped with his daughter and he employed us to snatch her back. When we discovered she was a KGB agent, we had to beat a hasty retreat from Poland before we ended up in a Russian jail. But we were younger then and thought we were invincible. Besides, when you're working as a pair, it's very different to being alone in a strange city. No wonder I felt edgy, wishing Bill had still been alive and on hand to share my worries.

Bells still rang out from various parts of the city reminding me it was Sunday and I wondered if the internet café would be open, this being a holy day. Then again, judging by crowds teeming the square and wandering into gift shops, everything seemed to be in full swing. And I remembered from our eighties Polish expedition how the devout Poles charged into churches for a swift prayer in the lunch hour, genuflecting and dabbing themselves with holy water before snatching a hasty sandwich and dashing back to work. Every day was holy in Poland, so I assumed the internet café would be open for business.

My guidebook told me the internet café was near a shopping mall called Galeria Krakowska near the railway station. I walked through the square, passing horses slowly pulling an open buggy of tourists, towards a small park from where I could see the railway station. I was surprised at the volume of visitors thronging the streets this being late October, but many of them looked like retired couples, although there seemed to be a fair amount of young students of every nationality, probably on gap years or school trips.

Close to the railway station I found the internet café sandwiched between a gift shop and a shop selling mobile phones. I suddenly realised I had no phone charger with me, and after all the calls I'd made from Sevenoaks and Gatwick yesterday evening, I guessed my mobile would soon be out of charge, so I determined to buy a pay-as-you go mobile after my preliminary reconnoitre of the Russian's internet café.

Almost everywhere you went, restaurants and cafés advertised the easy availability of wireless connection, so I guessed this Eclipse character used public computers to avoid being traced to his own computer. I found this strange. If he was such a computer expert, he would surely know enough about computing to make his own computer safe from enemy infiltration. And even though he was cautious enough to use a public computer, Shapiro had managed to trace his whereabouts, so his vigilance had been easily compromised, and in just over half an hour while I waited in Brad's kitchen. The whole world of internet and computing seemed mysterious - and deadly. But then, what did I know about it? Other than how dangerous and threatening it had become to me and my family, and I almost wished I was back in the dark ages when I used to watch Roger Moore in *The Saint* on a black and white telly and the best invention was a Teasmaid.

When I entered the internet café, I could see it was well used. There was a long glass counter displaying a variety of cakes and biscuits, and at the back of the serving area an espresso machine, and a fridge cabinet containing soft drinks and bottled beers. Computer booths and flat screen computers were placed next to one another in rows - there must have been twenty or more - all of which appeared to be in use, and in the centre of the café a small space was set aside for tables and chairs, several of which were taken by young customers presumably waiting their turn on a computer.

Standing behind the counter attending to a customer was an attractive young girl with dark hair, and at the far end of the counter was a man in his thirties, designer stubble and spiky hair gelled upwards into a trendy clump. He talked on a mobile, and the way he leaned over sideways as he spoke, I guessed he was about to end the call. If he was in charge, I could either approach him now to ask about the Russian or spend a bit more time surveying the customers. But what good would that do? I wouldn't know who the hell I was looking for. The only way to find this Russian, I decided, would be through a generous bribe with the zlotys I had changed from sterling at the airport.

The man clicked his phone off, slid it into the breast pocket of his shirt, and I could see he was about to exit through a door behind the counter. I hurried over the other end of the counter and waved a hand at him.

'Excuse me,' I said. 'Are you the manager?'

He stopped, his hand on the door handle, and stared at me poker-faced, but with a suspicious gleam in his eyes. I waited for his reply but he continued to stare at me without moving. I smiled to ease the tension.

'Do you speak English?'

He nodded slowly. 'I spend many years in England. Muswell Hill.'

I laughed nervously. 'Ah yes. Know it well. Been drinking in many pubs there. Are you the manager here? '

'Yes, but what is it you want?' he asked impatiently, shuffling from one foot to the other.

I leaned closer to him across the counter and lowered my voice. 'I'd like some information.'

His eyes narrowed. 'What about?'

'About one of your customers who comes in here regularly.'

He shrugged and pursed his lips. 'Why should I...?' he began, but seemed distracted, looked towards the door, and changed his position again.

'I'm willing to pay,' I said. 'One hundred zlotys, just to point out a regular customer to me.'

He stared at me without speaking, strain showing on his face. 'OK. You wait there. And I come back in a minute.' He started to open the door, then looked back over his shoulder and half smiled. 'A call of nature, as you say in England.'

Then he was gone, leaving me feeling slightly more relaxed and amused having discovered my clandestine operation was suspended by someone bursting to go to the loo. I turned and leant back on the counter, surveying the internet customers. At a nearby booth, a pair of eyes caught mine. Then he looked down at his keyboard again. It may have been curiosity but I thought it unusual. Nearly everyone working on a computer concentrates on the screen, paying little attention to their surroundings. Except the one person in the café who had caught my eye.

Could this be Eclipse? I wondered. And if it was, why was he expecting me? Had someone in the UK warned him I was on my way over? And who the hell could that person be now that Chapmays was dead? But I'd be stupid to think there were only two of them. After all, Tim Bayne had been heavily involved in something illegal and dangerous up until the time he was murdered.

The man who had caught my eye continued to work on his computer, but I got the impression it was false, a pretend concentration, taking care not to look in my direction again. He had steel grey hair, was maybe in his late-forties, a smooth clean-shaven man wearing a blue blazer on top of a yellow polo shirt. I watched as he moved his computer mouse several times, clicked the computer off and stood up. He came over to the counter. The way he avoided looking in my direction was so studied especially as he passed within a few feet of where I stood. No one could have walked so close to someone and avoided catching their eye, which gave me an even greater reason to be suspicious.

'Only ten minutes today,' the young girl behind the counter said as he gave her money. 'Very expensive way to use computer.'

He laughed nonchalantly, patting his blazer pocket. 'A text on my mobile from my wife. And when she hollers, I have to drop everything.'

He was an American.

'Please, keep the change,' he said, then without a glance in my direction he turned and left the building.

For a moment I debated whether to follow him or not. I decided against it. I was here to find a Russian named Alexei. Maybe the brief eye contact with the American was me being paranoid, seeing spooks everywhere. Perhaps it was at that very moment I looked in his direction that his mobile alerted him to the text, and not wanting to disturb the concentrated peace of the internet users, he happened to look up and made eye contact with me.

The manager of the café returned. He leaned close to me and dropped his voice. 'A hundred zlotys you offer just to point out a customer. Why do you want to know about him?'

'I'm a private detective. He got a girl in England pregnant three years ago. She had a child and she wants me to find him.'

He nodded and looked amused. 'If he did not give her money when child was born, what makes her think he will do it now?'

I shrugged. 'That's what I told her. But she still wants me to find him.'

I took the hundred zloty note out of my pocket and slid it across the counter. I kept my hand on it as I waited for him to accept my offer in return for details about the Russian.

'Does this man have a name?'

'His name is Alexei.'

'Popular name.'

'It's a Russian spelling. The man is Russian.'

He looked up at the ceiling momentarily, then said, 'I think I know who you want. Yes, he comes in here often. But not today. Maybe tomorrow. Maybe not. Maybe the next day. But he is often here. He spends a long time on the computer. A good customer.'

I let go of the zloty note and he shoved it into the pocket next to his phone.

'Thank you...what's your name?'

'Ludwik.'

'Thank you, Ludwik. I would be grateful if you would keep this just between you and me. Please, whatever you do, you mustn't warn this Alexei. If I come back tomorrow, and if he happens to be here, perhaps you can let me know who he is. There'll be another hundred zlotys in it for you. I need to try and find out where he lives. On behalf of my client.'

The manager looked amused. 'The mother of his child, yes?'

'That's the one,' I said.

'OK, you come back tomorrow. He will be here.'

'How can you be so sure?'

'He is here every day. I don't know why not today. You come here tomorrow.'

I smiled, guessing he wanted more easy money. 'Let's hope he's here for both our sakes.'

***

I came out of the mobile phone shop with a brand new Nokia in my pocket. As a potential customer it gave me leverage to ask them to set it up ready to make calls, dispense with the packaging, and put a two-hundred zloty credit on it, which was roughly equivalent to forty pounds' worth of calls. At least I could go back to the hotel now and phone home, then speak to Nicky to see if there was any news from Alice. But it was only eighteen hours since the shooting, so the police questioning was likely to be at full throttle, and I pitied poor Alice after all she had been through, being thrown into a police cell, then questioned as a criminal rather than a victim.

I decided to walk back along the Planty, a ring of parkland surrounding the Old Town. As I reached the tree-lined walk I heard a screech behind me and looked round as a young skate boarder almost collided with an elderly woman. Had I not turned around at that moment I wouldn't have spotted him. He was a long way back and it couldn't have been a coincidence. I wondered what the American from the internet café was doing following a hundred yards behind me. He froze for a moment then dodged sideways behind an embracing couple. It was a stupid thing to do because if he'd ignored me and carried on walking, I might have believed his presence in the park was nothing more than a coincidence. Now I was certain he was tailing me.

I turned away quickly and carried on walking, hoping he didn't realise I'd spotted him. As I walked briskly along the path, weaving in and out of Sunday dawdlers, I was at a loss to know what I should do. I was desperately vulnerable, a stranger in this Polish city, powerless to expect any help and, although I was surrounded by hordes of visitors, I had never felt so alone before.

I strolled slowly towards the main square and the Cloth Hall, deciding my best bet was to sit outside a café in a public place, and calm myself with an ice cold beer. That way I could keep my eye on the man following me.

As I sipped my beer, I spotted him in a souvenir shop, turning a carousel of postcards with pretended interest, just a few buildings along from the café in which I sat. It seemed obvious he wasn't going to let me out of his sight, and would try to find out which hotel I was staying at. Was he one of Eclipse's men? If so, how was it he knew where to find me? Someone must have told them I'd left England and was here in Krakow, and guessed I'd head for the internet café. Then he must have overheard me making enquiries from the proprietor and followed me. But none of it made much sense. No one, other than Alice and Nicky, knew I was in Krakow. What the hell was going on? I was stuck in a maze where no exit seemed possible and the walls seemed to be closing in on me.

I stared across at the Cloth Hall and saw crowds flocking in and out of both entrances of the ground floor of the huge rectangular building. I looked it up in my pocket guide book and saw a photograph of the inside, an enormous market place with stalls selling linen, folk art and local sculptures. I decided my best bet would be to enter one end of the Cloth Hall, try and lose him in the crowd, exit the other end, then try to shake him off by dashing along some of the narrow streets leading from the square.

I paid for the beer, hurriedly left the café and quickly crossed the square without looking back to see if I was being followed. I turned into the Cloth Hall, breathing in a heady aroma of incense and wood, and weaved in and out of the shoppers, heading for the opposite end of the building. I stopped halfway across, pretending to examine a carving of a Madonna and child. From the corner of my eye I saw him enter the hall, clearly scanning the area until his eyes met mine. I knew then he wasn't worried about being spotted and was unlikely to let me out of his sight. I started to panic, worried about Eclipse and his men finding my hotel, visualizing the late night visit and the sudden attack. I began to sprint, dodging between the shoppers. I barged into an overweight man, and felt his heavy gasp as he was winded, but kept moving as fast as I could for the other exit. I got to the wide open doorway, glanced hastily over my shoulder, and saw the American elbowing his way through the crowds after me, and only a five or six yards behind. I dashed out into the square, but the concourse was wide. There was only one thing for it. I ran full pelt for the nearest street which was probably a good 150 yards away. I had covered half the ground, glanced over my shoulder, and saw the American was also running flat out. As soon as I got to the street, I saw it was short and narrow and there was an alley leading off it to another street. I turned quickly and ran into the alley, then turned right into the next street. I ran past restaurants, bars and shops. Up ahead it looked like a main street and I could see a taxi rank. As I put on an extra spurt, I saw people staring at me in amazement. Nobody in Krakow dashed anywhere on a Sunday which was a day for a leisurely pace.

Panting heavily I reached the taxi rank and climbed into the back of the cab at the front of the queue. He said something to me in Polish and I replied breathlessly in English.

'Can you take me to the castle by the Vistula? I'm in a hurry. I have to meet someone there and I'm late.'

I remembered seeing in my tourist guide a castle near the river bank but I couldn't remember it's name. As he pulled out into the road, the cabby said, 'Wawel castle.'

'That's the one. I forgot the name.'

I glanced out of the rear window and saw the American climbing into the next cab. I took a hundred zloty note out of my pocket and held it up so the driver saw it in his mirror. 'The man in the taxi behind is following me. Here's an extra hundred on top of the fare if you can lose him.'

He changed into a lower gear and revved the engine. The taxi shot forward and crossed dangerously close in front of a tram, which let off a warning clang. The taxi driver grinned. 'Hey! Am I in a movie?'

'Nothing so exciting,' I said, glancing at the road behind. There were no taxis following. 'Just the woman's husband, and he has every reason to want me in hospital.'

The cabbie sniggered. 'I hope the lady was good. Dirty.'

In spite of my fear, I laughed, which was partly out of relief; because when I looked out of the rear window, I saw we had lost him.

'You still want the castle?' the driver asked.

I thought about it for a moment. Although I was not in the mood for sightseeing, there was very little I could do until the following morning and needed to kill some time. 'Yes,' I said. 'Take me to the castle. It's a nice day for it.'

Chapter 30

Monday 14 October 2013

As I walked along the park that bordered the Old Town at nine that morning, I felt nervousness rising in my throat like a dry stone. I was a fish on dry land. This was not my territory, it belonged to this Russian and his henchmen. Even if I found him, it was doubtful I stood much of a chance of defeating him. Who was I trying to kid? I asked myself. This was not some stupid computer game, a fantasy I could just shut down when the game ended. I knew there was little chance of getting to Eclipse, especially now I knew his American sidekick was there to protect him. I decided it was time re-evaluate the situation.

I sat on a park bench to think things through. Alice had warned me not to take any risks and had even suggested a visit to the British Consulate if necessary. Fortunately I still had the flash drive and I thought I could convince someone at the consulate that this Russian needed immediate investigation then arrest by the Polish police. But in spite of all the evidence on my flash drive, as far as officials were concerned, it could have been fiction. It wasn't evidence, merely a written statement of events by Alice and me. And Eclipse was smart at concealing his identity, as he had been for many years. My only glimmer of hope was in my conviction that there is always someone smarter, and if Brad Shapiro could disclose his true identity...

While I sat staring into space, wondering what action to take, my mobile vibrated in my pocket, which I answered immediately. It was Michelle calling. I had rung her last night, given her my number and wasn't expecting a call back so soon. It was at least an hour earlier in England, so I wondered what was so important for her to ring at this hour, as she was about to run Olivia to school.

Her voice was loud and clear, as if she was calling from nearby.

'Freddie! That bastard's started harassing Olivia again.'

I felt a jolt in my head where the laptop had hit me. 'What? Tell me exactly what happened.'

'As she got ready for school, Olivia checked her email. The bastard said he's going to... to... '

'Calm down, sweetheart. Tell me what he said.'

I heard Michelle sobbing, then she cleared her throat to control herself.

'He said he's going to snatch her and take her to his dungeon where lots of older men will... will have sex with her. She'll be a sex slave and he'll soon be coming to get her. Freddie! What the fuck is going on? You said this American bloke had sorted the problem.'

'I thought he had. But now I'm going to sort it myself.'

'What d'you mean? How can you?'

'I know where this bastard operates from, Michelle. From an internet café here in Krakow. I've been there, and I know how to find him.'

Catching her breath, Michelle shouted, 'He's dangerous, Freddie. This man is dangerous.'

'No, he's not,' I lied. 'He's a sick-minded geek, and I'm going to follow him home and beat the shit out of him.'

'Oh, God! I can't believe this is happening. Isn't there anything else you can do? Can't you call the police over there?'

'If I can't sort it myself, I will. I promise you. I'll get in touch with the British Consulate and get them to call the Polish police. But first I'd like to find out where he lives, and see if he's got all kinds of child porn at his place.'

'Why not let the police do that, Freddie?'

'Because they'll need search warrants, and before they can get warrants they'll need some proof. And there isn't any proof, Michelle. That's the problem.'

I heard her crying again. 'Oh, Freddie. This is a nightmare. I can't believe it's happening.'

'I'll sort it, sweetheart. I promise you, whatever happens it'll be sorted. And I'm going to get straight on to it, right away.'

'Oh, Freddie! Be careful!'

'I will, Michelle. Please try not to worry. I'll do everything in my power to stop this bastard. I love you, sweetheart.'

'I love you too, Freddie. Please be careful.'

'I will.'

I hung up and pocketed the phone. My anger was white-hot and I wanted to leap up, run all the way to the internet café, identify the Russian, and punch his lights out. But I knew I needed to calm down and think it through. I decided my original plan to pay the manager of the café to identify the Russian, then follow him home, might be wrecked if the American was present. If that was the case, then I could jump in a taxi and go to the British Consulate and try to involve the police.

But first of all I wanted to take a good look at this evil bastard.

***

The café was not as busy as the day before, with less than half the internet booths occupied. As I entered, the girl came forward to serve me, but stopped as the manager, at the far end of the counter by the door, said something to her in Polish. She gave me a smile and I carried on to the end of the counter, ready to part with the one hundred zloty note if the Russian was here.

The manager grinned and shook hands with me, acting the part of an old acquaintance. 'Ah! How are you, my friend?'

'Not so bad,' I replied. 'Good to see you again.'

His grin widened, enjoying the deception, and I became anxious in case he gave the game away by not taking it so seriously. But then I had given him a different story about why I was looking for the Russian, one which he found amusing about the pregnant girl. Then his smile vanished, his eyes became hard and businesslike and he leaned towards me, his elbows on the counter.

'He's here,' he said conspiratorially. 'Be careful not to turn round. He is in booth number ten, over by the window. But first let us discuss money.'

'I thought we had agreed on one hundred.'

He tapped the side of his nose and the grin returned. 'What I find out is worth double. I make enquiries and I have more information to give you.' Seeing the worried expression on my face, he added reassuringly, 'Don't worry. My enquiries were...' He made a circular movement with his hand as he struggled to find the right word. 'How do you say it?'

'Discreet?' I suggested.

He nodded. 'Yes, I make discreet enquiries. And what I find out will take you to his home. Worth two hundred zlotys, yes? And I will throw in a large espresso so it looks like you are here for a friendly chat.'

'OK,' I agreed. 'It's a deal.'

'Maria!' he called to the girl. 'Large espresso for my friend here.'

It was said loudly, and I got the impression he enjoyed the duplicity, putting on an act for his own satisfaction, as if indulging in a private joke.

I got another hundred zloty note out of my wallet and discreetly slid both notes across the counter towards him as if I was paying for coffee. They vanished under the counter this time into his trouser pocket. He leant forward again, and lowered his voice almost to a whisper.

'I found out this Alexei lives in Nowa Huta.'

I shook my head and stared questioningly at him. 'Means nothing to me.

'It is a town on the outside of Krakow, built by the Soviets, and this Alexei travels by tram every day. A half hour ride on trams number 4 or 15.'

'Right, so if I followed him out to this...'

'Nowa Huta.'

'I've never been to Krakow before. If I go by tram, like other European cities, do I need to buy a tram ticket in advance?'

He jerked a thumb to the back of the café. 'Behind this building there is a kiosk. You can buy tickets there. When you get on the tram you punch ticket in machine. Go and get the tickets now, then come back and have your coffee. This Alexei usually spends all day here. But today he must have other business, because he only books one hour of internet.'

As I crossed towards the door, I glanced at the Russian in booth number ten. Because he was staring intently and closely at the computer screen, I couldn't get a good look at his face, but his head I could see was as hairless and smooth as an egg, and he wore an American-style windcheater in bright red with a yellow baseball style motif and number on one side. Good. It would make tailing him easier without fear of losing him.

Once I had purchased my tram ticket, I hurried back to the café, where my coffee sat on the counter in front of Ludwik.

'Enjoy your coffee,' he said, and smiled as he watched me taking a sip. 'It's good coffee, yes?'

'Yes,' I agreed. 'But not worth ten pounds.'

He laughed, and I got the impression we had run out of things to say to one another now that our business was concluded. There was nothing to do but wait another half hour until the Russian's internet booking expired. My biggest worry now was that if the American should turn up. Although the American hadn't seemed like a typical tough-guy, and had looked more like a college-educated businessman, it didn't mean he wasn't the Russian's bodyguard and someone to be reckoned with. He had looked like an American secret service agent, one of those suited-and-booted clones straight out of a Hollywood movie.

I felt nervous and glanced at the door every time a new customer entered. Sensing my anxiety, the manager seemed amused by it, and broke the silence with a deluge of London reminiscences about Soho and Covent Garden pubs. I felt so disconnected from this shared small talk on London watering holes, I was relieved to see the Russian closing down his computer ten minutes ahead of time. Without so much as a glance in our direction, he got up, nodded at the girl, said something to her in Polish, then exited.

I was slightly reassured by the Russian's height. He was short, no more than five-six, maybe shorter than that. I'm six foot, with quite a big build, but I wasn't going to kid myself the little Russian guy might not be as hard as they come. I was briefly reminded of Bill. There were very few blokes tougher than him.

'Good luck,' the manager whispered. 'Take care.'

I thanked him, waited until the Russian had walked fifty yards away from the café and followed. He walked back towards the Old Town but branched left along one of the main thoroughfares. He had no idea who I was, so there was no need to act furtively and pretend I wasn't walking purposefully in the same direction as him. He halted at a tram stop and I was pleased to see a queue of at least half a dozen other people. I got on the end of the queue, and we waited less than five minutes when a clang of a bell signalled the arrival of a number 15 tram. There were two boarding and exit doors, and when I saw the Russian climb aboard at the one nearest the front, I boarded towards the rear and punched my ticket into the machine's slot. Although I knew nothing about our destination and where to get off, because the café manager had told me it was a thirty minute ride, I thought I could relax and study the pocket guidebook for a while, which described the town as vast working-class district which had become something of a tourist attraction. Originally an enormous steelworks development, paid for by the Soviet Union, the area housed hundreds of thousands of people, and is the only complete socialist-realist town in the EU in an architectural style typical of the Communist era.

The tram stopped at various districts, passing anywhere estates that looked like retail parks in most parts of the world. As passengers got on and off the tram, I glanced over my guidebook every so often, keeping an eye on my quarry, but also vigilant in case his American minder got on at another stop. I found it odd, if not highly suspect, that the man who had followed me so obviously, not wanting to let me get away, hadn't reappeared at the internet café.

After twenty minutes I spotted the blast furnaces of the steelworks in the distance, and then we approached the town where in the past most of the residents had been employed producing steel. The tram came to what looked like the central square of the town and I saw everyone on board about to alight, including the Russian I was following. I took my time tailing him, as the streets were not so busy as in Krakow. He walked determinedly along what looked like the main thoroughfare, from which branched many streets at angles like the spokes from a wheel or central hub. As I left the square I noticed it was named after Ronald Reagan, and guessed it might have had something to do with the Poles giving their Soviet rulers the finger after the glasnost era. I didn't think it was to honour him as an actor.

Although I had to concentrate on following Eclipse and was determined to end his nasty hobby as an online paedophile, I did notice how in this district teeming with small apartments wherever you looked, the grass verges were well kept, and there was hardly any litter or graffiti.

Halfway along the wide main thoroughfare, Eclipse crossed the road and turned right. There were a few people walking in the same direction as him so I didn't think it mattered if I walked close behind him, because I had made up my mind that as soon as he disappeared into a block of flats I would be right behind him to find out exactly where he lived.

When he was only a few yards in front of me, and still oblivious to being followed, he turned towards one of the entrances leading to a block of flats. I saw him take out a bunch of keys to unlock the main entrance, and I knew the only way I could get in and find out where he lived was to pretend to be one of the tenants, and hope he might not say anything to me in Polish as I followed him in. As he pushed open the door I leapt forward stretching my arm out to stop it from closing. There was no way he wouldn't have noticed me now and he turned, nodded and gave me a polite smile. I returned the nod and smile, although it took me a huge effort, because I really wanted to flatten the little pervert. But that could wait, because I would soon know where he lived. After giving him a few minutes to get his breath back, I would surprise him and put an end to his nasty little empire of sleaze.

The flats were not high rise, and I might have been mistaken but as I walked along I noted they were five or six storeys high. I didn't know if there was a lift. If there was, I decided I would brazen it out and join him for the ride to his floor. But I couldn't see any lift, and I saw him walking towards the stairs, so I followed close behind, our footsteps echoing in harmony in the stairwell. It must have been obvious he was being followed. Strange. He seemed unaffected by my close proximity. If someone had walked close behind me all the way from the tram terminus, I'd have at least felt inquisitive enough to turn around to see who it was.

At the first floor he turned into a passageway and marched along to his front door. I carried on walking past him, noting the number on the door, and continued past all the flat doors to the other end of the corridor. I heard his keys rattle as he unlocked the door, then went inside and shut the door.

Good. I had him. It had been easy. Now all I had to do was work him over and scare the shit out of him, so he would think twice before embarking on anymore perverted troll behaviour. I knew I was going to have to be ruthless, make him suffer, so that he might need medical attention. But it was the only way to stop this monster from scaring young children. I braced myself, walked back along the passage, took a deep breath and knocked on his door.

It opened after a moment and the little pervert stood in front of me grinning cockily. His unflinching, arrogant attitude stirred in me a heaving anger and I stepped inside, ready to grab the sick deviant around the throat. It was then I noticed he wasn't alone. There were three others, and one of them was the internet café proprietor.

He suddenly lunged forwards, spinning me round so I faced the other two, then locked my arms behind my back. A rock-hard fist smacked into my diaphragm knocking the breath out of my body, and another fist punched the side of my head. I blacked out.

Chapter 31

I couldn't have been unconscious for more than a few minutes because I became aware of Polish being gabbled frantically, the voices excitable and questioning. They had sat me on a hard wooden chair, and hands fumbled behind me, tying my wrists together. My legs were already tied to the chair legs. My head throbbed from the blow to its side, the same spot as the laptop injury, and my stomach felt hollowed out and queasy. I heard footsteps on bare floorboards walking from behind me. Then I stirred and blinked, and they all four stopped speaking. As they swam into focus through my fogged vision, I saw the four of them standing in a semi-circle in front of me like a welcoming party. How stupid I'd been. Obviously I'd been set up. The Russian knew I planned to follow him here, Ludwik would have told him, and presumably the proprietor jumped in a taxi as soon as I'd left the internet café.

'Who are you?' Ludwik demanded. 'What do you want with us?'

I stared at the Russian. 'You must be Alexei, otherwise known as Eclipse.'

They exchanged looks, wondering how I might have known about this closely guarded secret. 'There is no one here of that name,' Alexei said. 'You have made a mistake.'

I glanced around at the flat, and was shocked to find I was sitting strapped to the only chair in an uncarpeted room, devoid of any other furniture. Alongside one wall was a pile of neatly stacked cardboard boxes, which left me to conclude that the flat was used for storage purposes only. I wondered what was in the boxes, thinking it might be child porn, and my rage bubbled to the surface. I glared with loathing at the Russian.

'You disgusting bastard. How many children have you scarred and abused? Whatever you do to me will be nothing compared to what happens when they eventually catch you and stick you in prison. You know how much other prisoners hate paedophiles. Well, I hope you suffer for what you've done. I hope they crucify you. Fucking slowly over many years.'

The Russian threw the other three men a genuinely puzzled expression, shrugged hugely and muttered something in Polish. I got the impression that two of them, both lean, fit-looking men in their early thirties, spoke little or no English.

He turned back to me and shook his head.

'I know nothing of what you say. So now you tell me who you are. Which agency you work for?'

'I don't work for an agency. I work for myself.'

'He told me a lie about being a private detective looking for a man who got a girl with child,' Ludwik told the Russian. 'You want me to get him to tell the truth?' He stepped nearer, his fists clenched. The Russian stopped him with a restraining hand.

'Not yet. First of all he will tell me what he is doing in Krakow.'

'Looking for Eclipse,' I said, locking eyes with him.

The Russian frowned. 'I don't understand. Why you look for Eclipse?'

'Because Eclipse has been threatening my daughter on the internet. And if you're Eclipse, I think you had Tim Bayne killed.'

My accusation hit him like a thunderbolt. He opened his mouth in surprise and made a gurgling noise.

'How much did you pay Chapmays to kill him?'

'I don't know anyone of that name.'

'But you knew Tim Bayne.'

He paused thoughtfully, wondering what to tell me. 'Yes, Tim was my partner...' He laughed nervously. '...in crime. For years we make a fortune, and everything was good.'

'Stealing from banks?' I suggested.

He shrugged and smiled. 'Yes, but customers do not lose. Banks collect insurance.'

'Which raises their premiums and they pass on the extra charges to the customers.'

'And the bank executive's rob the customers by getting fatter bonuses.'

Ludwik sighed impatiently. 'We are not here to argue about banks. We want to know why you accuse Alexei of being a paedophile.'

The way things were going, I was starting to feel less sure about this. When they had knocked me out and tied me up, I thought at first these were ruthless men who would think nothing of torturing or killing me. Now I wasn't so certain.

'Because this all started when Bayne's daughter Alice employed my detective agency to find out why her family was murdered. At the same time my daughter received sex threats from a man - someone in Poland using the name Eclipse.'

The Russian slammed a fist onto his chest. 'Not me. I do not harm children. Never. It is someone who pretends to be me. Tim Bayne found out who he was and was going to... blow the whistle on this person. That is why he was killed.'

Just then we heard marching feet in the corridor outside, followed by a loud banging on the door.

'Policji!' came a yell from outside, then more words in Polish which I presumed were demands to open the door. The four men froze for an instant. Then the Russian and Ludwik turned to look at me, glaring menacingly, and even started to move towards me.

'This has nothing to do with me,' I said. 'I couldn't have known about this address before I followed you here.'

More door banging and yells from outside. The Russian looked towards the cardboard boxes and spoke in Polish to Ludwik. The four of them started to panic and Ludwik, moving towards the door, yelled something in Polish, perhaps demanding a search warrant. This was followed by angry cries from outside, more door banging, and then a loud splintering noise as the door burst open on its hinges and three uniformed policemen entered, their guns drawn. The four men in the room stepped back involuntarily and half-raised their hands. Stepping across the threshold past the broken door came two men in suits, one of them balding and middle-aged; the other much younger with spiky hair similar to Ludwik's. I guessed they were plain clothes Polish detectives. While two of the men and Ludwik were handcuffed by the three uniformed policemen, the younger detective handcuffed the Russian, while the older detective spoke in a Polish monotone, words he had clearly said many times before as he delivered the statutory caution.

As he droned through the litany in a bored voice, a figure appeared in the doorway, like an actor stepping onstage and waiting for an entrance round of applause.

It was the American who had followed me from the internet café yesterday.

Ignoring me, he walked over to the cardboard boxes, raised the lid of one of them, nodded with satisfaction and addressed the senior Polish detective. 'ATM skimmers. Hundreds of them.' Pretending to notice me for the first time, and with eyebrows raised in mock surprise, he instructed the police to untie me. One of the uniformed cops untied my legs, while another undid the cords behind my back. The American came and stood in front of me when this was done.

'Who the hell are you? And what business do you have with these men?'

'That one there...' I nodded towards the Russian. 'He calls himself Eclipse on the internet, and he's been targeting young children; he's a sex predator. My daughter was being threatened by him.'

'That's not true,' the Russian yelled. 'I come from a large family - a happy family - and I have many brothers and sisters. I love children.'

The American flicked his head towards the Russian and told him to shut up. Then he spoke to me again. 'It's true that Alexei Varushkin is Eclipse, but I don't understand where you fit in to this jigsaw. We've been after Eclipse for years, but...'

'Who is we?' I cut in.

He looked down at me like a specimen on a plate. 'My name is Jackson Headley.' He took out his wallet, flipped it open and showed me his badge.

I stared open-mouthed for a moment. 'FBI!' I said. 'What the hell has this to do with the FBI? Is this some sort of security issue?'

He smiled for the first time, like someone confronting total naivety. 'This has nothing to do with security. It is theft, plain and simple. These men have distantly robbed banks in America of millions of dollars over the years.' He inclined his head towards the Polish detectives. 'And along with the co-operation of the Polish police, I've been sent over to see if we can put an end to this drain on our resources. Not just in America, but globally. But the question still remains, where do you fit in to this scam?'

'I told you, this Eclipse is a sex predator.'

'Not true!' Alexei yelled.

'I find this hard to believe,' the FBI man went on, 'because we've had him and his accomplices under observation for some time now.'

I fumbled in my pocket for the flash drive and offered it to him.

'What's this?'

'It's a complete transcript of our investigation into Eclipse's affairs. If you don't believe me, read it and you'll see I'm telling the truth.'

He took the flash drive and pocketed it. Then he nodded to the Polish detectives.

'Search him, gentlemen.'

The detectives pulled me into a standing position, and a stab of pain streaked through my head where Ludwik had walloped me. I gasped, but they ignored it as they frisked me. They found my passport and flipped it open.

'Frederick James Weston,' said the senior Polish detective. 'And your occupation is given as company director.'

The FBI man snorted. 'Which means nothing.'

'So what happens now?' I said.

He raised his eyebrows as he stared at me. 'These men will be taken, questioned and charged. But I assume you're asking about your own predicament. I will read through the details of your investigation into Eclipse, and we will hold your passport to make certain you stay in Poland until our own investigations are complete. Which hotel are you staying at?'

'The Golden Tulip.'

'I suggest you stay there until we contact you.'

'When will that be?'

'Hopefully, tomorrow some time. Meanwhile you're free to go.'

The Russian stared at me as I shuffled towards the door. His eyes were defensive, pleading with a childlike innocence. But I knew how manipulative and cunning paedophiles could be and I dismissed his imploring look as that of a scheming bastard.

I stopped at the door and turned back. 'What happens if I'm stopped and asked to show my passport?'

'Mention that it is in my possession,' said the senior detective. 'Inspector Jakub Dabrowski.'

And that was that. There was nothing for me to do except to catch the next tram back to Krakow, wondering how long I might be kept in Poland.

Chapter 32

Tuesday 15 October 2013

I awoke with another bad headache and felt like something a dog might have regurgitated. My sleep had been disturbed by fearful thoughts following my phone call to Michelle. I told her Eclipse was now in a police cell, but she went on to tell me that Olivia received another threatening message around 5.15, and as the Russian was in police custody from mid-morning it seemed doubtful he could be the culprit, unless he had another accomplice helping him. I gave Michelle a feeble explanation, telling her not to worry, because sometimes internet servers can be slow responding, and perhaps it was one from when I observed him on the computer in the café that morning. But I found it difficult to reassure her, mainly because I was not convinced myself. I went to bed with a bruised head and brain, knowing I would spend a fitful night seeking answers.

Because I eventually fell into a deep sleep in the early morning, I almost missed breakfast. I had just finished a croissant and coffee when Jackson Headley, the FBI agent, loomed over my table.

'Mind if I join you?'

I nodded and gestured to a seat opposite. 'Coffee?' I offered.

'No, thanks. It's coming out of my ears.' He slid a hand into his inside pocket as he sat down, took out my passport and flash drive and placed them on the table in front of me. 'I read the report, and made copies, and we have no reason to keep you here.'

'What about the Russian? What have you done about him?'

He sighed deeply. 'He's rich, with a healthy Swiss bank account. He'll get the best defence lawyer available. The skimmers we found at that flat he'll either deny knowing anything about, or he'll plead guilty to possession, claiming he had no intention of selling them or using them, and was merely storing them on behalf of another mysterious Russian national.'

'I don't care about him stealing from banks,' I began, but he raised a hand to stop me.

'After an intensive interrogation of all four men, we don't think they had anything to do with this other business - the murders and the internet threats.'

He dropped his voice to a soft spoken and sympathetic level. 'I know this is hard to accept, Freddie, but I think there's someone still out there masquerading as Eclipse.'

'And did you discover from the real Eclipse why Tim Bayne may have been killed?'

'Alexei Dabrowski has a theory, although he can't prove it.'

'OK. Let's hear it.'

'Tim Bayne as you know partnered the Russian in their criminal activities, making millions by scamming banks and controlling a huge ATM skimming empire. Then he thinks his partner stumbled on something really nasty on the internet. He thinks it may have been something to do with child abuse and Bayne was working to expose it and destroy it.'

'Which is what got him and his family murdered.'

'It looks like that, although we only have Dabrowksi's word for it.'

I sighed. 'Well, at least Alice Bayne will know her father was trying to do the right thing, even if he was a crook. But now we're no nearer to finding out who this monster is and I'm worried about my daughter's safety.'

'How old is your daughter?'

'Fourteen. Why?'

The FBI man frowned deeply. 'More difficult to keep an eye on them at that age. They need their independence.'

'Thanks,' I snapped, 'for you words of comfort.'

'I'm sorry, Freddie. I truly am, but it looks like it's a case of back to the drawing board in trying to find this other Eclipse.

I wish I could help. But my remit is to stop cyber thieves from stealing millions of dollars, not catch internet trolls who may or may not carry out their threats.' He saw I was about to object and continued hurriedly. 'You want my advice for what it's worth? Go back to England and talk to the police?'

'The fucking police,' I spluttered indignantly. 'Didn't you read about my interview with the manager of Tim Bayne's software business, when the firm was visited by who he thought was a high-ranking police officer both before and after Bayne's murder?'

'Sure I did. And there may be one or two rotten apples in the barrel, but they can't all be corrupt, Freddie.'

'But how do I recognise the corrupt or honest cop? How am I supposed to know who is honest and who's not?'

'You have to start by trusting someone, Freddie. Believe me, it's the best way, and I'm sure your wife would agree with me. Involve as many police officers as possible.' He picked up the flash drive and waved it in front of me. 'Add the rest of the story to this and go armed with what you've got to the police, telling as many people as possible. I'm sorry, it's the best advice I can give you.'

I thought over what he said for a moment.

'Well?' he said. 'You know I'm right, don't you, Freddie?'

With some reluctance I had to admit what he said made sense. There was nothing to be gained by attempting to sort out the investigation privately. It might even be time to go public and involve the press.

'Yes,' I agreed. 'I'll get to the airport, see how soon I can get back, and Nicky our secretary can help me to compile the rest of the story. Then it's down to the cop shop to shake a few skeletons.'

He glanced at his watch and stood up. 'I wish you the best of luck, Freddie.'

I rose and we shook hands. 'Shame we hadn't met under better circumstances,' he said. 'We might have enjoyed a few drinks and reminiscences together. But that's life.' He smiled before turning away, then walked across the dining room without looking back.

In less than half an hour, I was in a taxi heading for John Paul II International airport.

Chapter 33

I managed to get a mid morning flight with a window seat, fell into a deep sleep for a good hour, and arrived at Gatwick just after one o'clock. As I sat on the train heading for Victoria, I sent Michelle a text telling her I was on my way home just as soon as I picked up the hired car from where I'd parked it next to the office.

I got back to Chalk Farm just after two-thirty, dashed into the office and was greeted by Nicky, who got up and gave me a hug, an expression of concern on her face.

'What's wrong?' I asked.

'Michelle has rung several times because she was worried. She knew you were on your way back and your phone would be turned off. Apparently Olivia's been getting more and more threatening emails, even though you told her this Eclipse is in jail. She thought I might be able to offer an explanation and set her mind at rest. But apart from telling her that maybe the servers were slow in delivering the messages, I didn't know what else to tell her.'

'Which is exactly what I told her, Nicky. Talk about clutching at straws. Shit! It looks like there's still someone out there masquerading as Eclipse.'

I gave Nicky a garbled version of what happened in Poland. When I finished I felt exhausted and frustrated by the complexity of this horrendous assignment and a spasm of fear coupled with fatigue ran through my body. I knew I had to pull myself together, so I went into our inner office, slumped into the chair behind the desk and put my head in my hands.

'You OK, Freddie?' Nicky asked as she followed me into the office.

'It's a fucking nightmare,' I mumbled helplessly. 'I don't know where we go from here.'

She put a hand on my shoulder and squeezed. 'I don't want to make you feel worse, Freddie, but you look like shit. Why don't you go into the loo and freshen up while I brew fresh coffee? Just take a minute to calm down.'

My shoulders ached from stress. I rolled them, raised my head and sat back. 'I don't know what to do next, Nicky. I really don't. And do you have any idea what's been happening with Alice?'

'Her solicitor contacted me. She's in court today for the preliminary hearing and charge. She's got a top lawyer representing her, and she's not short of bail money. So any time now we might be hearing from her. Of course, she hasn't a clue about what's been happening with you in Krakow, and the way you hit a dead end as far as Eclipse was concerned.'

'At least I found out a few things about her father which might make her feel differently about him, seeing as he was on a mission to expose child abusers.' I stood up and felt a twinge of pain in my shoulders as I removed my coat and slung it over the back of my chair. 'That coffee sounds like a great idea, Nicky. I'll just freshen up.'

I went into the bathroom to see if I could improve my appearance, though I doubted it was possible when I stared into the mirror above the washbasin. I looked like an extra in a zombie movie. I washed my face, wet my hair, and brushed it into a presentable likeness of my former self, although the improvement was marginal. When I stepped out of the bathroom, a steaming mug of fresh coffee awaited me. I blew on it and had just taken a sip when my mobile rang. I saw it was Michelle and answered right away.

She screamed in my ear. 'Freddie! She's gone. Olivia's been taken. They've taken our daughter.' Even through her frantic sobs I could hear a babble of voices in the background. 'I'm at the police station,' she gabbled. 'I went in early to school, wanting to have a word about what's been happening with her computer, and they told me she never came to school today.'

214

I was numb with a feeling of dread, the sort of feeling no parent should ever experience. Eventually I found my voice. 'Didn't you drop her off this morning?'

'Yes,' Michelle sobbed. 'And we'd run out of juice at home for her lunch box, so she asked me to drop her by the corner shop. Oh God! Why did I do that? I should have dropped her right outside school.'

'Don't blame yourself, Michelle. That's not going to help.'

'But she's gone. She never arrived at school. What are we to going to do?'

'What are the police doing about it?'

'They're going through all the internet stuff at the moment. They said they normally wouldn't consider her missing until...' I heard Michelle crying, then someone in the background asking if she was all right. 'Yes, I'll be fine. I'm talking to my husband.'

'Michelle, listen to me,' I urged. 'Can you hear me?'

'Yes, yes. What?'

'Give me Olivia's internet password.'

'Freddie! The police are on to it. They're doing everything they can.'

'Michelle!' I pleaded. 'Just do it, will you? Give me her password. I want to check the last message she got.'

Nicky stood over me, her eyes brimming with concern, a pen and notebook in her hand, ready to offer practical help.

'Her password is "pirhouette6".'

'Thanks, Michelle. "Pirhouette6".' Nicky wrote it down as soon as she heard me say it. 'As soon as I check her email, Michelle, I'll call you back, then I'll come over to the police station.'

I hung up and reached for the computer keyboard.

'Don't waste time booting it up,' Nicky urged. 'Use mine.'

I dashed into the outer office and sat at her desk, typed in BT Yahoo mail, followed by Olivia's email address and her password. The latest Eclipse email had no attachments or graphics. But the message was chillingly understated.

'Time has run out and I promised you to some men. We have a cozy little dungeon waiting for you. See you later today. Eclipse.'

After reading the disturbing message, I looked up at Nicky. 'How do you spell cosy?'

'C-O-S-Y.'

'This one is spelt with a Z.'

'Which is an American spelling.'

Our eyes met, and we both realised instantly who was behind it all.

'Jesus!' I said as I stood up hurriedly. 'Of course he could stop the emails being sent, because he was the one sending them.' I tapped my trouser pocket. 'I've got my car keys. I'm going to Sheppey right now.' I walked quickly to the entrance door. 'I'll kill the bastard when I get to him. I will fucking slaughter him.'

'Wait, Freddie!' Nicky shouted as she dashed into my office, returning with my leather coat a moment later.

'I don't need it, Nicky. I'm already boiling hot as it is.'

She grabbed my arm and started to slide it into a sleeve. 'Don't be stupid. It'll help protect you, Freddie. Please! Wear it for my sake.'

I hadn't a clue what she meant but I was too overwrought to argue. I slipped into the coat and stepped into the street. As I dashed towards the car, I yelled back to Nicky, who stood in the doorway, 'Call Michelle, tell her what's happened, and to get the police on to it.'

'Right away, Freddie!' Nicky shouted as I climbed into the car.

I tried not to drive like a maniac and risk being pulled over, but as far as flashing speed cameras were concerned, I was about to find out how many speeding convictions I could chalk up in the next ninety minutes.

***

Shapiro's brightly-painted house looked much the same as it had the first time I visited, forbidding and lacking in humanity. In spite of the sunshine yellow of the paintwork, it had the cold aura of a twilight dwelling, an empty shell of a computerised mausoleum. As I screeched to a halt by the kerb outside his driveway, then leapt out of the car and ran up the path toward the front door, I realised his Volvo estate was gone. Where the hell was he? And where had he taken Olivia?

I banged the door over and over, kicking it frantically, shouting and swearing uselessly. Some passers-by in the street stopped to watch my futile display of frustrated anger as I ranted and kicked the door hard. Eventually I calmed down, staring at the passers-by, who moved quickly on in case I might attack them.

I knew because his car was gone, the house must be empty. I tried to think what I could do to get inside, thinking I might find a clue to his whereabouts. But the only way inside this impregnable fortress was by police SWAT battering rams, and I hadn't a clue how long the police would take to make a decision for unwarranted intrusion, in spite of the urgency of Olivia's abduction.

As I'd neared the Isle of Sheppey, I'd taken a call on my mobile. It was from Michelle. Nicky had rung her about Shapiro being the abductor, but it took her some time to convince the police. And when they did eventually accept the gravity of the situation, knowing they had to move fast to avoid a tragedy, the Met still had to work in conjunction with the Kent police. However urgent the situation was, a strict protocol still had to be met.

Feeling more and more helpless as the minutes ticked by, I cursed the police, even though I was aware of how much I needed them at this moment. I felt tears spring into my eyes as I thought about Olivia, how she must be feeling, imagining how terrified she must be as her nightmare became a reality. Nightmare! The word clicked in my head as I made some sort of association. It was the word "night" that did it. I remembered poking around in Shapiro's kitchen and finding details of the derelict nightclub he'd bought. At the time I'd put it down to an innocent expansion of his computer business. Panic swept through my brain as I guessed what the nightclub was used for.

I got in the car and drove like the clappers, and it took me less than ten minutes to get to the road leading to the nightclub. As I got nearer, I could see there was a middle-aged man in a three-piece suit, standing outside the entrance to the nightclub. He looked as if he had just arrived and took a mobile phone out of his pocket, about to key in a number. But he stopped as I drove at speed into the weed-sprouting car park, and screeched to a halt next to a silver BMW parked near Shapiro's Volvo. I noticed the rusting Mondeo had been removed.

I got out of the car hurriedly and marched towards the man. He seemed nervous, said something short and hasty into the phone, cut the call and put it back in his pocket. He walked towards me, intending to walk by me to get in his car, but I stopped him with hand on his chest.

'Hey!' he exclaimed. 'What the hell d'you think you're doing?'

His face seemed familiar, and he spoke in the haughty tone of an aristocrat talking to a peasant.

'Where is Brad Shapiro?' I demanded. A glance at the lock on the entrance told me it might be tricky to get inside without permission. 'And how do I get inside the nightclub?'

He shuffled around me, taking car keys out of his pocket. 'I have no idea what you're talking about. I got lost, pulled over, and have been trying to phone for directions. So if you don't mind - '

Before I could stop him, he'd run to the car, got in and locked the door. I ran after him and banged on the window. 'Stop, you bastard! I want to know...'

I saw extreme fear in his expression. He panicked as he revved the engine, accelerating without bothering to see if a car might be coming along the road. His BMW shot forward at speed, almost colliding with another car. An angry blast from a car horn as he ignored the near collision and sped off down the road.

I went back to the club's entrance. The lock was strong and unassailable as were the tightly-fitting doors. I knew there must be some sort of delivery entrance, so I ran around the back, looking to see if Shapiro had installed any CCTV cameras. Either he hadn't got around to it yet or he didn't want to give the impression the nightclub was anything other than derelict.

There were two doors at the back of the building, with no locks on the outside, and I guessed these could be opened only from the inside by metal bars, the sort you have on cinema exits. There was only one way to get inside this building and I knew what I had to do.

I climbed back inside the Renault, and drove towards the rear of the club. Behind the delivery doors at the back was a run in of about twenty yards. I straightened the Renault up so it faced the doors head on, fastened my seat belt, put it into first gear, and pressed the accelerator to the floor as I let out the clutch. The car shot forward and hit the double doors with a mighty bang. The seat belt jarred against my chest as I was propelled forward and the vehicle shuddered with a metallic grinding noise. The bonnet buckled and concertinaed with a sandpaper sound of grating steel as the car cannoned through the doors with a loud splintering of wood as the doors caved in, dust and debris flying like splintered glass.

I unclipped my seatbelt and threw open the car door. The dust from the impact swirled around, and steam rose with an oily smell from the shattered radiator. Inside the club it was dark, like the entrance to a cave. But I had no fear now I knew Olivia was being held somewhere in this hideous nightclub. I stepped over the rubble and entered. I was in what had once been a large kitchen, with old rusting cooking ranges and work surfaces, old pots and pans, burnt and caked with grease. At the far end of the kitchen there was a swing door with a porthole at head height, the glass in it cracked across the centre. I dashed forward, pushing my weight against the door, thinking the hinges might be rusty, but it swung open easily and I found myself in a long corridor. At the start of the corridor, to the right of the door leading to the kitchen, there was a staircase, partly blocked with rubble and litter. Two rooms branched off along the corridor, and I guessed they might once have been the club offices. I hurried to the end of the corridor, to another door which looked as if it might lead into the main body of the club. As I pushed it open, I called my daughter's name, desperately hoping I hadn't been mistaken in assuming Shapiro had brought her here.

'Olivia! Olivia!'

'Dad!'

My stomach lurched. I've never felt so relieved in all my life. Olivia was still alive. As I stepped inside the club, I turned to where I heard her voice and saw her sitting upright in a chair beside a double bed, her hands tied in front of her. She leapt up and ran into my arms, sobbing and moaning. I was relieved to see she was still dressed in her school uniform, but then it flashed through my mind that that was how they wanted her.

'Olivia sweetheart, it's OK. I'm here,' I said as I felt her distressed body trembling against mine. 'It's going to be all right, I promise. Everything's going to be fine.'

I heard someone coughing lightly from a little distance away. It was Shapiro. He stood in the shadows beneath an old mirror ball in the ceiling, wearing an expensively-tailored suit, as if he was an executive chairing a board meeting. Behind him stood a table laden with bottles of spirits, wine, champagne in a bucket and glasses. This main area of the club had clearly been made habitable, and was a mixture of dungeon and Parisian bordello, lit mainly by dim red lights.

'Shapiro, you bastard,' I said. 'I see you don't have a weapon of any sort. What makes you think...?'

He didn't let me finish and screamed angrily, 'I don't do weapons, guns or otherwise. I leave that to the muscle.' Then, as if embarrassed by the sudden outburst, he chuckled. 'I mean, why keep a dog and bark yourself? I leave all the rough stuff to Peter there.' He nodded towards a raised area in the shadows, and I saw a broad-shouldered, shaven-headed man in a black raincoat, holding a machine pistol.

'Peter?' I questioned.

'That's right. Peter Chapmays. The other Peter won't be needing the false ID anymore, so it seemed a pity not to recycle.'

'I suppose,' I said to the armed man in the shadows, 'you realise just how expendable you are.'

'Save it!' Shapiro snapped. 'He knows the risks and he's prepared to take them.'

'But is he prepared to spend a lifetime behind bars? Or will he go the same way as the other Chapmays and fall on his sword? If that's the case, I suggest he does it soon, before the police get to Sheppey.'

'Don't kid yourself, Freddie. The police are not coming to save you. I can guarantee it.' Shapiro smiled grimly. 'I have friends in high places. And some of them will find recent events rather upsetting. You frightened off an influential customer, for a start. Just as he was about to become acquainted with your daughter. Maybe you recognised him.'

'His face did seem familiar.'

'He's been on *Question Time* more than a few times, and is highly influential. And rich. As are most of my potential customers. Now your daughter here was blindfolded when I had her snatched, so she had no idea of where she was. As soon as she had satisfied some of my distinguished customers, we would have blindfolded her again and eventually let her go. And now, because of your interference, your daughter knows where we are. So I'm afraid we will have to find another way out of this mess.'

I held Olivia tighter as I felt her shaking.

'Listen, you bastard!' I said through gritted teeth. 'How could I not do everything in my power to stop my daughter from being taken and abused? And why the hell did you target her in the first place? Was it because Alice Bayne assigned us to investigate her family's murder?'

'Spot on, Freddie. I had hoped, like Jack Dawe, you might be persuaded to drop the case. Especially once you found out your daughter's internet abuse was connected to Alice Bayne's enquiries. And still you carried on, thus endangering little Olivia here. Why did you do it, Freddie? Was it the money? Was Alice Bayne paying you handsomely for your services? You see, in the end it all boils down to money.' He looked down and spoke to Olivia like a much younger child. 'I'm afraid your daddy has sealed your fate by the age old story of greed, my darling.'

'That's not true, Shapiro, and you know it. Alice wanted justice for her family and my partner Bill and I were committed to helping her.'

Shapiro gave me a slow hand clap. 'How very noble of you. But it helps when you have a million bucks in the bank, yes?'

'There's something I don't understand, though.'

'Go on,' he said impatiently, glancing at his watch.

'Once your hitman was dead, and I went chasing wild geese in Poland, the trail leading to you would have gone cold. Until you threatened and abducted Olivia.

That's when I discovered it was you.'

'So how did you find out?'

'American spellings on Olivia's computer. It doesn't matter how clever a criminal might think he is, he nearly always makes a mistake. And you're no exception, Shapiro. So why didn't you just drop it and leave us alone once you knew I'd hit a dead end?'

'I suppose it was because you managed to track down Peter and kill him. It was irritating.'

'Irritating!' I yelled.

He stared at me impassively, and I realised I was staring at the face of another psychopath. This man felt no sympathy for another human being. His only concern was in achieving enough power to provide for his own needs and gratification.

'I don't know where you think this will end, you bastard. You may have friends in high places but...'

'Like you would not believe, Freddie,' he cut in. 'Some of my customers are cabinet ministers, chief executives of major organisations, high-ranking military and police officers - not to mention some upstanding members of the cloth. If I go down, because of what I know, they all go down with me. And they're not going to let that happen. So I'm sorry to disappoint you.'

'You really think they'll stick by you, Shapiro?' I said, then turned to look at his minder. 'Do yourself a favour, Peter - or whatever your name is - get out now while you've got the chance. Your boss may have friends in high places, but do you honestly think they'll stick by you? You'll be their Lee Harvey Oswald. The fall guy. They're the untouchables, enjoying champagne at Claridges while you're stuck in a six-by-five, terrified in case the nonce-haters get hold of you.'

'Shut it, Freddie! I'm beginning to find your conversation tedious and we need to bring this meeting to a close.' He nodded towards the man with the gun. 'And I may not use guns or weapons myself, but I know something about them. Peter has a Mac 11 aimed at you and your daughter. It can fire 32 rounds in only two seconds, enough to cut you both in half before you even think about...'

He stopped and listened intently. We all heard a small clinking sound from the corridor leading from the kitchen into the club, as though someone had kicked a scrap of metal on the floor.

'Who the fuck is that?' Shapiro whispered.

Both men were alert, straining to hear any other sound. I hadn't a clue who it could be. If the police were on their way, I doubted they'd sneak in the back entrance. It wasn't the way it worked. Armed marksmen would surround the building and then would begin a process of negotiation. But the police only had Shapiro's address which Nicky would have passed on to Michelle, and the only way they could find this nightclub was if they rummaged through his kitchen drawers, the same as I did, and then make the connection. I thought it might be some schoolchildren on their way home and, spotting the car crashed into the rear entrance, decided to investigate. But the noise had sounded too furtive to be young kids. Youngsters would giggle and egg each other on. It might have been an animal of course. A hungry, opportunist fox. But a fox, I realised, wouldn't push its way through the kitchen swing door. Whoever it was though, I was thankful for their intrusion, knowing it was our one chance to stay alive, using the disturbance as a distraction. Providing the person didn't enter the main area of the club, I guessed the gunman would have to go and investigate, leaving me alone with Shapiro. And if I could get to the American quick enough and get his neck in a lock...

'You'd better see who that is, but keep your eye on these two,' Shapiro told his gunman, who started backing away towards the door on my left, his gun aimed at my head. I felt Olivia trembling and thought I could use her fear to mask my instructions.

I leant over, holding her tight, speaking loudly with my head against hers. 'It's OK, Olivia. Everything's going to be...'

'Shut it!' Shapiro hissed. 'Shut the fuck up!'

As Shapiro spoke, with my mouth close against Olivia's ear I whispered, 'When I say "now", run! Hide under the bed.'

Shapiro, his eyes like lasers, glared at me, but he couldn't have heard what I said. His gunman eased the door open slowly as another noise, this time a dull thud, came from one of the other rooms off the corridor. The only way the gunman could investigate was to walk through, leaving the door propped open so he could turn back quickly and spray me and Olivia with a burst of gunfire if we made a move. I saw him looking round for something with which to prop open the door, but the nearest chair was over by the bed on my right.

'Just take a fucking look,' Shapiro snapped impatiently, the tension unsettling him.

Holding the door open with his foot, the gunman slid sideways through the gap, turning his machine pistol now so that it was aimed at the first door along the corridor. Then from this room came another thump, louder this time. The gunman stretched his body towards the door his gun aimed at the open door of the room, and I could see he was off balance. This, I realised, was our only chance.

'Now!' I bellowed, pushing Olivia in the direction of the bed, praying she would dive underneath and out of sight, while the gunman was distracted by me hurtling towards his boss. As I ran towards Shapiro, I heard a shout from the corridor but hadn't a clue what it was. At the same time Shapiro shouted an instruction to the gunman, 'Over here!' But he was just too late. I grabbed him round the neck and spun him to face the door, and out of the corner of my eye I saw Olivia's ankles wriggling as she pulled herself beneath the bed. A spray of bullets, probably half the magazine, sputtered across the club's ceiling, some of them shattering glass in the mirror ball, as Alice wrestled with the gunman's arm. I saw her bring his arm down hard on her knee, the gun clattered onto the floor, while she karate chopped him in the throat with her left hand, following it with a jab from her fingers straight into both his eyes from her right hand, then a fraction of a second later another jab in the eyes with her left hand. He screamed with pain and his hands covered his eyes as Alice finished him off with a rabbit punch on the back of the neck and he fell in a heap on the floor.

I had Shapiro's neck squeezed tight in both my arms, his head twisted round in the crook of my right arm. It was a lock designed to break a man's neck, though I doubted I still had the strength to execute this move at my age. Not that it was necessary as Shapiro stopped struggling as soon as he saw his gunman was defeated.

Alice looked across at me, a triumphant glint in her eyes. It was only momentary, but it was enough time for the desperate gunman to stretch his hand out to where the pistol had fallen.

'Alice!' I shouted. 'Look out.'

She looked down and saw him raising the gun. He had his finger on the trigger and turned it towards her. But she was a lot quicker than he was and stamped on his hand with her right foot; at the same time her left foot kicked him just above the mouth. His head slammed into the floor with a crack. It was over as far as he was concerned.

I let go of Shapiro and he stood facing me, his arms relaxed at his sides. His thin smile and vacant eyes were like the worst nightmare I've ever experienced as he whispered, 'You know something, Freddie, I'm completely bulletproof. Untouchable. They'll never take me, my friend, because if they do...'

I didn't let him finish. My right fist caught him on the left of his jaw and he reeled backwards with a loud gasp and fell across the drinks table. Bottles fell on the floor with a crash and glasses shattered and splintered. I was relieved to notice the brandy was unaffected.

I walked towards the bed. 'Olivia, sweetheart. It's OK. It's safe to come out now. We're going to be OK.'

She slid out sideways, her eyes bewildered and frightened. I could see how weak she was as she struggled to stand up. I went to her and held her. She looked across at Alice questioningly, a frown of confusion demanding an explanation.

'Olivia,' I said. 'I'd like you to meet Alice, who came to our rescue.'

Alice smiled sympathetically. 'Good to meet you, Olivia. Everything's going to be all right now, and the police are on their way.'

It was my turn to frown. 'But how did you know where to find us, Alice?'

'It was Nicky's doing. She attached a personal tracker to you; stuck it under the collar of your coat.'

I grinned. 'Good for Nicky.'

'Yes, she knew an old geezer like you would need looking after,' Alice said as I struggled to untie Olivia's hands. 'After I was bailed from the court, I went straight over to the office and she told me what was going on. And here I am.'

'For which I will always be in your debt. But how did you know what the situation was in here, with an unarmed psycho and one gunman with a machine pistol?'

Alice tilted her head back. 'There's a back stairway leading to a balcony up there. I had a perfect view of what was going on. Then I came back down here and made a noise to distract them.'

'And there's me thinking you were just being clumsy,' I said.

I heard a scuffling sound, and was distracted by Shapiro struggling to stand up. In the distance I heard the familiar wail of sirens as I walked over to him.

'This is it, Shapiro,' I said. 'Conspiracy to murder Alice's family, Rick Bishop, my partner Bill Turner and Jack Dawe. That must be worth six life sentences, quite apart from all the other charges like abduction. You'll be going down for the rest of your life, you bastard.'

He smiled but his eyes were dead. 'If I go down, there's a lot of the establishment I take with me, my friend. But at the risk of repeating myself, it is not going to happen.'

I had to stop myself from chinning him again, because I didn't want to provide him with the luxury of a hospital bed instead of a police cell.

The sirens were loud and close now. Soon cops would be swarming all over the disgusting nightclub - a building that almost became a living hell for my daughter.

***

Olivia snuggled closer to me on the back seat as we cruised along the inside lane of the M2 in the steady flow of rush hour traffic.

'You OK back there?' Alice asked.

'She'll be fine,' I replied. 'Olivia's had a terrible shock but, now it's all over, home's gonna be the most comforting place.'

After the police descended on the nightclub, Shapiro was arrested and handcuffed along with the gunman. They were taken in separate vehicles, the gunman in a police van, and Shapiro in an unmarked car with two detectives, an inspector and a sergeant. They wanted to send Olivia to hospital in an ambulance, to be treated for shock, but my daughter was having none of it. Her priority had been to phone her mother, putting on a brave face and giving her the news that she was well and unharmed. Even though Olivia had the phone pressed close to her ear, I could still hear Michelle crying with tears of joy. Then Jackie said she wanted to speak to her little sister. I watched as Olivia listened attentively to her sister, and then giggled before hanging up.

'What did Jackie say?' I'd asked her.

'She said some people have all the fun.'

I knew then everything was going to be all right.

I felt Olivia becoming restless. She sighed and sat up, staring at the brake lights of the cars every time we were forced to slow down, and I knew she found the journey strenuous, wishing she was closer to home instead of having to endure a long journey on top of everything she'd been through.

'Dad?' she said, blinking and rubbing her eyes

'What is it, sweetheart?'

'That American man, I heard him say no one can touch him. They won't let him go, will they?'

'Of course not. He's responsible for killing a lot of people, and he'll probably go to prison for the rest of his life. You needn't worry about that, Olivia. He'll never be released after what he did.'

Olivia leant forward and spoke softly to Alice. 'He killed your family, didn't he, Alice?'

Alice nodded. 'My father, my mother and my little brother.'

'I'm so sorry.'

'No, I'm the one who should be sorry. If it hadn't been for my father stealing millions of pounds, none of this would have happened.'

'That's where you're wrong, Alice,' I said. 'Admittedly he ran the cyber crime empire with Eclipse in Poland, but during his internet searches, he must have learnt about the ring of child abusers and he made it his mission to expose them and bring them to justice. That's what got him killed. It had nothing to do with the outfit in Krakow. So I hope that brings you some comfort. He may have been a crook, but where children were concerned, he did the right thing.'

I could see tension in Alice's neck and shoulders and I thought she might be crying. But I was mistaken, because after a short pause she spoke with determination.

'I need to finish what my father started then. And make certain no children suffer abuse in the future.'

Olivia frowned deeply. 'But I don't understand. You've already caught the man who was responsible.'

Alice didn't reply, and I knew she was struggling for an answer to give Olivia. We both knew that catching Shapiro was just a part of the problem, and there were still dozens of rich and powerful predators out there who needed to be stopped.

As the cars slowed to a twenty mile an hour crawl, a motorway sign lit up and informed us there had been an accident between Junction three and four.

'That's all we need,' I said, annoyed at the delay, but relieved at not having to say anything else on the subject of child abusers. 'We'll have to come off at Junction Four. Shit! That'll add more time to our journey, especially if we have to go through Chatham and Rochester.'

After we eventually reached the Junction Four exit, Olivia became silent and thoughtful, and I could see questions forming in her head.

'Alice?' she began hesitantly.

'Yes, Olivia?'

'Why don't you stay at our place tonight? We've got a spare room and I'm sure it'll be all right with Mum.'

'Well, I'm not sure...'

'You'll be more than welcome, Alice,' I added. 'And it's a long drive from Wanstead to Guildford.'

'Yes, I'd like that,' she replied.

I gave Olivia a smile and a hug, guessing that the invitation came from the compassion she felt from Alice's loss of her family eleven years ago.

As we drove towards Chatham, I felt a certain amount of satisfaction at bringing Shapiro to justice, although I regretted I would have to explain to Michelle that had it not been for Alice's investigation, Olivia would never have been put in any danger. But my biggest regret was that Bill was not around to appreciate the result.

Epilogue

Alice pushed the boat out and got us the biggest feast on the Chinese takeaway menu. It was quite late by the time we sat down to eat, and over dinner Olivia told Michelle and Jackie about how Alice had rescued us, using martial arts skills to overpower Shapiro's gunman. Alice blushed and shifted awkwardly in her seat as Olivia piled it on, portraying her as a comic book heroine or the main character in a movie blockbuster.

As I poured everyone wine, including a small glass for Olivia, I grabbed the remote and switched the television on for the *News at Ten*, with the sound turned off. I had just sat down again when I noticed the main news item was something to do with a motorway crash. I grabbed the remote and turned the volume up high.

The news report was rousing and dramatic, relating how two Metropolitan detectives, a uniformed police driver and a suspect being brought to London for questioning had been killed in a motorway crash between Junctions three and four on the M2. The newsreader said it wasn't known at this stage what had caused the car to crash, although it was believed the car was speeding in the outside lane when a tyre burst. Two other vehicles were involved but the drivers and passengers of these other vehicles sustained minor injuries. Nothing further was known at this stage.

I turned the volume down and we all stared at one another while we digested this news. Alice avoided looking directly at me, and I could tell what she was thinking the same as me. An accident? Huge coincidence.

Jackie was the first to break the sudden silence. 'So that bastard gets away with it?'

'How d'you work that out,' I said. 'The man is dead.'

Jackie shrugged. 'If he'd spent his life in prison, he'd have been punished. Whereas now - '

'And three policemen have been killed, Jackie,' Michelle pointed out. 'They didn't deserve to die. They've probably got wives and families.'

'Look, please don't take this the wrong way,' I began, looking around the table at everyone. 'It's happened now, and there's nothing we or anyone can do about it. And I don't want to sound selfish or hard-hearted, but at least it will give us breathing space.'

Michelle stared at me through narrowed eyes. 'How d'you mean?'

'Well, we are all, including Olivia, going to be spending a lot of time with the police giving statements. With what's happened with the motorway crash, and the death of their suspect, I reckon it'll be put on hold for a day or so.' As Michelle still stared at me frostily, I raised my hands. 'Please, I can't wish them back to life, and right now my main concern is my family.'

'Freddie's right,' Alice said. 'That should be the number one priority. I just wish...' She stopped suddenly and looked down at the table.

We knew she was thinking of her own family and we fell into an awkward silence. Michelle got up, cleared the remains of the takeaway and began loading the dishes in the dishwasher. Olivia yawned loudly.

'Mum!' she pleaded. 'I know I'm a bit old for it now, but will you come up and read me a short bedtime story like you used to do?'

'Of course I will.'

'I think I'll turn in as well,' Jackie said.

I kissed them both goodnight, finished loading the dishwasher, then took Alice through to the living room where I poured us brandy nightcaps. After we'd settled down, Alice looked at me and said, 'That was no accident, was it?'

'If it was, it was a hugely convenient coincidence for someone.'

'Could it have been a bullet fired from an embankment overlooking the motorway and hitting the tyre?'

'Possibly. Or from one of those B-road bridges spanning the motorway? And Shapiro told us if he went down, others would go down with him, and they wouldn't allow that to happen.'

Alice stared thoughtfully into her brandy glass as she said, 'There'll be an accident investigation.'

'A bullet from a powerful rifle fired from a distance would probably go through the tyre, and by the time the car lost control it may have covered several hundred yards. They'll examine the car thoroughly, but they're hardly going to close the motorway to search for a theoretical bullet. All they'll find in the car wreckage is a completely fucked tyre, and they'll conclude it was a blow-out.'

We talked around it in circles until Michelle came into the living room, saying Olivia wanted to see me to say goodnight. When I went into our daughter's room, I saw her eyes peering over the duvet, and for a moment I wondered if she still might be scared and traumatised. But I needn't have worried, because what she wanted was to ask me if I could, with Alice's assistance, help other vulnerable children and stop evil men from abusing them. Proud of her bravery and selflessness, I promised I would do everything in my power to track down the ringleaders of these horrendous crimes, however immune they thought they were from prosecution.

I kissed her goodnight, switched off the light, but left her door ajar so that light filtered through from the landing. When I got back downstairs, Alice had told Michelle everything, and apologised for involving us. I sank into the sofa next to Michelle.

'You weren't to know what would happen,' Michelle assured Alice. 'And Olivia made me promise not to stop you and Freddie from any further investigations into child abuse.' Then her eyes met mine. 'But I'm not going to apologise for the way I behaved and treated you, Freddie. Because you should have been open and told me everything that was going on, instead of keeping me in the dark about putting your family's life on the line.' I went to say something but she stopped me with a raised hand. 'No, let me finish. I promised Olivia I would let you carry on, and I will. But I'd like you to make me a promise.'

I grinned at her. 'Yes, I promise in future I will tell you everything along every step of the way.'

She leaned over and kissed me. 'And I'd like you to make me another promise.'

'Go on,' I said.

'I'd like you to visit Rick Bishop's wife and tell her the complete story. The poor woman mustn't go on believing he was murdered for money. Go and see her tomorrow.'

Seeing me hesitate, Alice said, 'It might be better if we both go. After all, it was my investigation that was indirectly responsible for his death.'

'Thank you, Alice,' I said. 'We'll make it a priority to speak to her as soon as we can sometime tomorrow.'

I must admit, it was an undertaking I dreaded. But it had to be done. And a promise is a promise.

Lightning Source UK Ltd.
Milton Keynes UK
UKOW03f0827150414

229998UK00001B/2/P

9 781783 335817